THE FIRE BETWEEN US

IONA ROSE

AUTHOR'S NOTE

Hey there!

Thank you for choosing my book. I sure hope that you love it. I'd hate to part ways once you're done though. So how about we stay in touch?

My newsletter is a great way to discover more about me and my books. Where you'll find frequent exclusive giveaways, sneak previews of new releases and be first to see new cover reveals.

And as a HUGE thank you for joining, you'll receive a FREE book on me!

With love,

Iona

Get Your FREE Book Here:
https://dl.bookfunnel.com/v9yit8b3f7

AMBER

As much as I loved my staff and how busy the bakery got during peak hours, I reveled in the silence of the afternoon when we shut down for the day. The staff usually left by three and then I spent an hour working on the business side of things. I gave the counters another wipe, though Joe, our cleaner, did a pretty awesome job.

From the corner of my eye, I noticed a blond-haired woman trying to open the front door even though there was a large sign that read 'Closed'. I tried to ignore her but she tugged at the door again. With a sigh I left the counter and unlocked the front door.

"I'm sorry, but we're closed." There were always customers who came after we had closed and as much as I hated turning people away, we really did have to stick to our closing hours.

Something about the woman's face seemed familiar and I narrowed my eyes and tried to place.

For her part she stared at me without speaking, before her eyes widened, and she let out a cry. "Amber Davies! Oh my

God. Wow! I can't believe it's you. Heck you haven't changed one bit." She grinned and the picture of a pretty, curvaceous girl sprung to my mind.

It was my turn to shriek. "Jesus Christ! Julie Watson!"

She was one of my closest friends in high school before she and her family moved away. We'd communicated for a short while, but slowly drifted apart over time.

"What are you doing here? Are you back in town?" I asked her.

She nodded eagerly. "Yes. I moved back here a couple of months ago and I went looking for you in your old neighborhood, but there was someone else living in your old house. I couldn't find anyone who remembered you or me. I thought you'd left town."

"No. My parents passed on a few years ago and Timber and I sold the house," I told her quietly.

The grief had lessened over the years leaving behind a dull pain. Whoever said that you never got over the loss of a loved one was correct. It didn't help matters that our adoptive parents had been the only children in their families. Once they were gone I had no other relatives other than my older brother, Timber.

I noticed the stricken look that came over Julie's features. "I'm sorry, I never heard."

"It's okay, it was a long time ago." It dawned on me that we were still out on the street. "Come in."

She saw the closed sign and made a comical face which made me laugh. "Oops, I'm sorry I didn't see that."

"I'm glad you didn't or else we wouldn't have met," I said, feeling giddy with a rush of happiness. Julie and I had always believed that we would be friends for life. She had been the closest thing to a sister I'd ever had.

I never did forge that kind of friendship with anyone again, even in college. I had friends but they were not that close and establishing the bakery had taken a lot of my time and energy.

"How are your parents and sister?" I asked her, leading the way into the bakery.

"All well, but back in Washington," she said, looking around. "This is really cute. You work here, of course?"

"Yes, Timber and I own it." I couldn't help the tone of pride in my voice. I loved my little bakery.

I co-owned it with my brother, but he was a silent partner and usually only helped out when he was in between his photography assignments.

Color bloomed on Julie's cheeks. "Uh, and how is he doing?"

A giggle escaped my lips. Julie had been hopelessly infatuated with Timber. I'd loved teasing her about it and each time she denied it, but whenever she was home and Timber was around, she would follow his movements with lovesick-puppy eyes.

Julie burst out laughing. "I made such a fool of myself. Did he know?"

I shook my head. "I don't think so."

"What happened to Josh," she said. "The guy you swore you'd marry and have many babies with?"

We spent the next fifteen minutes reminiscing and giggling, reminding me of how much I'd missed having a close girl-friend. The years melted away and we were young girls again.

"I've missed you," Julie said with tears in her eyes.

"I've missed you too." Impulsively, I went to her and pulled her into a hug as if the last decade hadn't happened.

We drew apart after several seconds and laughed self-consciously.

"I'm glad you're doing so well," she said, her eyes moving to the counter.

"Thanks," I said. "Want some cookies? On the house."

Her face sobered up suddenly as if she just remembered something sad. "Cake. I want cake. I had a lousy afternoon. My fiancé just broke up with me and moved out of the apartment we share. I need a big fat slice of cake to cheer me up."

I tried to imagine the pain she must be feeling. I'd never been so in love that I was ever heartbroken the way literature and movies showed it. When my last relationship ended, I'd actually been relieved. I'd gone out with Carson for a year. It had been nice at the beginning, and I'd loved having a man so obsessed with me that he even watched me sleeping and texted me almost a hundred times a day.

Yeah, I'd been that naïve. It hadn't taken long to realize that Carson had a problem. He didn't want to be my boyfriend. He'd wanted to own me.

"Oh, I'm so sorry, Julie," I said sincerely.

Tears swam in her eyes.

"**Y**ou need more than cake," I decided. "You need a drink. Can I treat you to a drink?"

"Yes please," she said gratefully. "I'd love to catch up."

"I just need to close up and then we can go."

Five minutes later, we were in an Uber headed to one of the trendiest bars in town. I loved it for the anonymity it offered and the band that played on Fridays and weekends. The residents of our middle-sized town in New Jersey were a mixed group of all ages but the majority were young people.

We chatted casually in the Uber, catching up on mutual friends we'd known back in the day.

It was a little early for the young professionals who frequented The Oyster Bar, and we got a nice table at the far end of the room.

"I've missed New Jersey," Julie said after the waiter had taken our orders for drinks.

"New Jersey has missed you," I told her, still amazed by how suddenly she had walked back into my life and it was as if no time had passed.

"I was contemplating returning home to Washington but now I'm having second thoughts," Julie said. "I just found a job that I love, and I hate the thought of leaving it."

"What do you do?" I asked her.

"I'm an interior decorator," she said. "I just got a job in an architectural firm, and I love it."

"Then stay," I urged, excited at the prospect of living in the same city with Julie again and strengthening our friendship.

Our cocktails were served and before I knew it, we'd drained our glasses and were ordering more. It was the best evening I'd had in a long time. I laughed more than I had in the last six months, and I told Julie stuff about Carson that I'd never told anyone.

"He was a bastard and I'm glad you finally got rid of him," she said.

"The court restraining order got rid of him," I said, my voice louder than usual. The five cocktails I'd taken were doing their work. Julie and I laughed uproariously.

A sad expression suddenly came over her features and even in my tipsy state I knew that she was thinking about her ex-fiancé. She needed a distraction. Something to help her forget about him even if it was only for one night.

"I know what you need," I announced.

Julie leaned forward and stared at me expectantly.

"A one-night stand," I said and stood up to get a better view of the people in the bar.

Julie laughed. "Are you serious? Is that your solution for my broken heart?"

"I read that the fastest way to heal from a broken heart was to sleep with another guy. What do you have to lose?"

"I will if you'll join me," Julie said with a twinkle in her eye.

I was glad to see that she still possessed the wild side she'd had in high school, but I wasn't really in the mood for a man, let alone a one night stand. I looked around disinterestedly. My eye was caught by a group of four men standing in a semi-circle at the bar. One of them, a dark-haired, utterly and totally edible looking man stared right back at me, holding my gaze.

My heart pounded in my chest and my legs turned to jelly. Heat pooled in my pussy and spread to the rest of my body. Lust burned a hot pit in my belly. My breath came out in gasps, as if I'd been running. I'd never been that physically attracted to a man. Maybe it was the alcohol talking.

I shifted my glance back to her and struck out my hand. She placed hers in mine. "Deal," I said.

Her attention was also drawn to the four guys. "They are hot," she said softly. "I can't remember the last time I admired a guy."

"Me neither." I didn't admit that I'd never had a one-night stand either. I'd wanted to, after Carson and I broke up, but I never worked up the courage. The idea was solely tempting.

I noticed movement at the corner of my eyes and when I turned the hot guy was headed our way. He moved like a panther, fluidly, unhurriedly, but full of suppressed power. All the air left my lungs as he got closer. He was seriously ripped, with his shirt stretched out across his wide muscular shoulders and chest.

I grabbed my glass and took a large swig of my drink. When I looked up, he was standing over me, a panty-melting smile on his panty-melting face.

"Hi ladies," he murmured in a warm deep voice.

"Hi," we both echoed back.

"Would you like to join us for a drink," he asked.

Julie and I exchanged a glance, communicating without words, just as we had when we were younger. We both stood up.

He led the way to the bar counter where his three friends were. They were friendly and welcoming. Introductions were made all round. The only name I heard was panty-melting Brody's. Brody. Oh my. That was a name for a cowboy. Well, he could have passed for one. He was soooo gorgeous.

Brody and I managed to move a little to one side, in essence secluding ourselves from everyone else. I didn't mind. He said something that I couldn't hear over the music. I moved closer. A mixture of sage and manly scents wafted up into my nostrils making my lust go a notch higher.

I had never been that physically affected by a man. Ever. He towered over me and stood so close; his breath fanned my face.

"I've not seen you here before," he drawled.

I tilted my head up, my gaze zeroing in on his lips. They were full and yet so masculine. It was easy to imagine him lowering them to mine. I didn't recognize the person I'd become with a few drinks in me.

Meeting Julie had awakened my hibernating wild side. In school we had been known as the opposite twins. Julie had been the crazy one and I'd been the one who tempered her wild side. Alcohol usually brought out the wildness in me. I was feeling so brazen as Brody and I feasted on each other with our eyes.

We chatted and had another round of drinks.

Then the band played a slow song that I loved, and I dragged Brody to the dance floor. Julie and one of the guys had beaten us to it and were wrapped around each other.

Brody slipped his hands around my waist and drew me close. I let out a sigh as I draped my hands around his neck and rested my head on his chest. God, it felt good to be held by a man.

My nipples hardened under my top, and I was sure he could feel them pressing against his chest. Unable to help myself, I caressed the hard flat muscles of his shoulders as we moved to the music. Brody's hands roamed my back too, increasing my need to kiss him.

I raised my head and as if he had been waiting for me to make the first move, he brought his lips to mine. Our mouths moved against each other, licking, discovering, before I parted my lips, and he slid his tongue in.

He tasted of heat and whiskey. A combination that made me dizzy with arousal. We kissed as if we had been practicing for years, without any awkward moments like scraping of teeth.

Heat poured through my body as Brody deepened the kiss and pressed me tighter against his body. I wanted more than making out on the dance floor. I wanted sex with a stranger. Someone I would never see again in my life.

A warning went off in my head. I'd promised myself to stay away from men after what happened with Carson. But I wasn't looking for a relationship, my brain countered. Just one night of fun.

That was all.

Then tomorrow, I would go back to my normal life.

BRODY

I couldn't believe Amber agreed to go home with me.

Was it really true what they said about red-haired women being crazy and wild? Dylan and I discreetly exchanged our apartment keys before I drained the last of my whiskey.

I watched Amber whisper something to her friend on the dance floor before she made her way back to me. With a slow smile I took her hand, and we left the bar together. I felt as if I'd won the lottery or better. Money couldn't compare with the feeling I had at that moment.

It was rare that I scored that fast with a woman as beautiful as Amber. The chemistry between us as we made out on the dance floor had been explosive. Her body had been like a liquid, molding against mine, making my cock so hard it had throbbed painfully in my pants.

The first thing I'd noticed about her was her smile as she spoke animatedly to her friend. She had the kind of smile that made you smile back for no reason at all. The way her heart shaped face lit up as she gestured with her hands.

I'd never been so mesmerized by a woman, and I'd watched her for hours before making my move. Talking to her had been like having a peek into heaven. There was nothing pretentious about her. She laughed with her whole body, throwing her head back, caring little for the impression she was making.

She wanted me as much as I wanted her, and she made no secret of that fact. She touched me when we spoke and held my gaze, telling me without words that the attraction between us was real.

I had to have her.

A cab was waiting right outside the bar, and we got in and I gave him Dylan's address. Unable to help myself, I pulled her towards me and kissed her, sucking on her lower lip before plunging my tongue into her mouth.

She moaned loudly as if we were already in the privacy of home. I loved a woman who didn't care for other people's opinions. Amber was clearly a woman after my own heart. We got to our destination too fast, just as we were really getting into it.

The cab driver didn't bat an eyelid as I paid the fare. He'd seen his fair share of half-drunk couples making out in the back of his car. I held Amber's hand and led her to the entrance of Dylan's building.

It had never made me uncomfortable in the past to pretend that Dylan's place was mine, but that time, as I pushed the door open to the apartment, I felt a twinge of guilt. There was a good reason for it, I told myself.

Except that Amber didn't seem like the kind of woman who would fixate on me because I was wealthy. But what did I know about her? We had hardly spoken in the bar, as we'd been too focused on our physical attraction.

"Nice place," Amber said, looking around Dylan's living room.

She was less tipsy than she had been in the bar and a wary look had come over her features. A shadow of fear went through me. What if she decided that she didn't want to do this after all?

"Thanks," I said and closed the distance between us and pulled her into my arms. "I've been wanting to get you alone from the first moment I saw you," I whispered to her in between kisses.

She moaned and I felt her body relaxing in my arms. I kissed her until her lips were swollen.

"Let's go to the bedroom," she said. "My legs can't hold me up any longer."

"They don't need to," I told her and easily lifted her and carried her down the hallway.

Her giggles of surprise bounced off the walls and I peppered her with kisses all the way to Dylan's guest bedroom. I was relieved that the bed was already made. Once, I had brought a girl and the bed had been unmade. Talk about a mood killer, having to make the bed first.

I laid her on the bed and crawled in after her, draping my body over hers. I went for the curve of her neck and sucked it before turning my attention back to her mouth. I teased her lips, licking and sucking before I lowered my mouth to her exposed cleavage.

I kissed the skin above her breasts and dipped my tongue in the valley that had teased me all evening. Her skin was soft and tasted of honey. I inhaled her sweet scent of vanilla and let my hand stroke the bare skin of her arms.

My cock lurched when I pulled her top over her head, leaving her only in her bra.

"Perfect." My words came out in a pant as I stared down at her round, full breasts.

Amber brought her hands to her bra and opened the front clasp that held it together. She shrugged it off and I helped slide it off her shoulders. Her nipples were large, hard and inviting. I took one into my mouth and teased it with my tongue and then sucked on it.

Whimpers left Amber's mouth as I showered attention on her sexy breasts. I lowered my kisses all the way to her navel. She raised her hips and I slipped off her pants and lacy panties. I wanted her completely naked.

I dipped a hand between her legs and let out a sharp breath at how wet she was. I stroked her folds nudging them open. Then Amber locked her thighs, imprisoning my hand.

I met her gaze.

"I want you naked too, Brody," she whispered harshly, her eyes gleaming with passion. She loosened her thighs and I got off the bed.

Her eyes didn't leave my body as I unbuttoned my shirt and threw it on the floor. One of the benefits of being a firefighter, even on a voluntary basis, was that we worked out a lot and my body showed it.

I unbuckled my belt and slid my pants zipper down. My cock bulged obscenely inside my briefs and Amber's eyes widened as she looked at it. My lips curved into a smile. I loved the reaction from women when they first saw my cock. Amber's reaction was no different.

I pulled down my briefs and stepped out of them. When I stood up, letting Amber see my cock, she let out a gasp. I wrapped my hand around it and gave it a few strokes.

I rejoined her on the bed and spread her legs apart. I let out a growl as I took in her glistening pussy, wet with arousal juices. I dipped my head between her legs and fanned her folds with my breath.

Impatiently, she raised her hips, and clasped the back of my head.

"Don't tease me Brody," she said, her tone harsh.

"I wasn't planning to," I said with a chuckle. I swiped her slit and she cried out. "I love how wet you are."

I swirled my tongue over her sensitive clit, teasing it and watching it swell by the second. She thrashed her legs and kept my head in place with a firm hold on either side.

I growled as I licked and sucked, loving her taste and the wild, loud noises that she was making. I'd never been with a woman as sexily noisy as she was. She said my name over and over again, making me feel like the greatest lover who ever lived.

I fucked her with my tongue, moving faster and faster until she screamed that she was about to come. I shifted my attention to her clit, clamped my mouth on it and sucked. Then I pushed a finger in and pumped in and out.

I felt it when the orgasm rocked her body. Her pussy walls clenched against my finger and her whole body trembled as if a tsunami had swept through her. I didn't wait for her to recover.

I reached for my trousers and dug for a condom in my wallet. I sheathed myself and returned to the bed. I met her gaze with a questioning one.

She nodded with a smile. "Nothing has changed Brody. I want you."

Pleasure swamped me as I gently spread her open and ran the tip of my cock up and down her still wet folds. I did this several times, spreading her wetness everywhere before sinking inside her tight pussy.

We both groaned loudly at the intense pleasure as I pushed my cock in until it filled her completely. She clamped her legs around my hips tightly and dug her nails into my arms. I pulled out almost all the way and then plunged back in.

Amber let out a series of moans and gripped her thighs tighter. Fuck, she was sweet. Her pussy was like a vice, gripping my cock and milking it with every thrust. I looked down at her and almost creamed myself at the sight of her full breasts bouncing and her lips slightly parted.

"I'm going to come, Brody!" she cried.

"Do it!" I growled, pounding my cock into her deeper and faster.

She came with a scream as her whole body convulsed. She jerked her head from side to side, her thick red hair flying as she did so. She was a vision to behold, and I couldn't hold my release back any longer.

I cried out in pure pleasure as I came in a rush of hot cream. My orgasm was sharper, more intense and drawn out. It was a different experience from other women. I couldn't define it but as we lay next to each other, waiting for our breaths to return to normal, I knew that Amber was a special woman.

I had a good feeling about her. I wanted to see her again.

She was the first to stir, sitting up and swinging her shapely legs to the side of the bed. She got up and padded stark naked out of the room, probably in search of the bathroom. I was in awe of her confidence as she strode off.

By the time she disappeared through the door, I had another massive hard on. I grinned like a fool, feeling as if I'd struck gold. She returned several minutes later. I made space for her on the bed.

Instead of getting back into the bed, Amber sat on the edge and reached for her panties. She straightened them and proceeded to put them on. She gathered the rest of her clothes and put them on as well.

"What are you doing?" I asked her, propping myself up with my elbow.

She turned to look at me. "Dressing. I need to go."

My brain unscrambled. "But I thought we would spend the night together." I felt like a complete fool as those pathetic words dropped out of my mouth. They were so not me.

She raised an eyebrow. "Why would you think that? We're strangers who met in the bar and decided to have sex. I don't want to see you again and I'm guessing you don't want to see me again either."

I opened my mouth to speak then promptly shut it. To be brutally honest, that was usually my line. I'd thought what I'd felt had been mutual.

Clearly not.

She finished dressing, got up and grabbed her purse. She smiled at me, and it hit me again how beautiful she was. It was a shame that she was colder than a fish inside.

"See you around," she threw over her shoulder casually before she disappeared from my life.

AMBER

It was four in the morning, and I was aroused as hell. Who does that? The pounding of the shower didn't ease the ache in my pussy. All I could think about was the last night and the feel of Brody's cock inside me.

I'd never had such wild sex and now, remembering it, I felt like an idiot for not staying the night for several more rounds. I'd not nearly had enough. It was as if a monster had been awoken and it now refused to go back to sleep.

Besides Carson, I'd only had one other lover and with both men, sex had been okay. I'd never enjoyed it as much as I did with Brody. It had been explosive, an out of the world experience, that I had no intentions of repeating. Every man had his thing. The one thing that drew women to him.

For Carson it had been his charm. He could convince a woman to give him anything. When he turned on his charm, you would forgive him for anything. It had worked with me up to a point, then he became undeniably obsessive.

Brody's thing was sex. He was the best lover I'd ever had, and I could have bet that I wasn't the first woman to say that after sex with Brody. My body had felt so good that it had tried to convince me that Brody was worth seeing again. Except I was wiser now.

I knew better. Beyond sex, the real Brody would emerge and who knew what sort of man he was underneath it. I wasn't foolish enough to think that all men were like Carson or that all relationships ended with a restraining order slapped against the man.

But I seem to attract the wrong type of man. I couldn't risk living with the kind of fear I'd experienced with Carson. I'd been careful and not asked Brody anything personal about himself and he hadn't offered. I didn't know what he did to earn a living or whether he had siblings.

Nothing. We had just flirted most of the evening. It had been better that way.

But my body refused to get the memo. I poured shampoo on my head and scrubbed my scalp, but still the image of a naked Brody standing over me would not leave my mind.

I stood under the water and let the shampoo rinse off. When the water ran clear, I grabbed my vanilla flavored shower gel and poured a dollop on my washing cloth. Everything went well until I got to my chest. My nipples were like two hard bullets and so sensitive they were almost painful.

I ran my fingertips over them, imagining that Brody's hands were on me. I tugged at them and let out a loud moan. The last time I'd touched myself had been years ago, but I couldn't stop myself. It was as if something had taken over my body, and I wasn't in control of my own actions.

I dropped one hand between my legs and skimmed my palm over my clit. The pleasure was sharp and sweet. I made soft, circular movements and when my pussy demanded more, I slipped two fingers in and pumped furiously. It wasn't long before my body was convulsing and trembling.

It was an unsatisfying orgasm, but it took the edge off my arousal. Enough to let me finish my shower and get ready for work.

As I dressed, I chuckled softly as I remembered Brody's expression when I told him that I was leaving. I'd read that in a magazine how-to article. How not to appear vulnerable and needy after a hook-up.

The writer of that article would have been proud of me. It had taken everything in me not to curl up to Brody after sex. The article had been adamant that cuddling with a stranger was a big no. It was not the proper etiquette.

I left my apartment soon after and as usual, the streets were dead quiet at that time of morning. The bakery was a ten-minute walk from my apartment, and I loved that early morning walk. It was an opportunity to plan my day and make a mental to do list.

The back door was open which meant that Joe, our every-thing guy was already in.

"Morning Joe," I said entering the kitchen.

Joe was already busy cleaning the counters as he did every morning apart from Sundays.

"Morning my dear," he said with a warm smile. "Coffee?"

"I'll get it, thanks." We exchanged the same words every single day. "One for you?"

"Later."

We exchanged chit chat as I made my coffee. I asked about his grandchildren who were the light in his life.

Armed with my first cup of coffee, I cleaned up and sipped my coffee as I measured the ingredients for the first batch of baking. Soon, the bakery kitchen was rich with the aroma of baking cakes and pastries.

The other guys come in later, in time for the morning rush. It was a busy day and all thoughts of Brody and the evening we had spent, completely left my mind.

I got a moment to relax with a cup of coffee and a sandwich at lunch time. The back door was wide open, and a shadow fell on it before Timber's huge frame filled the doorway.

"Hey sis," he said, walking to where I sat.

I offered my cheek. "Hey you."

He placed a backpack on the counter, poured himself a cup of coffee and pulled a stool next to me. He cocked his head to one side and contemplated me. "Something's different about you."

My face heated up as the memories of the previous night returned with a full force.

"You went on a date," he said.

"Close. I met an old friend. I don't know if you remember Julie Watson. We went out for a drink and had a really good time catching up."

Timber nodded. "How could I forget? You two were practically joined at the hip and if I remember correctly, she had a schoolgirl crush on me."

I laughed. "She would hate it if she thought you remembered it."

Timber laughed. "If I ever meet her, I'll pretend that she's a stranger."

"Don't go that far," I said and sipped my coffee.

"Speaking of the past, there's something I wanted to talk to you about," Timber said. He looked suddenly nervous, which piqued my interest.

"I'm listening."

"I was thinking that me and you could take some steps to find out whether we have any biological relatives." He stared at me earnestly, a vulnerable expression in his eyes.

I understood the fear and excitement he was feeling. We had toyed with this idea before, but it had always been the wrong timing. At least for me it had been, and I had a sneaking suspicion that it would never be the right time for me.

"With Mom and Dad gone, we won't be hurting anyone," Timber continued, raking his fingers through his sandy colored hair.

People were usually surprised when we told them that we were siblings. We were as different physically as ice and heat. There was an easy explanation for it. We had both been adopted at birth. Timber was first and then I'd followed two years later.

Our parents hadn't kept it from us, but they hadn't offered any other information and we hadn't asked for it. For me, I'd forgotten that I was adopted. It had always felt as though I had been born to my parents.

"What do you say?" Timber said.

The answer at the tip of my tongue was no but that wouldn't be fair to my brother. He had always had that longing to find our biological parents. I, on the other hand, had zero interest.

"Whatever you want is fine with me," I said.

A look of relief came over his features. "Great." He reached into his backpack. "I have these packs from lineage.com."

I laughed. "Were you so sure that I'd say yes?"

He grinned. "I'd have convinced you if you'd said no." He gave one of the innocuous looking packages to me. "You're supposed to spit into the small container inside, then I'll mail them back."

I followed the instructions and handed the package back to Timber, glad to have it over and done with.

When the contents were back in his backpack, he turned to me with glistening eyes. "Can you imagine discovering that there is a whole tribe of people related to you by blood? People who resemble you and think as you do?"

I smiled but I felt none of the excitement that Timber felt. My mind drifted off as he talked about the different possible scenarios. Guilt came over me. Our parents had been great parents and had never once made us feel less than.

"How long does it take before you hear anything?" I asked.

"A couple of days, I think," he said.

"You'll be a mess by the end of those days," I teased him.

"I would if I was home. I'm going on assignment tonight and I'll be gone for three weeks," Timber said and then grew serious. "I'll probably be hard to reach by cell phone but if you need me, talk to the agency, they'll know how to reach me."

I punched his shoulder playfully. "I'll be just fine, don't worry, mother goose."

"If I don't worry about you, who will?" Timber said.

A picture of Brody shot into my mind, uninvited and unwanted. I'd followed the first instructions in the article perfectly, but I wasn't doing the next ones well. My mind couldn't get over the fact that I would not see Brody again.

"You're right, but like I always tell you, I'm a big girl and I can take care of myself."

"Okay, fine," he said, raising his hands in the air in mock surrender. "Have you contacted the website guys? I'm taking the last pictures today."

"I haven't but I will before you get back," I said. I'd been putting off having the website done and other things that Timber had insisted would do wonders for the business.

I just wanted to bake cakes and cookies from morning to evening. I was the first one to admit that I didn't have a business bone in my body but as an entrepreneur, I had to develop business skills as well.

"No worries. Today I'm taking pictures of the front of the store," he said and carefully removed his camera from the backpack.

Timber handled his camera like an egg. His photography was everything to him and it took up all his time.

"Have you gone on a single date, like we agreed?" I asked him as he fiddled with the settings of the camera.

He looked up. "I haven't met anyone I like enough to want to spend an hour or two with."

I shook my head. We were both hopeless. At this rate, we were never going to fulfill our mother's wishes which had been that we'd settle down and have families of our own.

"I'll be outside," Timber said.

"Okay." I carried our mugs to the sink and cleaned them up.

My mind wandered to Brody, and I found myself wishing that I'd asked him what he did for a living or even his phone number. Maybe I'd been too hasty. It would have been nice to meet again for another night of passion.

Okay, I told myself. That was over and there was no use thinking about it. Brody had been a nice fun distraction for me and now it was time to focus on my business. The first thing I was going to do was to email the website people to get things rolling.

My cell phone had two missed calls from Julie, and I called her back. She was busy at work, but we agreed to meet up again over the weekend.

BRODY

"Undercover millionaire," Declan said, dumping a dirty mug into the sink where I was washing up. "Have you gotten another date with the mysterious Amber?"

"Don't call me that," I snapped.

His question compounded my bad mood. It was a reminder of how the evening with the sexiest woman I'd ever met had ended. I'd gone through it with a fine-tooth comb. I recalled everything I'd said. There was nothing that had offended her.

So why the fuck had she left as if she couldn't wait to see the last of me? I couldn't stop thinking about her which was frustrating as hell.

She wasn't the only cause of my bad mood, though. She was only a hook-up, nothing more. My father had said something to me that had gotten my blood reeling.

"Structure fire, 34 Moore Lane." The dispatch call was followed by the sound of the alarm before it came back again.

I was in the middle of cleaning up after we had a late lunch. I was glad for the interruption. I hadn't become a volunteer firefighter to wash dishes. Of course, it was necessary and part of the job, but that didn't mean that I had to like it.

Adrenaline coursed through my system as I hurried out of the kitchen to change into my gear. Less than two minutes later, we were in the truck, driving out of the fire station. The air was thick with excited tension. This was the reason why I'd become a volunteer firefighter. For the adrenaline.

Andy, the guy who was driving the truck let out a string of loud curses followed by a series of impatient, angry hoots. There were always idiot drivers who refused to give way to fire trucks. Those were the cause of our biggest headaches.

We got to the house which was already engulfed in flames. Andy brought the truck to a stop in front of a hydrant. As we jumped out of the truck, an older gentleman came rushing towards us.

"I thought she had gone out of the house in front of me, but she didn't. She's still in there. You have to help her. Please," he said, his voice laced with hysteria.

"Please try and calm down," I said to him. "Who is inside?"

"My wife." He turned to look at the house, with billows of smoke rising from it into the air and his legs seemed to lose all their strength. One of the guys caught him before he sank to the ground and led him to an ambulance that had just arrived.

"The roof may come down at any minute," Dan, our captain said.

I glanced back at the old man staring forlornly at the house and I made a split second decision to do everything I could to help save his wife.

My partner and I rushed into the house first, quickly followed by the guys with the hose. I adjusted my breathing equipment before dropping to the floor. We were the pack men whose job was search and rescue.

Outside the house, the guys had probably broken the windows and were already dousing the fire with water. Then I heard a blood curdling scream and froze for a few seconds.

"Where the fuck did that come from?" I asked my partner, Chad.

He pointed upwards and I groaned as I looked at the dense smoke seeping down the stairs. You could hardly see them apart from the last two. The scream came again, and it went straight to my heart. The plan was usually to fight the fire downstairs before going up, to give the guys time to make headway fighting the fire from outside.

"I'm going up," I said to Chad.

He grabbed my arm. "Don't do it man."

I shrugged off his hand. We had to get that woman out. The danger ceased to exist for me, and I rapidly crawled up the stairs. The screams didn't cease though they grew quieter.

I reached the landing and crawled down the hallway, following the screams which had turned to cries. As I pushed the door open to the back bedroom, I heard a crash. The ladder guys had taken out the window of one of the bedrooms. The smoke and the heat immediately began to lift as I belly crawled in.

"Can you hear me?" I shouted.

A faint cry responded, sounding close to me. I couldn't see a thing in the thick smoke and my only hope of getting to her was to probe with my hands extended. Deeper in the room, my hand came up against a soft body.

Hands gripped my hand and I murmured words of comfort before standing to hoist her onto my shoulder. Luckily, she was not heavy and the heat in the house had ceased somewhat. Still, I knew we didn't have a lot of time. The roof could collapse at any moment.

I hurried out using my memory of the layout of the house to find the staircase.

"I got her," I cried as I hurried down the stairs taking care not to bang her legs or head on the wall. When I carried her out, the medics were waiting and they quickly wheeled her to the ambulance, her husband close behind and seconds later drove off.

I was about to turn back when the captain came and placed a hand on my shoulder. "Take a rest. We'll handle the rest of it." He met my gaze. "Good work in there but next time, you are not to go in alone. We don't want to lose you. There's only so far you can push your luck."

I nodded. He was right and charging in there alone had been stupid and careless. Still, I couldn't have lived with myself if that woman had died, and I'd not given it my very best. Besides, unlike most of the guys, I didn't have a wife and children. It was easier for me to take risks.

An image of Amber arose, and I quickly shot it down. That was over and done with. It had been the best night of my life but like Amber had said, it was only sex.

It took all afternoon and evening to fight the fire and inspect the neighboring houses to check for any damage. By the time we left the scene, order had been restored and the reporters and their cameras had left as well.

I should have been tired, but I wasn't. Fresh adrenaline rushed through me as I thought through the plan I'd come up with. It was risky and dangerous. Even more dangerous than crawling up the stairs of a burning house to rescue an elderly lady.

Had things gone wrong, I'd have died a hero. What I was planning on doing that evening, could not only soil my reputation forever, but it could land me in prison for a very long time. But my anger overlapped any fear I felt. I believed in justice, in any form.

I took a shower and changed into my street clothes and as I excused myself from having coffee with the guys before I left, I experienced a moment of guilt. We had all spent the afternoon fighting a fire and we were physically and emotionally exhausted.

My plan would force the guys back to work for another shift. But it was for a good cause, I told myself. If it would rid the world of one more pervert, it would be worth it.

I waved goodbye to everyone and roared off on my motorcycle. The streets were quiet at this time of night, and I drove through the back streets rather than taking the direct route that would take me to my destination.

My heart thundered in my chest as I sighted dozens of lights from a restaurant parking lot. Excitement coursed through my blood as it dawned on me what it was. An illegal motorcycle race. I hadn't been to one in years, having been there and done that.

I changed directions and headed that way. The parking lot was filled with motorcycles lined up and the roar of engines. I knew the drill. I headed to the guy doing the registration and I gave my name.

He looked me up and down with a smirk, but I ignored him. The atmosphere was carnival like with the bikers throwing good natured insults at one another. I felt myself relaxing as I joined the line and waited for the race to start.

The scent of leather and smoke permeated the air. I grinned and revved my engine. I took it as a sign of good luck to come across a bike race. Chrome wheels glistened in the semi-darkness and waxed bodies of the bikes shone.

The whistle went off and everything grew quiet. On the second one, the bikes thundered off violently, the noise from the engines, deafening. My bike flew through the air and soon, I was way ahead. I had the advantage of having one of the most powerful bikes ever made.

Fifteen minutes later, I'd circled the route and made my way back to the starting point which was also the finishing point. Instead of stopping when I got to the finish line, I waved at the marshals and drove off. I had no need for the winnings. All I'd wanted was to race. The second-place winner was welcome to take the money.

I took in quick breaths and by the time I reached the back street of my destination, I was panting. I parked my bike a short distance away and patted my leather jacket. The matches were still there.

My steps were like that of a cat, light and fast. I stopped every so often to be sure that there was no one around. Not that I expected there to be. I reach the back door of the store and quickly fish my pocket for a pin. I quickly pick the lock and the door swings open.

It's dark inside but my eyes soon adjust to the darkness, and I begin to make out what I'm seeing. I was in the kitchen of the bakery and looking at lots of shiny, industrial sized equipment. What a waste.

I couldn't allow my heart to soften. He deserved to lose everything. Hopefully, this would make him leave town.

I fished into the pocket of my leather jacket and pulled out a canister of lighter fluid and aimed it at the walls. That done, I glanced at the door to make sure that it was still open and then struck a match. I stayed long enough to ensure that the fire had caught.

Outside, I looked at the building, the fire building up inside still unseen. "How do you like that, you sonofabitch?"

I strode to my bike, turned the ignition and drove home. Just as I'd predicted, my beeper rang as I was entering my apartment. It was the station. I turned back the way I'd come and hurried to the station.

"All hands-on deck," the captain shouted as I entered the packed station.

My muscles were tight with tension as we got on the truck and drove towards the store I'd just torched. Sweat dribbled down my face.

"It's the new bakery," Andy said. "It's owned by a woman from what I heard from my wife. Her cookies have become—"

I didn't hear the rest of the words. It couldn't be owned by a woman! There had to be a mistake. My father explicitly said that the owner was a man. A huge guy I'd seen with my own eyes, taking pictures at the front of the bakery.

"My wife goes there too," someone else said and my blood turned cold.

AMBER

Something was terribly wrong. I could feel it in my guts. The usual peace I felt as I strolled down the street at four in the morning was lacking that morning. There was nothing different about the morning. The skies were awash with hints of color signifying that dawn was on its way.

The streets were quiet as usual apart from the distant sounds of cars. I walked a little faster in an attempt to dislodge the feeling of foreboding in my belly. I saw it from a distance and broke into a jog. There was a weird light reflected in the display window.

As I got closer, it dawned on me with panicked horror what I was seeing. My bakery was on fire. The smoke alarms were going crazy, and I could hear sirens sounding from a distance. I was glad for the alarm that was connected to the fire station that Timber had insisted we install.

I rushed to the back and stifled down a cry at the billows of smoke rising from the building. Unable to wait any longer, I remembered the fire extinguisher in the kitchen. It could probably help. I dropped my bag on the ground and made for the back door.

I turned the lock, and it gave way. Inside, I was hit by a blast of heat, but it eased after that, and I stepped in. I couldn't see anything. The kitchen was full of black smoke and there was a smell of burning flour mixed with melting plastics.

I experienced a moment of panic as breathing became harder. I thought of how hard I had worked to make the bakery a reality. I had to try to save it. I inhaled deeply and stepped deeper into the room, using mental images to figure out where the fire extinguisher was.

My lungs burned as I inhaled smoke. I took another step and my eyes hurt so badly I was tempted to close them. I forced myself not to think of the discomfort I was experiencing. What mattered was the bakery.

I thought of Timber and how disappointed he would be. We had both sunk all our savings into the project. The bakery had picked up in the last few weeks and our hope for creating a profitable business had soared. And now this. Tears stung my eyes as I inched forward.

Then, a blast went off, the force of it throwing me to the ground. I landed on my back and groaned with agony as a searing pain shot through me. The temptation to close my eyes was great, but I knew that if I did, I would definitely die.

I pushed myself to the door inch by inch. I reached the door, and I simply couldn't move any more. My eyelids grew heavier. I would close my eyes just for a few seconds.

The next time I came to, I was lying on my back, covered with a white sheet up to my waist and an oxygen mask on my nose and mouth. I blinked several times as I took in a man in white looking down at me. He was saying something, and it took a few seconds to decipher the words.

"Can you hear me?" he said.

I nodded, glad that I could move my head. Confusion filled my brain and then the memories slammed into me. I sat bolt upright and ripped off the oxygen mask. "My bakery."

"Ma'am, please lie back down," he said and gently pushed me back.

"My bakery?" I wanted to cry as I recalled how smoke filled the bakery had been. "Is the fire out?"

"The firefighters are doing everything they can," he said. "You're lucky that Brody found you."

"Brody?" I murmured tearfully. I remembered everything. How something had exploded in the kitchen, knocking me to the ground.

Another face replaced the one looking down at me. A face I couldn't forget. What was Brody doing here? Nothing was making sense.

"Amber?" he said softly and took my hand. "Everything's going to be okay. You're safe now."

"I need to know," I said and clutched my hands together. "How bad is the damage?"

"It's bad but we'll find out more later. For now, we need to take you to the hospital. We don't know how long you were exposed to the smoke for."

I nodded and shut my eyes. Tears stung the corners of my eyes. I didn't open them even when the doors of the ambulance shut, and it started moving. What terrible luck, just when I thought things were finally starting to turn around.

Worst case scenario, Timber said, as if he was seated right next to me.

Thinking was hard but I made myself do it. Worst case scenario was the bakery burning to ashes. Then what? The answer came right away. It was insured. Which meant that in a couple of months, we would be back in business. It was painful to imagine all our equipment ruined but at least, we would be compensated by the insurance company.

It would be tough for everyone for the next couple of months, but we would survive. I was glad for the savings that I had. My parents had always insisted to us that we make it a habit to save a percentage of our earnings every month. I was glad for that advice.

As I waited for the building to be repaired, I wouldn't starve.

"We're here now," Brody said.

I snapped my eyes open. "You came with me." It was a statement more than a question. "Thank you."

"Don't mention it," he said in a kind voice.

Why was he being so kind to me considering how I'd treated him the last time we had been together? My face heated up with shame. I had used and discarded him.

"I'll be okay now," I said. "I'll call my brother. He'll be here soon."

"Can you give me his number? I can call him for you," Brody said.

I had no legitimate reason to say no. I reached for my bag automatically then stopped when I realized that I had probably left it outside the bakery.

"Is this what you're looking for?" Brody said, lifting my bag in the air.

"Yes," I said, pleased and grateful someone thought to grab it. "Thank you." I suddenly felt tired. "His name is Timber." I let my eyelids close again.

In the hospital, I was taken to the ER and after the doctors and nurses had probed me everywhere, I was admitted overnight for observation at the hospital. I tried to tell them that I was okay, but no one was listening to me.

The nurses were kind as they settled me in and so was the doctor when he came, but I was relieved when they left, and I was alone in my room. I allowed the tears to fall out of my eyes unchecked. I hated feeling sorry for myself but at that moment, my life sucked plenty.

I longed for Timber's common sense and optimism. A light knock came on the door, and I wiped off the tears with the back of my hand. I didn't answer but a second later, it opened several inches and Brody peered in.

It was nice to see a familiar face and I summoned a smile.

"May I come in?" he said.

"Yeah," I said.

He entered the room with my bag hanging from his shoulder. Giggles burst from me as I imagined what the people who saw him must have thought. God, he was hot with those ripped arms and impossibly wide chest. I would never have guessed when we met that he was a firefighter.

He met my gaze and grinned. A panty melting grin. I'd hoped that my memories of that night had exaggerated Brody's looks. Wrong. He was hotter than I remembered.

"What?" he said.

"You look cute carrying a handbag," I said, surprised that I could laugh after the morning I'd had.

"I'll consider making it a permanent fixture on my shoulder," Brody said as he came to stand by the bed. "How are you feeling?" he asked, a look of concern coming over his handsome features.

"A lot better. The doctor said I'm okay, just a few burns that will heal in a few weeks."

Brody nodded. "I'm relieved to hear that." He stared at me, and I knew he was remembering the night we had spent together.

A blush crept up my cheeks. A vision of a naked Brody popped into my mind. My panties instantly became wet.

"I've been going back to that bar hoping I'd run into you again," Brody said quietly.

All the air left my lungs. I hadn't expected him to say anything about our hook-up. I felt bad enough at the way I had left him.

"I don't go out a lot," I said, sounding breathless. "Work keeps me busy." Then I remembered I had no work anymore and panic rose up my throat.

"What is it? Breath Amber," Brody said.

I took deep breaths.

"I called your brother, but his phone was turned off," Brody said.

"He's a photographer and is out on assignment," I said and made a decision not to bother him.

I wasn't badly injured and there was nothing he could do about the bakery. Only the insurance could. I reminded myself that I wouldn't be starting from zero. I had a customer base, and we were beginning to make a name for ourselves. The imposed time off would give me time to brainstorm ideas for growing bigger.

"I'll be fine," I said to him, determined not to take up any more of his time. "I'll most likely be discharged tomorrow."

"I'd love to drive you home," Brody said.

I stared at him. "Why are you doing all this? I'm sure it's not part of your job as a firefighter to escort people home."

He smiled. "We do sometimes but that's not why I want to do it. I like to think that we're friends despite the ruthless way you used and dumped me."

"I did not use and dump you," I said, my face heating up again.

"Oh, then what do you call what you did?" Brody said.

I couldn't meet his gaze. "It was just a sex thing for both of us. There was no use pretending that it was any different."

"It wasn't for me," Brody said quietly. "I thought and still think you're special and I want to see you again."

My heart pounded so hard, I thought it would fly right out of my chest. He wanted to see me again! Before I could break out the champagne, I reminded myself that it wasn't Brody's decision but mine.

And there had been a reason for not wanting to get tangled up with another man so soon after Carson. I needed a long break from men to build up my trust again.

"I would have said no," I said to Brody. "I'm not interested in relationships right now. I want to concentrate on my work, that's all."

"I wasn't interested in a relationship either but meeting you changed that. Maybe I can convince you," he said with a twinkle in his eyes that made me smile. "I love a challenge."

I shook my head. "You'll be wasting your time." I'd never met a man who was unashamed to admit how much he wanted me in his life. It was beyond flattering.

He wasn't just any man either. Brody had to be the hottest man I'd ever met. He could have any woman he wanted. My stomach exploded with nerves. I wanted to say yes so badly but thoughts of Carson stopped me from making another mistake.

It didn't matter how hot Brody was. I was not looking for a relationship.

"Let me worry about that," Brody said.

BRODY

Fuck, fuck and fuck. I couldn't believe that I'd made such a stupid mistake. I had just torched an innocent woman's business. I had more or less ruined her life.

I replayed the scene with my father in my head. We had come from his lawyer's office to sign some legal documents. As we had driven past the bakery, he had instructed his driver to slow down.

Outside the bakery had been a man taking pictures of the display.

"That's the owner," my father had distinctly said, pointing at the man with a camera. "He's new in town and a bad sort. The kind we don't want here."

I hadn't been surprised that my father knew about the stranger. He was chummy with the powers that be who ran our town, and he kept his ear on the ground. That was part of his success in the real estate industry.

He had then gone on to say in a low voice that the man was a suspected pedophile. The police were keeping an eye on him, but he had everyone worried. My blood had boiled. No way was he settling down in our town and in a white-hot rage, I'd made the plan to drive him out of our town.

I needed to find out from my father how he could have made such a serious mistake. It wasn't like him at all. We didn't get along, but I respected his sharp brain and memory.

I drove my bike to my old childhood home, driving faster than I usually did. It was a wealthy suburb and I passed one massive house after another before turning onto Edge Road. Like most homes, my parents' home was gated, and I punched in a code and the gates swung open.

I stopped my bike near the front door, killed the engine and marched to the front door. I pushed the front door open and stepped in. Silence enveloped me but as I moved down the hallway, muted voices came from the dining room.

My parents were in the middle of breakfast and my mother looked up with slight irritation on her face. She hated surprise visits, even from me or my sister.

"Brody, you gave us a fright. Why didn't you ring the bell?" A warm smile replaced the frown. "Come here, you naughty boy."

I went to her and dutifully kissed her on the cheek.

"Maria," she said. "Kindly serve Brody some breakfast."

"Hi Maria," I said to the maid who had been with my parents for years. "No breakfast for me. Just coffee, thanks." I was too pissed off to eat. "Hello Father." I pulled out a chair and plopped down.

"Hello Brody, what brings you here so early in the morning?" A wary look came over his features.

"I'm sure you know why I've come," I said.

"Is it too much to ask you two not to talk business over the breakfast table," my mother said.

"That's the reason I came Mother," I said.

Maria chose that moment to bring my coffee. I murmured my thanks and waited for her to leave the room before continuing.

"Father, you lied to me about the owner of the bakery. It's owned by a young woman by the name of Amber," I said, clenching my fists tightly under the table. The enormity of what I had done was sinking into me with every passing hour.

Guilt flashed in his eyes before a hard look replaced it. "If she had accepted my offer to buy the space, it wouldn't have come to that."

Red hot anger gripped me. I made as though to stand up.

"Sit down Brody," my mother commanded. "There's nothing that cannot be resolved."

I turned to her in disbelief. "What is there to resolve Mother? It's too late."

My father told her the whole tale. "I knew that Brody's temper would take care of that little problem and it did. All's well that ends well."

If he hadn't been my father, I wouldn't have hesitated to punch his nose. What a fool I had been. I was the one to blame for the loss of Amber's livelihood, not my father. He had merely accused a man of being a pedophile and I had allowed my temper to take over.

He knew which of my buttons to press. He had known that just mentioning the word pedophile would set off my legendary temper. The past caught up with me again and sadness washed over me.

It had been more than twenty years, but the pain was still as fresh as the day Martha's mom had come banging on our front door asking if we had seen Martha. She had been eight years old, and my younger sister Liz's best friend. We had stayed back while my parents and the other grownups in the neighborhood had gone searching for Martha.

Her body had been found two days later, dumped in a field almost an hour from where she had been picked up. A known pedophile had murdered her. That word had stuck in my brain, and I'd hated people who harmed children with something that came close to an obsession.

When a child went missing, I was always the first to volunteer in the search party. I never forgot Martha and the pain her loss caused her family and friends. And all because of one evil human being.

"Brody does have a point David," my mother said after hearing the whole horrible tale. "Someone's life could be ruined by this."

My father narrowed his eyes. "You seem to know her quite well."

"I had gone on a date with her," I said between clenched teeth. "I didn't know at the time that she owned a bakery. If I had, this would not have happened."

"What you mean to say is that you were more interested in getting into her panties rather than getting to know her," my father mocked.

"I'd appreciate it if you would keep profanities from the table," my mother said, tightly.

We were getting nowhere. I'd already found out what I wanted. I pushed my chair back. "This is the last time that I'll ever believe anything you say," I said, pointing a finger at my father.

"Get her a job with one of our friends. Her business would have collapsed anyway. Eighty percent of all startups collapse within six months. You probably saved her the humiliation of failure."

I looked at my mother. She quickly looked away, which shouldn't have surprised or disappointed me, but it did. She never called out my father, no matter what he did. I hated that she valued maintaining her lifestyle more than doing the right thing.

"Speaking of which," my father continued. "Are you ready to join the company now? You told me to give you a year to think about it. A year is up."

My mother looked at me with beseeching eyes. She wanted me to say that I was ready. Her life's ambition had been to get me to start working for my father. "I'll let you know." I marched out of the house, shouting goodbye to Maria as I shut the front door.

I gunned my motorbike and headed back to the bakery. Smoke still smoldered from the building and the air was heavy with the scent of burning. The captain saw me and headed my way.

"How is she?" he said.

"She's okay. The doctor wants to keep her overnight for observation," I said, and he nodded. I noticed a guy with a file going around the building. "Is that the insurance guy?"

The captain nodded. "It doesn't look like good news for your friend. The police are pretty sure that it's arson."

I inhaled a deep breath and fisted my hands to stop them from trembling. This was going from bad to worse. I'd been so careful not to leave any signs that someone had torched it.

I thought about Amber waiting to hear that the insurance would compensate her for the loss. How would she react to hearing that someone had torched her business and the insurance company was not going to pay? What if they're investigations pointed back to me?

No, there was no way. I'd planned it well and there were no CCTV cameras on the back streets I'd used. The building didn't have any security cameras either. I made myself calm down.

We talked about the damage. Thankfully, it was just the interior that had been destroyed. The structure appeared sound. That was good news, but Amber still needed capital to restart her bakery.

I joined the other guys and listened as they threw possibilities back and forth.

"It could be a sour past lover," Jim said. "There are some crazy people out there."

I hated that I was the subject of discussion and speculation. I was supposed to be an example of upholding the law, but now I was no better than a criminal. I had committed arson, driven by my own stupid temper. Sweat trickled down my back.

I had to do everything I could to make things right for Amber. As I drove towards home, my mind was hard at work. I definitely had to do something to help her get her business back on its feet.

The first thing that came to my mind was to write her a check for a hundred thousand dollars. Easy enough to do. She wouldn't accept money from me though and besides, what reason would I have for giving her money?

Fuck. I was a fool. I had walked right into the trap that my father had laid for me. It was easy to piece together what had happened. The bakery was in a prime location in town. My father must have approached Amber with an intent to buy it from her and she had said no.

He would go to any lengths to get a property he wanted, but I'd not thought him capable of destroying a person's legitimate business. And I had helped him accomplish his goal. Or so he thought. I was going to do everything to make sure that Amber got her business back.

I drove my bike into the parking garage of the high-rise apartment where I lived. I headed to the elevator and pressed the button for the penthouse. As I rode the elevator up, an idea came to me. What if I told Amber that the money was a gift from the fire station?

That we had a fund to help people struck by misfortune. Would she believe that? It was easy enough to set up a fund so that it wouldn't look as if it had come from me. Then the trust would write her a check.

My heart thumped with excitement as I gave more thought to the idea. My father thought that Amber would sell the building to him now that she was close to destitute, and at a throw away price. I would be more than happy to beat him at his own game.

The elevator stopped on the thirty-ninth floor. As much as I hated the negative attention from women that came from being wealthy, the trust fund my maternal grandparents had set up for me was useful at a time like this.

My father was super wealthy in his own right, but it had been my mother who had given him the capital to grow his business. She came from the wealthy Copper family and had married way beneath her, according to her family.

I crossed the huge marble landing and headed to the master bedroom. With a housekeeper who came every day apart from weekends, everywhere I passed was sparkling clean.

As I passed by the only door that I kept shut in the apartment, my step faltered, and a fleeting feeling of sadness came over me. I hadn't stepped into that room in years. I shook my head and proceeded to my bedroom, to take a much-needed shower and rest.

AMBER

The paperwork was done, and I could get the hell out of the hospital and go home. The first thing I wanted to do was go to the bakery and see for myself how bad the damage was. I finished dressing and was about to grab my bag when a knock came on the door.

Julie had come by in the morning and even though she had been to the bakery, she hadn't told me enough details of how the bakery looked.

"Come in," I said, hoping that whoever it was would not delay me.

The door swung open and Brody's smiling face appeared. He had a box of chocolates in his hand. "Hi."

"Hello," I said, struck anew by how handsome he was.

I bet he picked up different women in bars every single day. He had the kind of looks that dampened your panties without him uttering a single word.

"Is that for me?" I said, gesturing at the box.

"It depends," he said, a twinkle in his eye.

"On what?"

"On if you let me take you home," Brody said.

"Okay," I said. "Now, give it to me. How did you know that I love chocolates?"

Brody laughed as he handed me the box. I peeled it open and removed one perfect round chocolate and popped it into my mouth. I closed my eyes as chocolaty flavors burst in my mouth.

When I opened my eyes, Brody was staring at my lips and when he raised his gaze, his eyes brimmed with lust. Awareness lit up my skin and the air seemed to sizzle with sexual tension.

"I guessed," Brody said, his voice coming out husky and a little weird. He cleared his throat. "So, are you ready?"

I gestured at my bag. "Yeah, I guess I am."

The playful atmosphere had disappeared. Brody took my bag and led the way out. We passed by the nurse's station to pick up my prescriptions and then left.

I inhaled fresh air greedily when we stepped out. The overnight hospital stay had been my first one ever and it had felt like I'd been in a prison. Brody chuckled as he watched me inhale and exhale.

"Have you ever spent a night in a hospital?" I asked him.

He shook his head. "Fortunately, no."

"It was my first time. Those four walls felt closer with each passing hour," I said.

"I'm glad it's over," he said and led the way to his truck.

"Thanks for offering to drive me home," I said when we'd settled in the car and fastened our seatbelts.

It was times like those that I felt the loss of my parents deeply. The nurses would have had a hard time convincing them to leave for home. I glanced at Brody and gratitude washed over me. His presence had driven away the loneliness that had crept into my heart.

"Where do you live?" Brody asked.

I gave him my address.

He turned to me sharply. "That's not too far from the bakery."

"No. I usually walk to work," I said.

An odd look came over his face, but he didn't comment.

A rumbling sound filled the air. To my embarrassment, the source turned out to be my stomach. I let out an embarrassed laugh.

Brody didn't laugh. "You must be starving. Do you like Chinese? I know this great place where we can get take-out on the way home."

My belly rumbled again. "I love Chinese."

He smiled at me, and my heart did somersaults. "Done."

We didn't talk a lot on the drive home. Brody called the Chinese restaurant to order our food and when we got there, it was ready for us.

"I'd like to pay for the food," I said, digging into my handbag.

Brody held my hand. "Please. I'm the one who offered."

Pinpricks of awareness lit up my skin. "Thank you." My voice shook slightly. I'd never been so physically attracted to a man or had such explosive chemistry.

"I won't be long," he said, killing the engine outside the restaurant.

I stared at his ass as he walked away and swallowed hard remembering how it had felt to touch him. I had no business anymore and all I could think about was how hot Brody was. I had been a fool to leave his apartment after only one round of sex.

Because now, I had no intention of sleeping with him again. And not just him. Any man. The reality of my situation hit me afresh and a tremor started from my feet and rose. Panic threatened to overwhelm me.

Taking a deep breath, I concentrated on breathing in and out. I could do it. I had done it before. I knew everything there was about running a bakery and what was needed and what was not. It would be easier the second time round.

More importantly, I was in a position to start again. The business was insured which was what mattered. There was a lot of work ahead of me, but I was no stranger to work. I loved working and I wasn't fazed by the thought of getting the bakery up and running again.

Joe, Caroline and Tracy had called me that morning wanting to come and see me at the hospital, but I'd convinced them that I was okay and there was no need to. We had agreed that they would come and see me at home once I'd been discharged.

The restaurant door swung open, and Brody appeared. I noticed the admiring looks that the women he passed gave him. He seemed not to notice. Perhaps he was used to female attention.

What had he seen in me? I had no problems with my self-esteem but there were millions of women who were more beautiful than me. Brody could have had any of them.

"I hope I wasn't too long," he said as he entered the car.

"Not at all," I said.

The scent of delicious food filled the car and my belly rumbled again.

"This is beyond embarrassing," I said, clutching my stomach, hoping to keep it quiet.

Brody laughed. "You shouldn't be embarrassed. Not in front of me anyway."

To my surprise, my body relaxed, and I slumped deeper into the car seat. I glanced out and noticed that Brody was taking a longer route that was away from the bakery. I understood he was doing it to protect me, but I really needed to see it for myself.

"Do you mind passing by the bakery?" I asked.

He muttered what sounded like curses. "I was hoping you wouldn't ask. Are you sure about that?"

"I have to see it eventually," I said. "It might as well be now."

"Okay," Brody said. "Just remember it looks worse than it is. Structurally, the building is still sound."

"I'll remember," I said.

My stomach muscles tightened as we got closer. Then I saw it. It looked as if someone had poured black paint on the bottom half of the building. Luckily, it was only one story and the buildings on either side of it had not been affected.

Still, staring at my beloved bakery that looked like a charred piece of barbecued meat made me want to cry. How long would it take to get it back to a habitable condition? What would I be doing while I waited? Counting the fingers on my hands?

Brody brought the car to a stop in front of the building. A yellow tape went around the building.

"Why is that there?" I asked Brody. "Do you know?"

"The police are still investigating," he said. "They have to rule out a couple of things before they can remove the yellow tape."

That made sense. I'd already concluded that an electrical fault had probably caused the fire. Timber and I had made sure that everything had been customized for heavy duty electrical use, but you never knew. Maybe someone had been careless. All it took was one small mistake somewhere.

"Let's go." I'd seen enough. There was no way anything had survived that fire.

I was lucky that I'd been found alive and was removed from the fire in time. Brody parked the car and we got out. I liked that he sprinted around to open the door for me. There was something about gentlemen that turned my legs to jelly. He insisted on carrying my handbag and the takeout.

At the door, he held open my handbag while I fished for my house keys. His nearness dominated my mind, making me want to kiss him. I was glad that he could not read my thoughts. He would have concluded that I was a sex starved, desperate woman.

I opened the door, and we took the stairs to the first floor.

"This is where I live," I said, throwing the door open. "Come on in."

I was proud of my small one-bedroom apartment. It was homey with bright colors and cushions and throws. Over the years, I'd collected all sorts of pieces of décor which all worked to create a relaxing environment.

"It's very pretty and feminine," Brody said.

"Thank you." It felt so good to be home and even better to have Brody in the house. It would have been a little sad to get home alone. "Make yourself at home, I'll just pop into my bedroom for a few minutes."

He smiled and nodded.

I wondered if his eyes were on my ass the way mine had been on his as he walked to the Chinese restaurant to get our food. I swayed my hips a little more than I normally walked.

I dropped my handbag on the bed, went to the adjoining bathroom and ran a comb through my hair. Peering at my reflection, I looked the same. No bags under my eyes even though I hadn't slept well at the hospital.

I re-tied my hair with a band, brushed my teeth for the second time that day and splashed water on my face. I'd already showered at the hospital, but I picked out fresh clothes and changed into them.

"You look refreshed," Brody said when I returned to the living room. His gaze swiftly went over my shorts and t-shirt.

"I feel refreshed," I said, glancing at the food. "Looks like you found everything."

The plates were on the table as well as the cutlery.

"I took your words literally," Brody said and at my blank look, he explained. "When you said, feel at home."

I laughed and sat down. "I'm glad you did." I unpacked the food and served myself a generous helping of everything. "You bought the whole restaurant." There seemed to be a bit of everything.

"I wasn't sure what you liked, so I bought as much as I could," Brody said looking adorably sheepish.

"Thanks, but you didn't have to. I'm not a fussy eater."

"That makes you a lot different. People who work in the food industry are known to be very picky about their food."

"I agree a hundred percent. You should hear my employees when we're ordering food. It takes an hour to get everyone's order," I said with a laugh.

Brody was easy to talk to. We kept the conversation light and didn't talk about the fire until we'd finished eating.

"I'm sorry about the bakery," Brody said. "But you'll rebuild it, right?"

I was touched by how much my misfortune had clearly moved him. "I will. Baking is the only thing I've ever wanted to do."

He nodded.

"I'm hoping to hear from the insurance company soon and then I can start sorting out that mess. Timber might be back home as well, which will be awesome," I said.

"I love your attitude," he said, staring at me intently. "Nothing can knock you down."

I thought of how close Carson had come to knocking me down and shuddered inwardly. Men could be dangerous. Even Brody with all his hotness and charm. I hope he wasn't expecting anything romantic from me. That part of my life was over for the next couple of years.

He seemed to sense a shift in the atmosphere because he stood up.

"I'm glad you're back home and I wish you all the best. Everything will be just fine," he said.

I stood up and walked him to the door. "Thanks for being there for me Brody. You went beyond your professional duty."

He leaned forward to kiss me. I thought he would kiss me on the cheek, but he went for my lips. It was a light brush of the lips, but it left me tingling all over.

BRODY

It was eleven in the morning, and we had already responded to an MVA involving three vehicles and a medical emergency at the nursing home down the street.

As a firefighter volunteer, I was usually called in when there was an emergency, and they needed more hands or to cover someone. I was working the entire shift to cover Brad. I was under the truck checking for some noise I'd heard on the last call.

Amber sneaked into my mind without me being aware of it. It'd been happening more and more often. I found myself thinking about her a lot and wondering what she was doing at that time of the day. I'd never felt that way about a woman.

Usually, they bored me after a date of two. Amber was different. I wanted to know everything about her.

Deep in thought, I didn't hear the pair of feet standing next to the truck until a deep voice spoke.

"That's him."

"Thank you."

I froze. That sounded like Amber. If it wasn't her, then I would know that I was losing my mind. I slid out from under the truck. I grinned like a fucking idiot when I saw Amber. She looked so pretty and so perfect with her hair flowing down her shoulders and a beautiful smile on her face.

"Hey you," she said.

I stood up and wiped the grease on my hands on my overalls. "Hi. What a nice surprise."

She suddenly looked ill at ease. "I came by to say thank you to everyone now. I even brought some muffins, but I doubt you'll get any."

"That's sweet of you," I said, my gaze dropping to her lips. It wasn't a muffin I craved. It was her lips. I still remembered how sweet it had been to suck on them. I imagined them wrapped around my cock and hardened.

Shifting my feet to cover my growing erection, I tore my eyes away from her mouth.

"They told me that if it hadn't been for you reaching the bakery so fast, I'd definitely have died in that fire," she said, tears sprouting into her eyes.

"Hey, it's okay." I opened my arms and she stepped into them, not caring that my overalls were not the cleanest.

I held her tightly and inhaled her feminine scents. God, she smelled good, and her body felt so soft. I knew how it felt to bury my cock inside her tight pussy and the memory was torture. I wanted to rip off her skirt and blouse and turn her around to place her hands on the truck. Then fuck her from behind.

She drew back and I reluctantly dropped my hands.

"Thank you, Brody," she said, holding my gaze.

"You're welcome." Guilt slammed into me, and I could barely get the words out.

She would hate me if she knew I was the one who had destroyed her life. I reminded myself that I would replace everything she had lost. The check was written and ready for her. I was relieved I hadn't given it to her before she came to the station.

The guys would have thought she was crazy when she thanked them for the check from the fund for fire victims.

"Can I take you out for dinner tonight?" I asked her.

She didn't hesitate. "I would love to but it's my treat to say thank you."

"You'll take me out when the bakery is up and running again," I said. "Tonight, the treat is on me."

"Okay, fine," she said.

"I'll pick you up at seven?"

"Sounds good," Amber said and took a step forward. To my surprise, she kissed me on the mouth and then with a wave, she left.

I stood staring at her curvy ass as she left the bay and disappeared into the station. I was sweating and my breath came out fast, as if I'd been running. I could hardly wait for this evening to come to see her again.

I checked my reflection in the rearview mirror before hopping out of my truck. I hoped I looked good. I'd settled for gray slacks and a white shirt with a light sweater to complete the casual smart look.

I rang Amber's bell and a few seconds later, she buzzed me in. I took the stairs two at a time, clutching the bouquet of roses I'd bought for her. The door creaked open just as I reached the landing.

I inhaled sharply at the sight of Amber. She looked beautiful and innocent and like a fucking dream. She wore a knee length dress with a plunging neckline that gave me an instant hard on. How had I gotten so lucky? Then I remembered that I wasn't lucky yet.

I'd slept with her only because she had wanted a hook-up that night. I wanted more. I wanted a relationship. I'd never felt that longing for permanence with a woman. Worse still, a woman I knew very little about but that didn't matter.

I wanted her in my life, and we would have time to slowly get to know one another. First, I had to convince her that we could be more than a one-night stand.

"Are those for me?" she said, her tone amused.

I loosened my grip on the flowers. I'd probably crushed them. I grinned sheepishly. "Yes, of course."

She took the flowers and turned. I followed her into the kitchen.

"Thank you, they're beautiful," she said.

"Not as beautiful as you are." It was a corny line, but I meant it. Amber had perfect features.

She didn't crack a smile as I expected her to. Instead, she stared at me with a serious expression. That's when I noticed there was an aura of sadness around her.

"Are you okay?" I asked.

"Yeah," she said with what appeared to be false cheer. "I'm fine and looking forward to dinner."

She got a vase and arranged the flowers in it. Then she paused to admire them before declaring them to be perfect. She made me smile. A lot. I'd seen guys behaving the way I was and I'd always poked fun at them. If I'd had an idea of the kind of happiness they felt, I would have been envious of them.

"I'll just grab my purse and we can leave," Amber said.

She was talkative as we headed downstairs to my truck. I must have imagined the sadness in her eyes. We made light conversation on the way to the Palm restaurant. She joked about sleeping in because she had no reason to get up now. Behind the joking tone was the same sadness I'd seen. I hadn't imagined it.

"We're having dinner at the Palm?" she asked me as we got out and I handed my truck keys to a valet.

"Yes," I said, without giving it any thought. "It's one of my favorite restaurants. I hope you like it too."

I loved the rustic atmosphere in the restaurant. The hostess greeted us warmly and led us to a nice table where we had a view of the whole restaurant. A server followed closely behind with the menus.

When we were left alone, we opened our menus, but I noticed that Amber wasn't reading hers.

"This place is so expensive," she said. "You didn't have to bring me here."

"I wanted to," I said, amused by her reaction. Most women would have been glad of the chance to eat in the famous Palm restaurant. "And don't worry. I can afford it."

"I'm not questioning your ability to afford it, but I'm a simple girl."

"More's the reason for me to take you to a nice restaurant," I said.

She didn't say anything else and turned her attention back to the menu.

"Are you okay with a chardonnay?" I asked her.

"Yes," Amber said. "I'm off the pain medication now."

The server came and took our orders. I ordered a steak and Amber hesitated but finally asked for a salmon dish.

I patted the check in my pocket and mused over whether to give her the check tonight. Maybe it would cheer her up. I mentally went over the little speech I'd practiced that afternoon.

Amber let out a loud sigh and before I could ask what had brought it on, she explained.

"The insurance company called me this afternoon," she said. "They won't pay for the bakery. They said that the police are suspecting arson."

I should have expected it but hearing her say the words out loud rendered me speechless for a few seconds.

"I called the detective in charge of my case, and he confirmed what the insurance guy had said. He asked me who would do something like that to me?"

I held my breath. "What did you say?"

"My ex," she said, misery coating her voice.

"Your ex? Why would he want to burn your bakery?" I didn't want to be found out but neither did I want the blame to fall on an innocent man.

"I have a restraining order against him," Amber explained. "When I ended our relationship, he refused to accept it. He called me like a hundred times a day, came to the bakery I worked in and stood outside for hours and bombarded me with social media messages. That kind of thing."

"That's a sick person." My heartbeat raced to near explosion. There was a man walking around the city who wished to harm Amber. "Has he contacted you since the restraining order?"

"No. It worked. He has kept away," she said.

That gave me some relief.

"So yeah, he's a suspect now."

I decided it was the best time to give Amber the check. "I have some good news for you." I fished the check out from the pocket and handed it to her.

"What's this?" she said, taking it and holding it up to read it. Her eyes widened and she shifted her gaze to me. "I don't understand. A check for a hundred thousand dollars, written out to me. Why and from who?"

Admiration for her flooded me. Most people would have already pocketed the check and then asked questions later.

"We have a fund at the station for victims of fires whose means of earning a livelihood has been affected," I said with a straight face.

"Oh," she said. "I've never heard of such a thing, but how kind." A conflicted look came over her face. "I don't feel right taking it. There are more deserving people than me. I will easily get a job Brody and with time, Timber and I will reopen the bakery. It will just take a little longer, that's all."

I'd not anticipated that she would refuse. My knee jerk reaction was to beg her to take it, but that approach wouldn't work. I had to convince her that it was people like her that the station supported.

"I have a feeling that the muffins softened their hearts as well," I said and smiled to show that it was a joke. "Seriously though, it seems that a lot of the firefighters' wives know your bakery and not just them. Your business plays a big role in our community. We want to have it back, feeding the people of this city."

Tears filled her eyes. I felt guilty that my speech had touched her, but I hadn't been lying. A lot of the guys' wives bought the cookies at Amber's bakery.

"I don't know what to say. You've been so kind. All of you," she said.

"Does that mean that you'll take it," I said, holding my breath as I waited for her answer.

She nodded. "Yes. With many thanks. I should come by the station and thank them."

My heart skipped a beat. I let out a forced chuckle. "The captain anticipated that you would say that. He said to tell you no need. Reopening the bakery will be thanks enough."

She let out a shaky laugh. "I can do that."

AMBER

I'd eaten dinner in what was probably the most expensive restaurant in the city, and I couldn't remember how my dinner had tasted. All I could think about was my bakery. It had been a roller coaster of emotions for me.

First the insurance company had broken my heart when they'd said they were not going to pay for the damage. Then Brody had put it together again when he gave me the check from the fire station fund. I had a feeling he had a lot to do with me being chosen to get that check.

"Thank you for dinner," I said as we were preparing to leave. "It was lovely." It made sense why he had picked such an expensive restaurant to take me. It had to be a sort of ceremony to hand over the check.

"You're welcome," Brody said, taking my hand as we walked out together.

It felt too good having my hand in his. Too warm. The heat spread from my hand to the rest of my body. By the time we entered the truck, every inch of me ached with the desire to possess him.

We were both silent on the drive to my apartment. I wondered if Brody was feeling as aroused as I was. I had promised myself to stay away from him or any other man. After he had scratched my itch. The only way I was going to resist Brody was if he turned down my invitation to come up to my apartment.

"Do you want to come in?" I said when we got home. I could hear my heartbeat thrashing in my ears. His gaze met mine in the semi darkness of the truck. There was no secret as to why I was inviting him up.

"Sure, I'd love to," he said in a cool voice. "Don't move. I'm coming to open your door."

I laughed and waited. He opened my door and took my hand to help me out. Instead of letting go of my hand when I was on my feet, he pulled me against him and kissed me. A fast, hot kiss that made panties wet with arousal and my legs barely able to hold me up.

I reluctantly let go of Brody's hand to open the door. He stood behind me and slid his hands around my waist and stood so close I could feel his erection pressing against my ass.

A moan escaped my lips and I ground myself against him. I managed to step away from him to get into the house. He followed closely behind and slammed the door shut.

I expected him to draw me into his arms, instead, he took my hand and led me to the bedroom without asking. I shivered with need as I followed him. In my bedroom, Brody cupped my face, stared at me intently and then kissed me.

His lips felt like heaven on me. The kiss quickly deepened and soon I was clinging to him and grinding against his erection.

"You're so hot, so beautiful," Brody said, drawing back.

He ran his hands down my neck, leaving a trail of heat on my skin where he had touched. He attempted to slide the dress off my shoulders.

"How do you take this dress off?" he said, his voice laced with frustration.

I laughed. "From the bottom."

He scooped it up and lifted it over my head and threw it on the floor. He stared hungrily at me before taking me back into his arms. As he kissed me, his hands stroked my back and dropped to cup my ass.

He did things with his tongue and mouth that no man had ever done to me. I moaned and called out his name unashamedly. His hands left my ass to unclasp my bra. He didn't fumble and a second later, it had opened. He slid it off me and covered my breasts with his hands.

I arched my back as he rubbed his thumbs over my nipples.

"How does that feel, babe?" Brody said.

"Good. Too good." I wanted his hands everywhere.

He lowered his head and took an aching nipple into his mouth. He teased it with his teeth and tongue, driving me mad with lust. I pressed his head and urged him to move to the other nipple.

I'd seen people in movies make love with a passion that looked exaggerated to me. Now, I knew that it wasn't a work of fiction. It really did happen. I didn't want the night to end.

Brody dropped to his knees and spread my legs open. He covered my mound with his mouth, and I screamed. I whimpered as he made a circular movement with his lips.

"Oh God, Brody," I cried. "Please."

He drew my panties to one side. "So wet."

The tip of his tongue teased my folds, coaxing them open and then flicking my clit in rapid movements. I ground myself against him, desperate to come. Brody took my clit into his mouth and sucked on it. I gripped his head for support as I toppled over the edge.

"I'm coming," I cried.

He licked my pussy clean and when he was done, he looked up at me with a look of smug satisfaction. "You taste like candy."

My face heated up but luckily, Brody had other things on his mind. He stood up and pulled me to the bed. He lay down beside me fully clothed and I went for the buttons of his shirts.

He stayed still and watched me. He reached out and tucked my hair behind my ear. I ran my hands over his chiseled chest. It felt like touching a wall of muscle. Brody raised his upper body and removed his shirt, tossing it to the floor where my dress lay.

I turned my attention to his pants. I ignored the massive bulge of his cock and unhooked his belt. My mouth watered as Brody pulled down his pants and boxer briefs. His cock sprang free and unable to resist, I slid down until my face was level with it.

I wrapped my hand around it and brought it to my mouth. His masculine scent surrounded me, and I took all of him into my mouth. Brody groaned loudly as I milked his cock with my mouth. I teased the tip with my tongue and cupped his tight balls with my free hand.

I loved the sounds that Brody was making. Wild abandonment. A man who was clearly loving what I was doing. He rocked into my mouth harder and faster and then abruptly took his cock out.

"If you don't stop now, I'm going to come," Brody said. "Get on your knees."

I grinned. "Yes, sir." He made me feel hot and playful at the same time. Was that normal? My pussy flooded with more wetness and heat as I got in position. Brody moved behind me and spread my ass cheeks apart.

"Fuck," he said, inhaling sharply. "You're irresistible, Amber."

I wanted to be irresistible to him. I felt the tip of his cock on me, moving up and down my folds. I thrust my ass out and cried out at the pleasure that the friction generated.

I ached to have his cock fill me. "I want you, Brody. I want your big cock inside me."

He growled and held me still with one big hand. Then without hesitation, he plunged his cock inside me. It felt as if he had taken my sanity with him as alien sounds and unintelligible words left my mouth.

Brody thrust into me hard and fast, keeping a firm hold on my hips. We moved together, with me meeting each of his thrust with my own rocking movements.

"Oh God, yes," I cried, close to orgasm.

Brody's movements changed and I knew he was close to coming. He let go of my hip and slapped me lightly on my left cheek, toppling me over the edge. My body erupted in a series of tremors as the orgasm rocked me.

"Fuck," Brody growled and the next thing I felt was a flood of his cream filling my pussy.

I moaned low and long as waves of pleasure washed over me. When I stopped trembling, Brody slowly withdrew and pulled me to lie on top of him.

"I'm glad we're in your apartment," Brody said after a few minutes of silence.

"Why?" I asked him.

"There's no chance of you leaving," he said. "Like the last time."

I laughed, embarrassed at the memory. "I regretted leaving so early."

"Is that so?" Brody said.

I hit him playfully on the shoulder. As much as I liked him, I wasn't going to tell him that I'd masturbated to him in the shower.

"Thank you for dinner, it was lovely," I said. I hated that he had felt the need to spend so much money on me. It hadn't been necessary at all.

"You're welcome. Besides I needed an excuse to see you again," Brody said.

His words thrilled me for a few seconds, then I brought myself back to reality with a mental slap. I didn't want a relationship no matter how good Brody was in bed.

"Has your brother come back yet?" he asked.

"No," I said. "His assignment was for three weeks."

"Is he younger or older than you?" Brody asked.

"Older by three years," I said. "We were both adopted though." I didn't know why I had told him that. I rarely told people about that unless we were very close.

"Oh," Brody said, sounding shocked. It was a standard reaction from the people I'd told about our adoption.

"Our parents were the best though," I said, warmth flooding my chest. "I never felt any different from other kids. My parents loved us completely."

"What happened to them?" Brody asked.

"An accident. Timber and I were in shock for months. Long after we'd buried them, I still couldn't believe that they were gone." Talking about them had stopped being painful.

I missed them like crazy. I missed my mom's enthusiasm for anything that I did and my dad's practical advice.

"What about you?" I asked him. "Do you have a family?"

He sighed. "Yes. My parents and my sister. I'm closest to my sister and like you and Timber, she's my little sister. Liz is married to a great guy named William and they have the sweetest little girl. Her name is Amelia."

I loved how his voice softened when he talked about his niece. "How old is she?"

"Three. She has no filter in her mouth and says the funniest things," Brody said with a chuckle.

"I'd love to meet her." I cursed under my breath as soon as the words were out of my mouth.

"I'm going to dinner at my sister's on Friday. I'd love it if you came with me," Brody said.

I should have said no, and I intended to say no. But the wires in my brain had probably short circuited because what I said was 'yes'.

BRODY

"How do I look?" Amber asked when I picked her up to go for dinner at my sister's.

She twirled at the doorway and then came to a stop and smiled at me. She was so fucking gorgeous and sexy.

"What do you say we skip that dinner? Liz won't mind," I said, half-jokingly.

Amber stepped back as if I'd slapped her and put on a believable shocked expression as if I'd insulted her dignity. I laughed.

I waited outside the apartment for her as she went back in to get her purse and her shawl. I was excited to introduce Amber to my sister and her family. They meant the world to me.

I held her arm lightly as we made our way to the car. Just touching her gave me a happy buzz. I opened the door for her and sprinted around to my side.

Amber chuckled as I got into the car and cranked the engine.

"What?" I asked.

"I can't believe you're taking me to your sister's place for dinner and I've never had dinner at your's."

My pulse rate increased. I'd known that the topic would come up, but I hoped to delay it as much as possible. The first thing women wanted to know was where a man lived. If he was cagey, they assumed he was hiding something. Like a wife.

Dismay settled in my belly as it dawned on me just what little hope I had for convincing Amber to be my girlfriend. My place was the first problem. I'd lied to her by taking her to Dylan's house and pretending that it was my house.

How would I explain to her my house and my lifestyle without telling her who my father was? But that wasn't the biggest obstacle.

The biggest was meeting my father. She knew him. I had no doubt that Amber could remember the man who had tried to bully her into selling her piece of real estate. The day she would meet my father would be the end of us. We had no future. How long could I keep her away from my parents?

Then there was the other frightening thing that could not only make me lose Amber, but it could land me in jail. Luckily, I seemed to have gotten away with it. No one had seen me. But if Amber ever knew that I was the one who had torched her bakery, she would never want to see me again.

"I didn't know you wanted to have dinner at my place," I said casually.

"I'm just teasing," Amber said. "Tell me about your sister? Is she anything like you?"

I shot her an amused look. "How would you describe me?"

"Confident, you go for what you want, you love women, and they love you back," she said.

"What? Wait—that's not true. Well, I don't love women anymore," I said, taken aback by her accuracy.

I really did love women but meeting Amber and getting to know her had shown me that I could stay with one woman. Given a chance. Amber was special. I'd never met a woman who made me want to be a better person.

Amber was laughing. "There's nothing wrong with you loving women and them loving you back. That's how we hooked up, right?"

"Right," I said. It had been pure luck that I'd been at the bar with the guys that evening. When Dylan had invited me, I'd been on the verge of saying no as I'd wanted to go straight home, then I'd agreed, thinking to myself why not.

I'd have missed the chance to meet Amber.

We got to my sister's neighborhood, and I turned the car onto Court Road. It was a beautiful place to raise a family, with beautiful mansions with a large lawn that circled each house. I slowed down and turned left to take the circular drive that led to the front of the house.

"What a pretty place to live," Amber commented.

"It is," I said, bringing the car to a stop. I killed the engine and slid out of the car. I hadn't warned Liz that I was bringing a guest, but she was a good sport about such things, and she would enjoy meeting Amber.

I placed my hand on Amber's back as we walked to the front door. I rung the bell and while we waited, I stepped close to Amber and kissed her on the lips.

"Stop it," she said laughing. "I want to make a good impression."

Before I could tease her, the door swung open, and Liz's eyes widened when she saw Amber.

She hugged me first. "Brody, you should have told me you were bringing a guest. I'd have dressed better than I have."

Amber laughed. "Not on my account."

I draped an arm around Amber. "Liz, this is Amber." I turned to Amber and introduced Liz as my bratty little sister.

"Don't listen to him," Liz said. "I'm the one who carries all the common sense in our family."

"It's a pleasure to meet you," Amber said, trying to stifle her giggles.

Liz held the door and welcomed us in. She winked at me as I walked past. It was her way of saying that she approved of Amber.

"We're in the living room relaxing before dinner," Liz said as she closed the door.

I lead the way to the living room. As soon as I stepped in, Amelia let out a shriek.

"Uncle Brody," she cried and ran to me. She launched herself against me, but I was ready, and I caught her easily and lifted her into the air.

"Hello sweetheart," I said, hugging her tightly.

"I have a new doll Uncle Brody," Amelia said.

"Can I see it?" I asked enthusiastically. Amelia always had a new doll or toy to show me every time I went to their house.

"I'll bring it for you," she said, wriggling out of my arms. She took off as soon as her feet touched the ground.

"Amelia, you didn't say hello to Amber," Liz shouted after her.

"It's fine, really," Amber said, laughing. "She's so sweet."

"She's a ball of energy," Liz said.

William and I slapped each other on the back and then I introduced him to Amber. We all sat down, and Liz poured us each a glass of wine.

"I can't tell you how happy we are to meet you," Liz said to Amber. "Brody has never introduced us to any woman."

"Did I also mention that my sister talks too much?" I said to Amber.

Amelia chose that moment to come back tearing into the room clutching a doll which looked anything but new.

"Isn't she pweety?" Amelia said. At three years old, she still mixed up her words, but I found it endearing.

"She is," I said and winked at Amber. The barbie doll looked as though it had been chewed on by a puppy. But beauty was in the eye of the beholder and if Amelia thought that her doll was pretty, who was I to argue.

"Do you want to hole her?" Amelia continued.

"I'd love nothing more," I said and took the doll. "Did you say hello to my friend?"

Amelia's gaze shifted to Amber. She moved to her and rested her little hands on Amber's thighs. I loved the innocence of children. Amelia stared at Amber with eyes filled with wonder.

"You have red hair," she said, and we all laughed.

"My name is Amber."

"Amber," Amelia repeated. "Would you like to hold my doll?"

Amber nodded enthusiastically. "I'd love to."

The doll was taken from me unceremoniously and thrust into Amber's arms.

"I think you've just been replaced as a favorite," Liz muttered.

"Shiny new object," I said. "It'll wear off."

Amber glanced at the two of us and laughed. William was used to our banter and most times didn't pay attention to us.

We relaxed in the living room for half an hour by which time, it was Amelia's bedtime. She reluctantly hugged and kissed us good night and left with her mom. I asked William about work. He was in real estate with his own company.

Amber listened intently and asked a few questions which pleased William. A few minutes later, Liz returned to the living room and asked us to the dining room for dinner.

We headed to the dining room, and I pulled out the chair next to mine for Amber. Her face was flushed, and she seemed relaxed. I was glad that she was getting on well with my sister and William. They were closer to me than my own parents were.

With the help of a uniformed chef, Liz brought the food to the table as well as the plates.

"Can I help?" Amber asked, half standing.

"No, but thanks for offering," Liz said. "We're actually done. Dig in everyone."

Dinner at my sister's always resembled a buffet. I counted five different meats and the same number of vegetables and accompaniments. We served and proceeded to eat.

"How did you guys meet?" Liz asked.

Amber's face turned a deep shade of pink. I knew she was remembering the first time we'd had sex. It didn't make for a nice dinner entertainment story.

"We met in a bar," I said, rescuing Amber. "We met through friends of friends."

"How cute," Liz said and then turned to William with a loving look. "Almost the same way that William and I met."

I listened with half an ear as Liz recounted the story of how they met to Amber. I'd heard it enough times. Instead, I enjoyed looking at her and the fleet of different expressions that came over her face.

I lost track of the conversation until I heard my name mentioned again.

"Maybe you can convince Brody to go back to his sculpting," Liz said.

I froze. I glared at Liz. I loved my sister, but she spoke too much. I hoped that Amber had missed it.

"Sculpting?" she said.

"It's nothing. Just something I used to play around with," I said quickly.

I hadn't sculpted in almost three years. Right about the time I became a volunteer firefighter.

"I wouldn't call it something you played around with," William said in his deep baritone. "You sold very expensive pieces."

I shifted in my chair. I'd put sculpting behind me after being unable to do any work for weeks. Every time I passed the closed door of what had been my studio, guilt came over me. It felt as though by moving in another direction, I was cheating on my first love, which had been sculpting.

I hated when that topic came up and it was usually Liz who brought it up. I blamed myself though for not telling her not to bring it up in front of Amber.

"I thought you were a firefighter?" Amber said.

I turned and met her puzzled look. "Part time."

"So, what do you do the rest of the time?" Amber said.

Silence descended on the table. Liz, sensing the tension between Amber and me, quickly jumped in. "Anyone for dessert?"

It was a little weird and pretty obvious what she was doing but it worked. We all pleaded full stomachs and moved to the living room for a last glass of wine. The conversation moved to Amber's bakery and the fire.

Liz and William were horrified. As Amber told the story, it horrified me afresh. I could have lost Amber without ever knowing what I had lost.

"I'm so glad that Brody found you in time," Liz said.

Amber gave a shaky laugh. "Me too."

AMBER

I thought I'd figured Brody out but clearly, I knew very little about him. I couldn't wait to be alone with him even though the evening had been a success. He had a wonderful family but the fact that I knew so little about him had frightened me.

Why had he kept it a secret that he was a volunteer firefighter and why hadn't he answered the question of what he did the rest of the time? I shivered as we made our way to the car.

Ever the gentleman, Brody opened the car for me, and I entered but the shivering didn't stop. It had been the same way with Carson. He had kept a lot of things from me which I only found out accidentally from other people. Was it a warning that Brody was not who he seemed to be?

But even as that thought filled my mind, the instinctive part of me rebelled against the idea. He was close to his family. Weird, dangerous people like Carson were loners. They were not close to their families and they sure as hell didn't become firefighters.

"You're very quiet," Brody said. "Are you okay?"

I swallowed and chose my next words carefully. "I'm okay. I just realized how little I know about you."

He nodded. "What do you want to know?"

"Normal stuff. What do you do on a day-to-day basis if you're not a full-time firefighter?"

"I volunteer in other places," Brody said but I could tell by his tone of voice that he didn't want to say more.

It was on the tip of my tongue to ask him why he had stopped sculpting but his response at the dinner table stopped me. We had slept together and had been as close as two human beings could be, physically, but Brody had a wall of privacy that did not invite intimate questions.

"I'm not so mysterious after all," he said in a playful tone.

"Let me be the judge of that," I said. "What do your parents do?" I was beginning to sound like I was interrogating Brody. It wasn't fair but I needed to know that I was safe with him.

"My father owns a real estate firm," he said.

"Ah, I see." Obviously, Brody worked at his father's firm when he wasn't at the station. Why had it been so difficult to say that?

Relief surged through me as the mystery around Brody melted away. He was nothing like Carson. He wasn't going to stalk me when things between us came to an end.

Not that I had plans to keep seeing him. But maybe for just one more night. The silliness of it didn't escape me. I kept postponing the moment when I would tell Brody I couldn't see him again.

For the rest of the way, we talked about the bakery and the plans I had. I'd contacted a structural engineer and he would start work in the next day or two once the police removed the yellow tape that surrounded the building.

Brody brought the car to a stop in front of my apartment building. He leaned across and kissed me.

"Thank you for a lovely evening," he said in an almost formal tone.

"I enjoyed myself too," I said, confusion coming over me. "Do you want to come in for coffee?" God that sounded weak.

"Thanks, but I'll pass. There's something I have to do at home, but I'll call you tomorrow, okay?" Brody said.

His words stung. They were a carefully veiled rejection. My heart raced and it took real effort to act as if I was okay. Stupid, stupid, stupid, I chanted to myself as I walked to the entrance.

How could I have thought that Brody felt the same attraction that I did? He waited until I was inside before driving off. Bastard! Was that his modus operandi? Fuck a woman, take her to meet your family and then dump her?

To my anger, tears formed in my eyes. I wiped them off impatiently and unlocked my front door. I should have followed the rules of a one-night stand. If I had, I would not have felt the burning pain that was spreading across my chest.

I kicked off my shoes angrily and stomped to my bedroom. I was a complete fool when it came to men and even the past hadn't taught me anything.

~

"How have you been?" Julie asked me as we sat across from each other in the coffee shop down the block from my place.

I was glad that she had called me and invited me for lunch. My plan had been to spend my new unwanted free time to learn new recipes and read business books. Instead, I'd spent the morning thinking about Brody and what I could have done to offend him. Had I asked him too many personal questions?

Julie snapped her fingers together. "Hey, come back to earth."

I laughed.

"I'm glad to see that you've bounced back from that horrible experience," Julie said.

I nodded. "It helps that the firefighters donated a hundred thousand for me to restart it. I don't know what I'd have done." I took a bite of my chicken sandwich.

"I know."

Julie sipped her coffee. "Are you still seeing Brody?"

Sadness came over me, but I shook it away. I hadn't seen or heard from Brody in five days. I tried to think about him as little as possible and when he did slip into my mind unchecked, I felt like a piece of used and discarded tissue paper.

"No," I said, wondering how much to tell her. I ached to tell someone and finally I told her all of it.

"But he seemed so into you at the hospital," Julie said.

I shrugged. "He probably just felt sorry for me. What about you? Did anything come out of that hook up?"

Julie grinned. "I think so. So far so good. We've gone on a few dates but he's worried that I'm on the rebound."

"Are you?" I asked her.

She shook her head. "I don't think so. Liam is kind and sweet. Being with him has shown me how selfish my ex-boyfriend was. He just took and took and rarely gave. Him breaking up with me was the best thing he ever did for me."

As we chatted, I glanced at the door as a man walked in. I caught sight of a familiar figure peering into the coffee shop as he went past. The hair at the back of my neck stood up.

"Amber what is it?" Julie said. "You look like you've seen a ghost."

"I thought I saw Carson go by," I said and rubbed my eyes.

"Are you sure?" Julie said, looking at me skeptically.

"I could have sworn it was him with his black hair oiled back, clinging to his scalp." I shook my head. "Maybe it's just my imagination."

"I'm sure he's not stupid enough to come near you when you have a restraining order," Julie said.

I nodded and smiled. "I'm sure you're right." I didn't bother to tell Julie what the statistics were on women who had been stalked by ex-boyfriends.

I was going to feel a lot better when Timber came back to town. I felt safer when he was around, knowing that he was just a phone call away. We finished our food and then Julie had to go back to work.

"I miss working," I said as we stepped out into the sunshine.

"What's stopping you?" Julie said. "You could take orders and bake them at your apartment. Contact your large order clients and do those."

I looked at her as if she had struck gold. "You're a genius!" I shouted and hugged her tightly.

She laughed. "I know."

"That's exactly what I'm going to do. I need physical labor otherwise I'll lose my mind," I said.

I was already planning my next steps. I would be so busy that I wasn't going to have time to think about Brody. I'd make myself so exhausted that every night I would fall asleep as soon as my head hit the pillow.

We hugged and said goodbye. I felt happy for the first time since Brody disappeared from my life. I had a purpose as I waited for renovations for the bakery to begin.

I reached home and as I fished for my keys I froze as I saw him again disappearing round the corner. I gripped my handbag and took off after him, grateful that I was wearing sneakers.

I had an advantage. He didn't know that I was going after him. Even if he wasn't Carson, something was weird about seeing him twice within my vicinity. Breathing hard, I rounded the corner and almost ran smack into him.

"Carson!" I shouted.

He looked shocked to see me.

"Why are you following me?" I said, fear coursing through me. "And don't deny it. I've seen you."

He looked at me like a cornered rat. "I swear I wasn't following you," he said.

Anger and dismay filled me. Looking into Carson's red hooded eyes took me back to the year before he'd been slapped with a restraining order. I remembered the phone calls with threats to kill himself if I didn't take him back.

He alternated the threats with begging for forgiveness. I got a new number and then he switched to sending me emails. In a period of one year, Carson had sent me a total of four thousand emails.

The anger overrode the fear that I was feeling. I pushed his chest with an aggression I didn't know I possessed. First Brody left me without an explanation or excuse and now my sorry ass of an ex was stalking me. I'd had enough of playing the victim.

"I'm not playing any more of your stupid games, Carson," I shouted at him.

"Okay, okay," he said, raising his hands in the air. "I just wanted to talk to you."

"About what?" I snarled. "You and I have nothing to say to each other."

"Are you seeing someone else Amber?" he said.

I narrowed my eyes. "That is none of your business."

"I'm just watching out for you," he said feebly. "People are not good Amber."

I raised an eyebrow. "Tell me about it."

He took a step back. "Look I don't want to get into any trouble." He turned away and strode off at a rapid pace.

Still stewing, I decided I'd had enough of being the victim. If Brody thought he could get away with treating me like a rug he could discard, he had another thing coming.

Instead of heading back home, I flagged down a cab and gave the driver Brody's address. I had what was referred to as a photographic memory. I only needed to hear something once and it was ingrained into my memory.

I prepared my speech as the cab headed to his place. He had pretended to be my friend and lover but after he'd had enough, instead of telling me, he had disappeared with a promise to call me.

The cab drove up and stopped outside the apartment building I vaguely remembered. I paid the driver and hopped out. I jabbed the bell and a minute later, a buzzer went off and I pushed the main door open.

With my heart pounding, I took the elevator to the second-floor apartment. I was both excited and nervous at the same time. I got off and found Brody's apartment door open.

I didn't bother with knocking and went straight in. Disgust came over me at the untidiness in the living room. Two dirty plates that looked as if they were from days ago. There were clothes on the floor and the coffee table looked as if it could do with a scrub.

I couldn't believe that Brody lived in such messy surroundings. I followed the noises coming from the kitchen. A brown-haired man stood over the stove and when he heard my footsteps he turned around.

"You're not Brody," I said.

"I know," he said.

BRODY

I was so absorbed in my work that a sharp pain in my back was my reminder that I needed to stretch. I placed my point chisel on the table and surveyed my work. The bearded man was really coming along.

Pride and happiness came over me. I'd missed it. Now, it felt as if a hole in my heart had been filled. For three years I'd not stepped into my art studio. The only person who did enter was Hellen, my housekeeper, to clean it. The joy was so much, it threatened to overwhelm me.

How could I have let my father keep me away from sculpting, which had always been the one thing that made me feel alive?

On the way to drop Amber home after dinner at my sister's, something had awoken inside me. I'd been consumed by Amber's situation. Her beloved bakery had burned down, and she had to start from zero. Instead of feeling sorry for herself and thinking about what she had lost, she was soldiering on with determination.

I on the other hand had allowed my father to dictate my life. True, I'd held my ground by refusing to go and work with him. But it was a shallow victory because I still hadn't followed my heart's desire. I had allowed the words he'd said over the years to dictate my life.

Don't tell me you're still carving those pieces of junk.

Get a real job, a man's job at the very least.

You always were a sissy.

Slowly by slowly, his words had chipped away at my confidence until he had succeeded, and I had abandoned my calling. The result was that I'd walked around feeling lost, like a zombie, for those three years.

Not anymore. I made a vow right there and then that I'd never let anything keep me away from my calling. I loved sculpting. I always had. It satisfied something in me that nothing else could. When I was working, I lost all sense of time and space.

Nothing else mattered except the three-dimensional object I was creating from a lump of hardened clay. My stomach rumbled. I had no idea when the last time was I'd eaten.

It had been like that for the last five days. I'd breathed and lived for my work. If it hadn't been for my housekeeper, I'd have collapsed from hunger. Now, I remembered that it was Saturday and Helen was not coming.

Before I could move, the door buzzer reverberated around the house. A visitor. Who could it be? I'd informed the captain to take me off the schedule for a while. My parents rarely came by. I doubted that my father even knew where I lived.

Puzzled, I went to the intercom and picked up the phone. "Yes?"

"Sorry to bother you sir," the doorman on duty said. "But there's a lady here to see you. Her name is Amber Davies."

Amber? Fuck. How had she found out where I lived? I should have told her but how would I have known that she would find out. Fucking Dylan. He was the only one who could have given her my address.

"Sir?" the doorman said.

"Yes, sure, show her up." I went to the door and opened it. My hands were damp with sweat.

I was a fucking mess. Nervous as hell and filthy. I hadn't showered or eaten yet. The elevator chimed and seconds later, Amber emerged. She came and stood in front of me and skewered me with an unflinching look.

My heart rapped against my ribs and rung in my ears. Her facial expression did not invite pleasantries. "Do you want to come in?"

She nodded and entered the apartment. I shut the door and followed her in. I saw my apartment through her eyes and cringed. High ceilings, marble floor, Ceiling to floor windows with sweeping views of the city.

She whipped around to face me and crossed her arms across her chest. "This is your home, right?"

"Yes," I said and closed the distance between us. "I'm sorry Amber, I shouldn't have lied to you."

The hard mask she wore melted away and she looked at me with eyes filled with pain. It pierced straight into my heart. I longed to take her into my arms but first I had to convince her that the intention had not been to hurt her.

"Why did you?" Amber said, her voice wracked with pain.

My skin burned hot and cold. Terror gripped me at the realization of how close I was to losing her. I fisted my hands to stop them from shaking.

"Because of all this," I said, gesturing around the apartment. I'd been a fool not to tell her.

Her gaze darted around the apartment before returning to me. She shook her head. "I don't understand."

I inhaled a deep breath. I had to tell her the truth. It was the only chance I had. "I never bring a woman home. The reason for that is because once she sees how I live, I'll never know if she likes me for me or because I'm wealthy."

Her eyes widened. "And you're a part-time firefighter?"

I nod. "I got a trust fund from my maternal grandparents when I turned twenty-five. It means that I never have to work if I don't want to." I surprised myself by admitting that to her. No one knew this apart from my family.

Liz was turning twenty-five the following year and she was also going to have access to her trust fund.

"So, you thought that if I knew you were rich, I would do what exactly?"

"I knew you were different pretty quickly, but by then it was too late to tell you. I'm so sorry Amber. You're the most special woman I've ever met and the last thing I'd want to do is to hurt you."

Her eyes were wet. "Where have you been for the last five days?"

"Sculpting," I said. "Meeting you, seeing how brave you were being after your bakery burned down inspired me to go back to my passion. Sculpting."

She stared at me. "You can't lie to me anymore, Brody."

I nodded frantically. A voice inside my head reminded me that I hadn't told her about my father. Fear wrapped itself around my heart. I didn't want to lose her just when I'd found her.

I'd tell her with time and in my own way. If I told her now that my father was the man who had tried to get her to sell her building forcefully, she would walk out of my door, and I'd never see her again.

Tears dropped from her eyes. I took a step forward and waited for her permission to touch her. She nodded and I swooped in and took her in my arms.

"I've missed you," I said, holding her tighter than I probably should have. "Am I hurting you?"

"No," she said and clung to me. "I've missed you too."

It felt so fucking good to hold her. Her body felt as if it had melted into mine and we had become one. I buried my face in her hair and inhaled her sweet scent. I didn't know how it had happened. One moment we were fooling around, and the next, I couldn't bear to lose her.

I suddenly became aware of how filthy and stinky I was. Reluctantly, I drew back. Amber raised an eyebrow.

"I need a shower and a change of clothes. I've been sculpting all day and lost track of time," I said.

"Can I see what you've been working on," Amber said, her eyes twinkling.

I hesitated. It had been so long since I'd shown anyone my work. The last person to see a piece I'd been working on had been my father. I pushed away memories of his snarling expression as he had looked at it as if it was a pile of junk.

"You don't have to if you're not ready," she said.

"No, it's fine. Come." I led the way down the hallway to my studio. The floor was tiled unlike the rest of the apartment and the walls painted a stark white color. Light flooded the room from the extra-large window which was the reason I'd chosen it as my studio.

My muscles went rigid as I waited for Amber's reaction to the piece I'd been working on.

"Can I touch it?" she asked softly.

"Sure," I said. "Just be careful of the edges. They're still a bit rough."

Amber picked up my bearded man gingerly and stared at him. "He looks so real." No one could fake the awe in her voice. "As if he'll start talking at any moment."

Pleasure swamped me. "Thank you, that's the greatest compliment anyone has ever paid me."

She turned to look at me. "That means that you haven't shown your work to a lot of people."

She was right. I hadn't but before abandoning it, I'd had a gallery buy every piece I finished. The owner had made me promise that if I ever did go back to sculpting, I would contact them.

I told Amber about selling my pieces to the gallery.

"That must have been so awesome for you," she said, her whole face lit up. "Even better for the people who bought your pieces. They must be so happy to get to look at such art in their homes every day."

"I've never looked at it that way," I admitted to her.

"How long have you been sculpting for?" she asked.

"About seven years. I used to paint and draw until I discovered the joy of making something I could touch and hold. I've never looked back since then, until—" I stopped abruptly.

"Until what?" Amber said, carefully replacing the bearded man on my worktable.

I took a deep breath. "My father has never been supportive of my sculpting. At all. He was pretty vocal about his thoughts on art as a whole."

"Oh," Amber said. "What's the problem with art?"

"According to my father, it's for wimps," I said, my chest filling up with emotion.

"That's bullshit," Amber said harshly, making me laugh.

The tension I'd been feeling dissipated. "I think I agree with that now. I believed him for many years. But I realized sculpting was the only work that made me feel whole and purposeful."

"I don't like your father very much," she announced.

I was startled for a second.

"Even though I've never met him," she continued. "What about your mother? What does she think?"

"I don't know. She keeps out of it." My mother had no backbone. Not when it came to my father anyway. She agreed with everything he said and even when she clearly disagreed, she would never come out and say it openly.

It had always been that way for as long as I could remember. I didn't understand her, and I'd stopped trying.

"Well," Amber said cheerfully. "You have another supporter in addition to your sister. Me."

"Thank you," I said, her words touching me more than I could express. "And now I really do need to take that shower."

"Okay but I think you smell great," she said with a laugh.

"Liar." I blew her a kiss and left the studio.

I was flying to my bedroom rather than walking. That's how great I felt. A weight had been lifted off my chest. Amber didn't think I was a fool for thinking I could make sculpting my full-time job. If anything, she had looked impressed with my work. And that made me feel like a million dollars.

AMBER

I understood Brody so much better. The restlessness and the pieces that hadn't added up. Introducing me to this sister and not his parents. From the way he had described them, I wasn't surprised that he was reluctant to let me meet them.

It was odd to think of Brody as wealthy, but it really didn't matter. He was still Brody but knowing that he had this great big passion made me feel a whole lot closer to him. I got now why he always seemed as if he was in a rush. It was the restlessness that came from not pursuing your passion.

I lifted the bearded man again. He was so gifted. I couldn't believe he had carved such realness with his hands. Such beauty. I suddenly ached for him with an urgency that could not wait until he came from the shower.

Unfamiliar with the layout of the massive apartment, I went in search of his room. Following the sounds of the shower, I entered the master bedroom that was bigger than my living room.

I took in the French doors that led to a gorgeous patio and the huge bed that sat in the middle of the room. I longed to throw myself on it, but I had more urgent business. In the bathroom.

I pushed the first of two doors open and a blast of steam hit my face. I stepped in and shut the door. The bathroom was all glass, mirrors and marble. It felt like stepping into a five-star hotel bathroom.

Brody was in the gorgeous shower cubicle and as soon as he noticed me, he slid the door open and stood under the water. I couldn't take my eyes off his gorgeous body. I drooled at his muscled chest and arms, imagining them around me.

My attention was captured by his cock. It was thick and jutting out of his body. I couldn't wait to wrap my hand around it. Slowly I undressed, popping off the buttons of my blouse first before shrugging out of it.

Brody kept his hungry gaze on me and when I tossed my bra to the floor, he gripped his steel hard cock and stroked it with his right hand. My pussy throbbed with the urge to have him inside me.

"That is hot," I said as I lowered my pants, with my gaze glued to the movement of his hand.

He pumped his hand faster. Wetness seeped out of me and dampened my panties. I pulled down my panties and strolled to the shower. I made myself move slowly as though I wasn't in a rush.

Brody used his free hand to turn off the shower. "You are so beautiful."

I sunk to my knees and pried his hand off his cock. I replaced it with mine and kissed the tip of it. It was wet with water and precum. I stuck out my tongue and licked it dry.

Brody let out a deep, loud groan. I took his cock into my mouth and sucked it. It felt so good to take him into my mouth and to hear the sounds of pleasure coming from him.

I licked him everywhere, including the undersides of his balls and his inner thighs. His scent was everywhere. Masculine and sexy. I hoped that it would cling to me and not wash off.

Brody rocked into my mouth, moving faster and faster. His balls tightened and his moans turned to groans. I increased the suction in my mouth and squeezed his balls with my hand.

With a loud growl, Brody exploded into my mouth, and I greedily swallowed every last drop of his cream. When his cock stopped throbbing, I rose to my feet and Brody cupped my face and kissed me.

I draped my hands around his neck and pressed my aching nipples against his chest. He dropped his hands to cup my breasts. I almost came as he squeezed my nipples.

"That feels so good," I moaned, thrusting out my chest.

He tugged at them and pulled gently.

"Oh God, Brody." It had been so long since he had touched me.

He lowered his head and swirled his tongue around a nipple before taking it into his mouth. Jolts of pleasure shot straight from my nipples to my pussy. My thighs dampened as arousal juices leaked out.

I grasped his head and pushed him down. I needed relief in my throbbing pussy. He chuckled and followed my urging. He assumed the position I'd been in, dropping to his knees and spreading my legs apart.

"I can smell your arousal," he said, his voice gruff.

His first touch with his tongue had me screaming and gripping his head tightly. He held my thighs firmly as they quivered and threatened to give way.

"Fuck, fuck, fuck," I cried. The pleasure was almost unbearable.

His tongue probed my pussy, leaving nowhere untouched. He thrust it in and out, mimicking his cock when he fucked me. I rocked against his face, with a mounting desperation to come.

Just as I was on the verge of coming, Brody withdrew his tongue and stood up. He turned me around as I protested.

"Hands on the wall," he said.

I giggled. "Am I under arrest?"

"Yes," he said, the words leaving his mouth almost inaudible.

I inhaled deeply and did as he asked. "I can't wait for the punishment." I wiggled my ass and Brody inhaled sharply.

I closed my eyes when I felt the tip of his cock nudge my folds. Brody drove into me hard, and I cried out as pleasure swamped me. Strange noises left my mouth, but I didn't care. All that mattered was the heated steel rod that was driving in and out of me.

Wild sensations charged through me and moments later, an orgasm was rocking through me. I dropped one hand between my legs and played with my clit as I came, intensifying my pleasure.

"Amber," Brody roared before filling my pussy with his cum.

We rocked together until our bodies became still. Brody withdrew his cock and pulled me to him. He reached out to turn on the water and then held me tight as the sprays of water came down on us.

I lay my head on his chest and luxuriated in the feel of his hardness against me. I mused over what I'd learned about Brody and was grateful that I'd decided to confront him.

"Shower time," Brody said and reached for a bottle of shower gel. He poured some in his hands and rubbed it all over my body.

I loved how big and gentle his hands were. He cleaned me everywhere and as I rinsed off, he gave himself another quick wash.

"I can't tell you how many times I've imagined you in this bathroom," Brody said as he turned off the shower.

We stepped out of the shower and Brody wrapped a massive white towel around me. He gave me a gentle push out of the bathroom. I couldn't get over how big Brody's bedroom was. I hadn't paid attention to the views when I first entered but they were breathtaking.

I moved to the windows and just stared out in awe at the sweeping views of the city.

"This is the reason why I chose this apartment. The windows," Brody said, coming to stand behind me.

He placed his hands on my shoulders.

"It's beautiful. If I lived here, I'd never leave it," I said and sighed contentedly.

Brody laughed. "I doubt that very much. You couldn't bear to be away from your cookies."

"True," I said. "Speaking of cookies, someone gave me the idea of baking from home to service my bigger clients before the bakery is back on its feet."

"Hey, that's a fantastic idea Amber," Brody said enthusiastically. "If you like, you can even use my kitchen."

I turned around to face him and slipped my hands around his neck. "That's kind of you but I don't need a lot of space."

Brody's stomach growled. He made a sheepish face. "Can you tell that I haven't eaten since breakfast?"

"I'll whip up something fast," I said, already excited at the thought of cooking in what was sure to be a well-equipped kitchen.

Brody's kitchen was better than I had imagined. Stainless steel appliances, marble countertops and an industrial sized stove that wouldn't have looked out of place in a hotel kitchen.

His fridge and cabinets were well stocked too. "Do you cook?" I peered into the fridge and settled on omelets. Brody got the pan and spoon out.

"I like cooking," he said. "Though I haven't been doing much of that lately during the weekends."

"Weekdays?" I asked as I took the knife and cutting board from him. I washed the tomatoes and onions.

"Hellen cooks during the week," Brody said.

I raised an eyebrow. "Hellen?"

"Yes, she's my housekeeper and does a little of everything."

I shouldn't have been surprised that Brody had a house-keeper. People who lived in penthouses had housekeepers and chefs. If they could afford to buy such apartments, they could definitely afford to pay for the staff.

"Does it bother you that I have a housekeeper?" Brody asked me.

"No, of course not, it's exactly the kind of lifestyle that I'm used to," I said, adopting a posh accent.

Brody laughed.

"It doesn't matter, honestly," I said, meaning every word.

While I cooked the omelets, Brody turned on the coffee machine and made us some coffee. When everything was ready, we set the food on the island and sat down on the stools.

Brody locked his gaze onto me. "How is the fire investigation going?"

"It's going. They are pretty sure that it's arson," I said. "And they are also almost a hundred percent sure that my ex had something to do with it." I inhaled deeply as I remembered running into him earlier. "I'm starting to think they might be right."

"Why?" Brody said.

"I ran into Carson today. Twice in the space of an hour. The first time I was having coffee with my friend Julie, I thought I saw someone like him. The second time I was walking home. I ran after him and confronted him." Saying it out aloud upset me again.

A hard look came over Brody's face. "That asshole is stalking you again?"

"I'm not sure," I said. "But this time I'm not going to play victim." I'd cowered from him the last time. I had no plan, but I knew that I wasn't going to be a hunted mouse.

"Move in with me," Brody said. "I'll feel safer knowing that you're near me. Plus, the security in this building is top notch."

That was the kind of thing I wasn't prepared to do again. The last time, before Carson was slapped with a restraining order, I'd moved in with Timber. I wasn't ready to leave my home again because of him.

"That's sweet of you to offer but I'll be fine. I can take care of myself," I said.

"I wish you'd consider it," Brody insisted. "Such people are unpredictable. I wouldn't forgive myself if he hurt you."

"Brody, as attracted as we are to each other, we haven't known each other for long. I can't move into your apartment. That's too much," I said.

"Okay then, I'll move into yours," he said with a straight face.

I stretched my hands. "And leave all this?"

He didn't smile. "In a heartbeat."

His words brought unexpected tears into my eyes. "Thank you. I appreciate the thought but really, I'll be fine. Besides, it could easily have been a coincidence, else I'd have noticed him following me before."

I could see that Brody was not pacified but he didn't pursue the matter further. We stacked the dishes we had used in the dishwasher and carried our coffee to the living room. We lay on the couch and sipped our coffee while talking, getting to know one another.

AMBER

Gordon, the contractor, was still doing his estimates when I got to the bakery. I walked around, taking care not to step on debris and pieces of charred and broken equipment.

I couldn't get used to seeing my bakery in that state and my throat tightened with emotion. I checked to see that Gordon was still doing his estimates and went out through the back door and walked to the entrance.

I was so lost in thought, that I didn't see that horrible real estate gray-haired man from weeks ago who had come, wanting to buy our retail space. The smile on his face did not reach his eyes.

"Miss. Davies, I was hoping to run into you," he said, his beady eyes boring into mine.

"Hello." I'd been taught by my parents to always be polite no matter how annoying a person was. My father had firmly believed that everyone deserved to be heard.

I tried to remember his name and failed. When he had first come to the bakery with the proposal, I'd been impressed by my first impression. He was clearly wealthy going by the well-cut clothes he wore.

He was tall and had a commanding presence with a booming voice that spoke of someone clearly used to having his orders obeyed instantly. When I'd turned down his offer, his features had turned ugly, and he had almost threatened me. I didn't want to let my imagination carry me away by linking him to the fire.

I made myself remember that the city was full of aggressive and greedy people in the real estate industry.

"I'm sorry about the fire," he said, sounding anything but sorry. "I bet you lost hundreds of thousands of dollars."

"We did, yes," I said, wishing he would just go away.

"Are you willing to be more reasonable now?" he said. "I can take all this headache away from you and give you enough to start your bakery elsewhere."

"Enough to start a new bakery elsewhere?" I said, raising an eyebrow.

"Yes," he said. "Surely, you don't think I'd offer you the same as the last time. This property is practically worthless now."

"I wouldn't sell even if you offered me a million dollars," I said, thrusting out my chin in defiance.

He shrugged as if it didn't matter either way. "It's your loss young lady. If you ever do change your mind—"

"I won't," I said and took a step inside the kitchen.

He took my cue and left, pausing at the corner to glance at me. Relief surged through me when he turned to go without another word.

～

"**W**hat the hell happened here?"

I whipped around to find Timber staring at the charred remains of the bakery kitchen, a shocked expression on his face.

"Who is this?" Gordon said.

"He's my brother," I said, hurrying across the ruined floor while cursing internally. I hadn't thought that Timber would come straight to the bakery when he came home.

He stared around him in disbelief. I hurried to him and wrapped my arms around him. "You should have called me."

"I wanted to surprise you by coming home a few days early," he said, the horror he was feeling reflected on his face. "Why the fuck didn't you call me Amber?"

"Because there was nothing you could have done and nobody got hurt Timber," I said.

He pulled me close and held me. "You should have called and asked them to find me. What happened?"

He frowned as I recounted the events from the night of the fire. I hated that he had found out in the way he had. I squeezed his hand as I spoke, reminding him that everything had worked out okay.

"I'll tell you the rest of it," I said, after giving him a summarized version. "Let me wrap up with the contractor and then we can go somewhere for coffee."

Gordon and I spoke for a couple of minutes and went through what the fire had affected structurally. Timber recovered enough to contribute a little and ask questions. When we were done, Timber and I left and headed to the coffee shop down the street.

"I'm still in shock," he said after we had ordered coffee. "The insurance company will pay though?"

I shook my head and took a deep breath. "They are suspecting arson."

Shock and anger drew themselves on Timber's face. "Do they know who it is?"

"No, but they suspect Carson," I said.

Timber looked thoughtful for a moment. "Why would he do that? I don't see him doing that. After he was served with the restraining order, he has pretty much kept away, hasn't he?"

"Sort of," I said and told Timber about running into him.

"Fucking asshole," Timber said. "This time you can't convince me not to give him a beating and you have to move into my place. I'll feel safer knowing you're nearby."

"What about when you go away on assignment?" I asked.

"I won't. I'll ask for local assignments," Timber said.

"You can't do that," I said. His most lucrative assignments were those which involved travel and staying out of civilization. He was getting more of those now which was great for his career.

He stared at me. "You're my only family Amber. I'll do anything for you."

I decided that it was a good time to tell him about Brody. "I know, thanks." I reached across the table to squeeze his hand. "It won't be necessary. Brody keeps an eye on me and to be honest most days, I'm either at his place or he's at mine."

"Who is Brody?" Timber asked.

I grinned. "Sort of a boyfriend. He's a part-time firefighter and an artist." I felt so proud to add that last part.

Warmth spread through me as I recalled what Brody had said about me inspiring him to go back to his sculpting.

"Wow," Timber said, looking intrigued. "That was fast. I've only been gone for what? Three weeks?"

I giggled. "I'd sort of met him before you left but it was too soon to say anything."

"I want to meet him," Timber said. "But I'm happy for you. Really happy."

"Thanks. Speaking of which, did the lineage guys get in touch with you?" I asked him.

"No idea," Timber said. "I had an urgency to see you when I got back, so I came straight here. Now, I understand why." He reached into his pocket. "I'll check now."

He fished out his phone and typed into it. I sipped my coffee and allowed my mind to drift to Brody. Things were happening so fast between us that it was almost frightening.

But more than the fear was an excitement for the future that I hadn't felt or wanted to feel in years.

"Fuck," Timber mattered. "I can't believe that this is happening." He looked up and stared into nothingness, and then glanced down at his phone again.

"What?" I asked. Nothing fazed my big brother so whatever he was reading had to be huge.

"They've sent both of our results. They've found our relatives, Amber," he said, his eyes dazed.

My heart pounded so hard I could hear it thrashing in my ears. After we'd sent off the DNA samples, and Timber had left town, I hadn't given much thought to it. "Oh," I said.

I changed seats and went to sit by Timber's side. I read the email. Apparently, they had found Timber's relatives, a mother and two sisters. As for me, they had found a woman named Janice, who was my cousin.

"Are you going to write to her?" Timber asked me.

I felt as though all air had left my lungs. I wasn't ready to write to anyone but seeing the excitement on Timber's face, I couldn't say no.

"What about you?" I asked him. "They found your mother and sisters Timber."

A look of vulnerability came over his features. I could see how badly he wanted to reach out to them.

"Let's write to them. We can copy one email to all three of them," I said.

His Adam's apple bobbed up and down as he swallowed saliva. "Okay. Let's do it but not to my mother. Let's email my sisters as feelers," he said and stared at me. "It's odd to say that and not be talking about you."

I laughed. "I know but I'm good with sharing. As long as I'll always be your first little sister."

He grew solemn. "I promise." He opened his email. "What do I say?"

"Introduce yourself and tell them how you found them. Then ask them if their mother would be willing to get in touch with you," I said.

"Okay but on one condition. After we finish with mine, we'll write to your cousin Janice. She probably has a lot of information about your birth mother," Timber said.

I wished we could have dropped the whole thing. Finding out that I had a cousin hadn't changed anything. I wasn't interested in connecting with my blood relatives. They were strangers as far as I was concerned. Being related by blood did not make strangers your family.

"Fine," I said.

"You won't regret it," Timber said, returning to his email.

I raised an eyebrow and took out my phone. It blinked with a new message and when I clicked on it, I saw that it was from Brody.

Brody: *Can I coax you into coming for lunch? I make a mean Chicken stir fry.*

I smiled, stupidly happy at hearing from him as well as the invitation. Plus, I desperately needed to speak to someone other than Timber.

Me: *I'm sold. I'll be there as soon as I can.*

"Done," Timber said and stared at his phone as if he expected his blood relations to pop out from it at any moment. "Your turn Amber. We're doing this together."

For the first time ever, I was relieved to part ways with my brother. All Timber could talk about was possible scenarios. I was happy for him, but I couldn't make myself excited about connecting with my cousin Janice.

If anything, I was hoping that she would not answer my email and that would be the end of that. I parked my car outside Brody's apartment building and made my way to the entrance. I had become friendly with all the door men and the one on duty smiled at me and gave me a friendly bow.

I entered the elevator and rode it to the penthouse apartment. Despite having been to Brody's place numerous times, I still couldn't get over how fancy and gorgeous it was.

The door was unlocked, and I entered and shut it behind me. I followed whistling to the kitchen where I found Brody setting the informal dining table.

"There you are," he said, grinning as if seeing me was the highlight of his day.

He made me feel special with the way he looked at me and spoke to me. It was the same for me too. He made me feel happy even though I had no reason to feel that way.

"Hi," I said, and went straight into his open arms.

I let out a sigh as his strong arms circled me.

"God, you feel so good," Brody said, pressing my body against his.

"So do you," I said, inhaling his manly scents.

He kissed the top of my head and drew back to look into my eyes. "How did the meeting with the contractor go?"

"Good," I said. "Until Timber came to surprise me."

"Oh shit," Brody said.

I nodded. "Let me wash my hands and tell you all about it."

I went on tip toe to kiss him and then headed to the visitor's washroom. I did my business and splashed water on my face. Back in the kitchen, I found lunch already on the table. Brody pulled out a chair for me.

"Thanks. That looks delicious," I said, eyeing the bowls of chicken stir fry and rice.

Brody spooned healthy helpings onto two plates and slid one in front of me. I took my first spoonful. "Perfect." Bursts of flavor filled my mouth. "You're a good cook Mr. Brody."

"Thank you," Brody said. "Timber must have gotten the shock of his life?"

BRODY

I felt sorry for Amber's brother as I pictured him expecting to find a running business and instead, he had found a burned bakery. Fresh guilt washed over me as Amber recounted the whole tale.

"That's not all." Amber wiped her mouth and pushed her plate away. "I told you I was adopted, right?"

I nodded.

"Well, before he left, Timber had convinced me that we should send samples of our DNA to this company that hooks up people with their relatives," she said and paused.

"Go on."

"We both did it and Timber sent off the samples. That was the end of it for me and besides so much happened after that. Timber checked his email today and there was correspondence from that company."

"How exciting." I searched Amber's face. She spoke like a robot, revealing nothing of what she was feeling or thought about the news.

"Timber found his mother and two sisters and for me, there's a cousin called Janice."

I guessed from her flat voice that it wasn't exactly good news. "Are you going to contact her?"

"I already did. Timber is so excited by the whole thing, but I'll be honest, I'm not. I've never been interested in finding my biological parents. Ever," she said harshly.

"Why? From what I've gathered over the years, most adopted kids' biggest wish was to find their biological relatives," I said.

Amber tapped the table with her index finger without seemingly being aware of it. A conflicted look came over her pretty face. Nothing could mar her beauty. Not even when she was in emotional distress as she was then.

"I met this girl at camp many years ago when we were both teenagers. Like me, she had been adopted at birth and her lifelong ambition was to find her birth parents. Unlike me however, she had horrible parents. They had their own biological daughter five years after adopting her and they treated her like a second-class citizen."

I knew there were heart-breaking stories in the world of adoption but hearing one from Amber made it even more painful. It made the stuff I went through with my father look like kids play.

"Anyway, she did find her biological mother and she got to meet her. Only, it turned out to be a disappointment. She had expected an instant connection, but she felt nothing and neither did her biological mother."

Understanding dawned.

"So, you see, a lot of times, it's not what you dream it will be and it ends up leaving you with a big fat hole in your chest."

The naked vulnerability on her face made my heart twist with pain. I pushed my chair back. "Come here."

Amber got up and came and sat on my lap. She threw her hands around me and buried her face in my neck. I held her tightly, wishing I could protect her from any and all the pain of the world.

"Maybe you should have told your brother that you were not ready to contact your cousin yet," I said after a moment.

"He would have been so disappointed and then there's also the fact that I'll never be ready," Amber said softly. "I might as well do it now."

Holding her with our clothes between us was not enough. I stood up and carried her with me.

"Where are we going?" she said.

"To my bedroom. I want to make love to you," I said. "Right now, it's the only way I can think of to make you feel better."

"I approve," she murmured.

I kicked the door shut behind us and set her on the edge of the bed. Grateful that she was wearing a dress, I knelt between her legs and caressed her thighs. Something powerful passed between us as we stared into each other's eyes.

I pushed her skirt up so that it bunched at the top of her thighs and spread her legs. I inhaled sharply at the visible wet patch at the front of her panties.

"I love how wet you are," I growled and dragged my fingers over the top of her panties.

A look of pure need filled Amber's eyes. She spread her legs further, giving me better access. I pulled her panties to one side and groaned loudly at the sight of her dripping pussy.

"Fuck Amber," I said as I lowered my mouth to her pussy.

Her womanly scents invaded my nostrils, and I flattened my tongue and swept along her folds, licking her pussy clean.

"You taste so fucking good," I said and went in for another taste and another. "I need these gone," I growled moments later.

I pulled down her panties and Amber raised her hips, giving me space to drag them all the way down. I felt as if I'd received the gift of a lifetime as she spread her legs again and bared her pussy for me.

I ignored the raw need racing through me and my painfully throbbing cock. I teased her clit, alternating that with fucking her with my tongue. Her fingers dug into my scalp and her moans filled the room.

I teased her and felt her orgasm draw nearer with every thrust of my tongue. When she came, her pussy tightened against my tongue, and she let out a series of whimpers that went straight to my cock. I licked her until her pussy stopped throbbing and then I gently pulled her dress over her head.

She unclasped her bra and shrugged out of it. I undressed and stared hungrily at her full breasts as Amber lay on the bed waiting for me. I wanted nothing more than to bury my aching cock into her sweet tight pussy but first, I wanted to relieve the ache in her nipples.

I joined her on the bed and wrapped my lips around one nipple. Amber groaned and raked her fingers through my hair. I loved how hard and pointed her nipples were. I sucked each nipple hard and swirled my tongue around it.

"I want you, Brody. I want your cock inside," she said, moments later.

My cock lurched as if it had understood Amber's words. She lifted her legs onto my shoulders, and I slid up until my cock was aligned at the entrance of her pussy.

Instead of plunging in like I desperately wanted to, I slid it up and down her slick pussy. Amber groaned and raised her hips, pressing her pussy to my cock.

"Please Brody," she begged.

I grinned. "I love hearing you beg for my cock."

She narrowed her eyes. "I'll pay you back for that." Her eyes rolled to the back of her head when I pushed my cock in inch by inch.

I drove all the way in until my balls rested on her ass. I pulled out and groaned loudly as her walls clenched my cock as though milking it. I wanted it to be slow but looking at her eyes wild and wide with passion, I lost all control and pounded into her.

She cried out with every thrust before her cries turned into whimpers. How had I gotten so lucky to meet her that day in the bar? And then again when I burned her bakery? I pushed away thoughts of the one of two secrets that would make me lose her if she found out.

I kept my hands on her thighs as I drove in and out of her. It felt as though I was fucking her deeper and harder than any other time. Sounds of our bodies slapping against each other filled the room, interspersed with our moans of pleasure.

I felt her pussy clench around my cock, and I knew that she was as close to coming as I was.

"Come for me sweetheart," I said, my balls tightening with the need for release.

"Oh God, yes," Amber cries, twisting her head from side to side. Her red hair covered her face and I reached down to smooth it away.

I wanted to see every emotion drawn on her face.

"Yes, yes, yes," Amber moaned as the orgasm thundered through her body.

I roared as I blew up inside her with the force of a storm. I gently lowered her legs from my shoulders and draped my body over hers and kissed her.

"You're so fucking sweet Amber," I said in between kisses.

She cupped my face. "So are you. I never knew it could be like this." Her cheeks pinked up.

Pleasure swamped me at her words. No woman had ever said anything like that to me. I had affected her in the same way she was affecting me. I'd slept with more women than I could count. That wasn't a brag. It was simply the way it was. But none of those women had made me feel like Amber did.

As if we had become one in that moment when our bodies were joined together.

I gently withdrew my cock and lay down on my back pulling Amber to lie on top of me. We held each other without speaking. A sense of peace descended on me. I was going to enjoy what we had as long as I could because I knew for a fact that it would come to an end.

Amber let out a sigh. "You've turned a horrible day into a memorable one."

I stroked her hair. "I think you handled Timber's surprise return pretty well."

"Thanks," Amber said. "I told him about you. He can't wait to meet you."

Guilt rose up my throat. In normal circumstances, I would have loved to meet anyone associated with Amber. But knowing the part I had played in destroying their business made me reluctant to meet her brother.

"Me too," I managed to say.

"That part wasn't too bad," Amber said, softly running her fingers over my chest. "But prior to that, this real estate person had come by. I'm not sure if I told you about him, probably not. He came by to offer to buy us out again. He's the most distasteful person I've ever met."

–the fuck?? My father had gone to see her again. I was so angry I could feel my muscles quivering. What the fuck was wrong with him? He knew that I was seeing Amber. Why would he do something like that without talking about it first with me?

The answer was straight forward. My father always did what he wanted without a care for how his actions would affect someone else. I thought of my mother and the emotional turmoil she had gone through over the years at her husband's hands.

It was no secret that my father lived like a bachelor until he got home to his wife in the evening. I hated that my mother allowed him to get away with it.

But I hated this more. If only he had stayed away. Maybe Amber would have forgotten how he looked when they eventually met. I couldn't keep them apart forever. At some point, Amber was going to meet my parents. And when she did, that would be the end of us.

"What did you tell him?"

"He had the audacity to tell me that the bakery was worth crap now and I was lucky he was willing to offer me something for it. I told him that I wouldn't sell it to him for a million dollars," Amber said.

Despite everything, I laughed. I could easily imagine how pissed off my father had been. He was not a man used to people opposing him.

AMBER

If there was one thing I'd missed about going to work very early in the morning, it was the sunrise. I stood outside my apartment building with a backpack strapped on my back and enjoyed the streaks of orange and purple in the skies.

Brody had asked me to be ready by six, but I'd been ready way earlier and I'd decided to wait for him downstairs. There was something about early morning, especially on Sundays, when it was silent and still. I loved hearing myself breathe and think.

I'd been busy in the last week, baking from home and meeting with the contractor. He estimated that the bakery would be ready for business in six weeks. Which was good news as I'd expected it to take months.

The noise of a car engine brought me back to the present and I smiled when I sighted Brody's fancy SUV cruising towards me. I went to the passenger door and opened it when the car came to a stop.

Brody's smiling face greeted me as I hoped in. I leaned across the console between the seats and kissed him.

"Hey, you, I've missed you," he said before swooping in for another kiss. He slid his hand along my jaw as the kiss deepened.

My skin lit up and my body got all sorts of signals, forgetting that we were in a car and there was no hope for any action. I shifted in my seat when Brody broke the kiss, in an effort to reduce the ache between my legs.

"Shall we forget the hiking and go up to your apartment?" Brody said. "We can always pretend the couch is a picnic bench."

I laughed at his facial expression. "Not going to happen. I've missed hiking. I was so glad when you suggested it last night."

"Okay, hiking it is," Brody said, putting the car into gear.

He had surprised me by texting me last night and asking me if I liked hiking. I'd done a lot of hiking before opening the bakery and probably knew all the hiking trails in and around the city.

"Did you finish the batch of cookies you were baking last night?" Brody said.

We hadn't seen each other for most of the week as we'd both been busy. Me, with my cookies and Brody with his sculpting work and volunteer work at the station.

"I did," I said. "They'll be ready for delivery on Monday. What about you? How's the sculpting going?"

Brody turned to me and grinned. "Very good. I contacted the gallery I used to supply pieces to, and they are interested in showing my work again."

"Congratulations," I said. "That is so cool."

"Thanks," Brody said. "They even said that they'd be willing to give me a show if my production is consistent."

"I wish I'd brought a bottle of wine or champagne. We have to celebrate this," I said. It was such a big deal to have a leg into the art world. It shouldn't have surprised me though.

Brody's work was exceptional. The details in his pieces were unbelievable.

"I do," he said. "We'll pop it open after our hike."

We were driving out of town but for once, I wasn't too concerned about which hiking trail we were heading to. My attention was on the skies. It was like watching a professional artist at work, playing with different hues, the brighter, the better.

It took us half an hour to get to the trail. Brody parked the SUV and we got our backpacks out.

"Do you want me to carry yours?" Brody asked.

I smiled, touched by his kindness. "No thanks. It's pretty light. Just water and a few snacks."

He took my hand and completely engulfed it in his large one. I liked the feeling of safety and excitement that I felt having my hand in his. We headed up a trail surrounded by woods and overgrowths.

"I chose this one because it's easy but still has that sense of being away from everything," Brody explained as he took the lead up the slim path.

"I've never been here," I said.

"I hoped you hadn't," he said.

I wish he knew it wouldn't have mattered. Brody had sneaked into my heart. I almost laughed out aloud at the memory of how determined I had been to keep it a one-night stand. And then a two-night stand. Anything, as long as my heart was not involved.

But I was coming round to the idea of soulmates. I'd never bought into it but how else could you explain how perfectly Brody and I fit together. I'd stopped being frightened that he would turn out to be another psycho like Carson and I was now just enjoying the ride.

Further along, the path widened enough for Brody and me to walk side by side.

"Has Janice written yet?" Brody said.

"Nope," I said. "And neither have Timber's sisters." We'd spent part of the morning at the bakery, and I could see how disappointed he was. "He's really down."

"I can imagine. I'm glad you don't seem too affected by the silence," Brody said.

"That's because I'd prepared myself for disappointment and unlike Timber, I really have no wish to meet these people." I sounded harsh and cold-hearted but the whole thing was like walking into a fire with your eyes wide open."

"Even if I found my close relatives, what difference would it make? They would be complete strangers and no amount of talking could make up for time not spent together."

Brody draped an arm around me. "I get it. I think you'd see it differently though if you met them."

I knew I wouldn't, but I had no wish to argue about it with Brody. "Maybe you're right."

The trail was beginning to slope a little but nothing too strenuous. "So, what made you decide to volunteer at the fire station?" I hoped that it wasn't obvious that I was changing the topic.

"I've always admired firefighters for the difference they make in people's lives," he said. "Cops as well."

"Why didn't you go full-time then?"

"Probably because subconsciously, I knew that I wanted to devote a lot of my time to my sculpting. I just got derailed for a few years."

"You can't let that happen again," I said with feeling.

"I won't."

"I can't tell you how grateful I was for the money from the Victim's fund," I said. "So was Timber. He wants to come to the station himself to say thank you."

"It's not necessary," Brody said. "Besides they think the bakery is yours a hundred percent. It will just bring on more explanations."

I didn't get the issue of explanations. All we needed to tell them was that my brother was a silent partner in the business. Still, Brody worked at the station and knew best how things worked over there.

A gently swirling sound reached my ears and I gripped Brody's hand and made him stop. "Listen, what could that be?" I whispered.

Brody grinned. "Come and see."

I begged him to give me clues but he wouldn't, and I kept guessing until we burst out of an opening.

"A waterfall!" I cried, staring in wonder at the water cascading down a rocky waterfall. "It's beautiful."

We went closer and admired the clear bed of water underneath. Brody helped me up a plateau of a rock and we plopped down on it.

"This is perfect," Brody said.

I was about to agree with him but when I met his gaze, it was on me. I flushed with embarrassment. I wasn't used to being showered with compliments all the time.

I busied myself with unpacking the sandwiches and water I'd brought. "Hungry?" I said, handing Brody a foil wrapped sandwich.

"Yes please," he said and took the grilled chicken sandwich.

I inhaled fresh air as a breeze blew across. I'd never gone on a hike with a date as I always deemed it as a bad idea. But with Brody, it was a natural experience. There was no awkwardness between us, and he was fit and clearly enjoyed hiking.

I wanted to know so much about him, but I'd noticed that he wasn't very forthcoming with information even after I'd found out that he came from a wealthy background.

"Are you still in touch with your childhood friends?" I asked him in between bites of my sandwich.

"No, not really," Brody said.

"How come?"

"I went to these fancy schools where everyone's big interest was who was driving what and where the next exotic vacation would be," he said.

"It doesn't sound half bad," I teased.

Brody didn't laugh. "It's a shallow life and it doesn't end with school. It follows you even when you're an adult. Those kids cared little for giving back or contributing to the community. I didn't like it then and I don't like it now."

Admiration flowed through me. I knew Brody was deep, but I didn't think that it went as far as shunning the kids he had grown up with.

"How do your parents take that?" I asked. "Your sister seems to be different too."

"She thinks as I do, thank God. My father suspects that our mother secretly adopted us." As soon as the words were out of his mouth, Brody gasped. "I'm sorry. That's a stupid and insensitive joke."

"Relax," I said laughing. "People say those kinds of things all the time. If I allowed myself to get hurt, I'd be hurting for five days out of seven."

"You're so cool," Brody said, looking at me as if I was the most exciting thing that had ever happened to him. "What about you Amber, have you carried your friends from your past forward?"

I laughed at the way he'd put it. "I didn't either but only because we all sort of drifted away from each other. I have Julie though. We were best friends when we were teenagers and then she moved away."

We exchanged stories from our past and then found ourselves talking about traveling. Brody had traveled extensively, and it was nice to hear his opinions of different parts of the world.

"As much as you dislike the world in which you grew up, it has enabled you to go to all sorts of exciting places," I pointed out.

"It's not the world that's a problem. It's the majority of people who occupy it," he said and reached for his backpack. "And now it's time for a glass of wine."

"I'm so proud of you," I said. "You're a professional sculptor now."

"It feels good." He uncorked the wine and poured it into traveling wine glasses.

We clinked glasses and I gave a toast to his future. We sipped the wine and kissed. His lips tasted of wine and freshness.

"Thank you for bringing me here," I said. "I could stay here all day."

"I could too, as long as we're together," Brody said, warming my insides.

The sun had come out and its rays resembled flecks of gold on the water. Suddenly I felt an urge to do something crazy. Something I'd remember for the rest of my life.

"How deep do you think that water is?" I asked.

Brody laughed. "I'm worried about where this is going. I imagine that it's quite deep. I've thrown quite a few stones in there and I've even been known to dip a long stick."

"Yeah?" I asked him and then drained the last of my wine. I set it on the rock and stood up. "Are you in or out?"

"As long as you're in, I am too," he said.

BRODY

I'd been described as crazy and even as a daredevil, but I'd never done anything as crazy as what Amber, and I were doing.

"This is pure insanity," I told her and took her hand.

"Doesn't it feel good though," she said and laughed when she saw me steal a glance around us to check if there were any peeping toms.

It did feel good to have the sun on my bare skin and to be perfectly honest, I felt the same thrill I usually did when I was bike racing illegally on the streets at night. Almost, except this time if we were caught, we'd be thoroughly humiliated.

"Ready?" Amber said.

It was a hot enough day that we were not cold at all, even with the slight breeze blowing. I tried to keep my eyes from straying to Amber's hot body. All our clothes were neatly folded and stored on the bolder we had been seating on.

"I can't believe you talked me into doing this," I said, staring at the inviting looking water.

"It didn't take much to convince you," Amber said.

"You know what surprises me about you Amber?" I said as we strolled to the edge of the water.

"What's that?" she said.

"The first impression I had of you was of a gorgeous, sensitive, quiet, albeit sexy woman," I said. "That quickly changed. You're wild and crazy and I love that about you."

She laughed and bowed. "Thank you."

I dipped my foot into the water. It was shockingly cold. I glanced back to where we had left our clothes. "We better make this fast before we get company."

"It's too early for company," Amber said.

She was right. No one was going to show up at the waterfall for the next couple of hours.

"At the count of three, we'll go in at the same, okay?"

Amber squealed. "I haven't had this much naughty fun in such a long time."

I counted down and we both went in. I pulled Amber along, laughing at her screams and shouts of how cold the water was. We moved deeper until the water was up to our waists.

As Amber was busy trying to make out what was at the bottom of the pool, I scooped water and poured it on top of her head. I took off towards the waterfall with Amber closely behind.

For the next few minutes, we horse-played in the water and ended up standing under the cascading water.

"It feels like a giant shower," Amber said.

I took her hand and pulled her against me. "You look so beautiful in the giant shower."

She draped her arms around my neck and then jumped up and wrapped her legs around my waist. I dropped my hands to cup her ass. Fuck she felt good. I lowered my head and our lips met in a hot, wet slide.

My cock grew harder as her pussy brushed against me.

"We should go home," I said, knowing very well that I was not fucking going anywhere. Not yet any way. Not before I fucked her tight pussy.

"I want you Brody," Amber said, her voice husky with need.

Any reservations I had about indecent exposure disappeared, and I gripped my cock and entered her. She whimpered and scraped my back with her fingers as I buried my cock to the hilt.

"Fuck Amber, you get sweeter each time."

My cock surged as her walls tightened around me. She moved her hips and met each of my thrusts. It didn't take long before we were both coming, fueled by the risk of getting caught.

When it was over, we stared at each other and burst out laughing. Then I lowered her gently and washed her pussy clean. I rinsed myself and we got out of the water. We lay on the boulder for a few minutes to dry off and then hurriedly dressed when we thought we had heard some noise.

Back in my apartment, we went straight to my bedroom and stripped off to warm up in bed. I made slow sweet love to Amber again and afterwards, we lay in each other's arms just talking.

"We really should get up and make lunch or something," Amber said. "I could do with a shower first."

I kissed her forehead. "Take a shower and I'll get started on lunch."

"Okay," Amber said and got up.

I ogled her as she strolled unselfconsciously to the bathroom. By the time she disappeared, my cock was beginning to swell. I shook my head. I couldn't fucking get enough of her. It was a new experience, and I was loving it.

I grabbed a pair of shorts and a t-shirt and pulled them on. I whistled as I headed to the kitchen. I flung open the fridge, stared at its contents, trying to figure out a quick lunch. There was leftover chicken which would do with a salad.

I was busy cleaning the vegetables when a loud knock came on the door, startling me. That never happened. The doorman would never allow anyone to come up without calling me first.

Frowning, I hurried out of the kitchen. I opened the door and groaned inwardly when I saw the visitor.

"Mom," I said, unable to hide my lack of enthusiasm. I remembered with a sinking feeling that my mother used to come to my apartment quite a lot when I first moved in.

Most of the doormen knew her and they would let her come up without informing me first. It hadn't bothered me then.

"Is that any way to greet your mother?" she asked as she stepped into the house.

"Sorry Mom, you caught me by surprise," I said. "You should have called to let me know you were coming."

She stared at me quizzically. "I've never called you before. Why now?"

It was at the tip of my tongue to tell her because I had a girl-friend, but I stopped myself in time. I needed her to leave. Pronto.

"Can we arrange to meet tomorrow, Mom?" I asked. "I'm kind of busy right now."

"I won't take much of your time. Is Hellen in? I could do with some coffee," she said, marching to the kitchen.

Panic rose up my throat. The last thing I wanted was for Amber and my mother to meet.

"Hellen doesn't come in on Sundays," I said, following closely behind her.

"Then you make me the coffee," she said and pulled out a chair while looking around. "You were cooking, weren't you? Are you expecting a guest?"

I turned on the coffee machine while calculating how long she would stay versus Amber's shower. Maybe she had decided to use the tub. That took longer.

"No," I said and left it at that.

"You never cease to surprise me, Brody. Why not just order a salad and have it delivered?"

My mother didn't believe in lifting a finger to do anything for herself when she could get other people to do it for her.

I gave her the coffee wordlessly and sat down on the chair opposite. "What's going on Mom?"

"Can't a mother visit her son without a reason?" she said.

I raised an eyebrow and swallowed down my impatience.

"All right," she said with a smile that made her look years younger. "I came to talk to you about your father. I think he needs to take it easy with work. He's not as young as he used to be. This working until late at night cannot be good for him."

Despite the bad blood between my father and me, I still loved him, and I wanted the best for him. "But that's how he's always been."

"I know but he's getting old and even his doctor is concerned about his heart. He needs to slow down or else…" my mother said.

"I see where you're coming from but Mom, I don't know how you think I can help. I'm the last person Dad would listen to. You know how things are between us."

"I'm not asking you to talk to him. What I want you to do is take up your responsibility at the company. That's the only way that he'll take it easy."

I shook my head even before she finished talking. "No Mom, I've told you and Dad countless times. There's no way I'm going to work at Orion. My path is different. As a matter of fact, I've gone back to sculpting and I'm already selling my pieces."

My mother stared at me as though I'd lost my mind. "And how much are they paying you for that?"

A few years ago, that would have gotten me rethinking my decision. Not anymore. I was a different person now. "It's not about the money. Thanks to my trust fund, I never need to work because of money. I'd like to use that privilege to contribute to the art world."

A throat cleared behind me. I stood up and smiled at Amber. The smile froze on my lips at the look of horror on her face. I followed her gaze down to her body. She was wearing one of my button-down shirts and she looked absolutely sexy.

"Sorry, I didn't know you had a visitor," she said.

I stood up and went to her. "It's okay. Mom, this is my girl-friend, Amber." I draped an arm around her.

My mother stood up and smiled at Amber. "It is a pleasure to meet you Amber and don't worry, I'm on my way out." she took her purse from the table. "You must bring Amber home for dinner to meet our family."

"I'd love that," Amber said. "I've met Liz and her beautiful family."

My mother stared at me with an accusing look on her face. "You took Amber to meet Liz and you haven't brought her home?"

That was the exact reason why I hadn't wanted Amber and my mother to meet.

"I'll bring her soon," I said and moved to the door.

"I'll see you soon my dear," she said to Amber, and I walked her to the front door. "I like her, Brody. For once, you've actually chosen a suitable girl."

"Thanks mom," I said. "I think so too."

"Don't forget dinner soon," she said wagging a finger and then leaned closer to me. "Women love stability. Think about what I said. Amber won't tell you this, but we like a man with a secure source of income. You'll want a family soon. The company will ensure that your family will live the kind of life that you yourself have always lived."

That was exactly the kind of life that I did not want for any family I would have in the future. My mother had completely misread Amber. She thought that she was from her privileged side of the world. A leisure woman who came from a wealthy family.

If she knew that Amber was a hard-working woman who earned her living with her own two hands, Mom would have been wary about her. She didn't understand people who were not born with a silver spoon in their mouths.

"I'll talk to you soon," I said and shut the door.

I returned to the kitchen to find Amber finishing up with the salad. She turned when she heard my footsteps. "I'm sorry. I didn't know your mother was here."

"It's fine. It's her fault for not letting me know that she was coming by." I shuddered as a thought struck me. What if it was my father who had shown up unannounced? A trickle of sweat formed on my forehead.

"Your mother is beautiful," Amber said. "She doesn't look old enough to be the mother of two grown children."

My mother would have loved to hear that. "She's had a bit of surgical help."

Amber's eyes widened. "Oh. I wouldn't have guessed."

I could see that she was shocked and understandably so. People from her part of the world didn't do such things. In the world I had grown up in though, it wasn't really a big deal.

Amber's shock however, highlighted what different worlds we came from. It didn't matter. As long as she and I understood each other.

AMBER

My phone rang as I was parking my car. I hoped it wasn't from the two customer's whose batch of cookies I'd just delivered. It had been a busy week, baking and delivering. It reminded me of how it had been before I got the bakery.

I couldn't wait for the renovations to be finished and I could return the operations to the bakery. It was inconvenient baking from home. I missed the open space in the bakery kitchen and the camaraderie that came from working with other people. I missed my staff.

I hadn't seen much of Brody either. I missed him though we spoke at least twice a day on the phone. He was busy with his work and from what I'd garnered, there was stuff going on at home. I'd caught a bit of the conversation the previous Sunday when his mother came in unannounced.

Something about Brody going to work with his father. I hoped that everything was okay with him. I'd hoped that he would invite me to go with him to dinner at his parents' place but so far, he hadn't.

His mother was different from the other women I knew but she had seemed nice, and I looked forward to getting to know her a little bit. I was usually pulled to women of a certain age as they reminded me of my mother.

I killed the engine but by then my phone had stopped ringing. I checked the screen. The call had been from Timber. I hit call. He picked up on the first ring.

"Gordon said I just missed you," Timber said after we had exchanged greetings. "Are you home?"

"Just got there," I said, detecting a note of excitement in his voice.

"Okay, I'm coming over," he said.

"See you soon." I left the car and headed to my apartment. I didn't have to think very hard about the reason why Timber had sounded excited. It had something to do with his blood relatives.

I'd written to Janice from an email I rarely used and since then, I'd not checked whether she had written back. I turned on the coffee machine and fished out my phone and logged into my email.

To my surprise, there was new mail, and it was from Janice. Panic swelled up inside me, threatening to swallow me belly first. My palms grew wet with sweat. I set my phone on the island and rubbed them dry on my pants.

I inhaled deeply and told myself not to be stupid. It was just an email and for all I knew, Janice could be saying that there was no one who had ever given up a child for adoption in their family.

The doorbell rang, saving me from reading the email just yet. I jumped and hurried to let Timber in. I waited at the door for the elevator to reach my floor.

"Hey, you," he said, bounding towards me.

"Hi," I said and kissed his cheek. I led the way to the kitchen. "I made some coffee. You sounded like you needed a cup."

He sat down. "I do, thanks."

I poured the coffee into two mugs and carried them to the island counter. "So, what's up?"

A huge smile broke on his face. "One of my sisters wrote. Apparently, they had gone on a short vacation together. That's why no one was answering my emails. They want us to meet. And the interesting thing is that they live less than twenty miles from here. Weird right?"

"Oh Timber, that is so awesome," I said, happy for him. It was what he had always wanted and dreamed of. "You said yes, of course."

He grew solemn. "Not yet. I wanted to hear your thoughts first."

"Are you crazy?" I asked. "This is what you've dreamed of for years. You have to meet them."

"It's one thing to dream of it but when it's the reality, it's a little frightening. What if we take an instant dislike to one another?"

I laughed. "That doesn't sound like you at all, Timber. You're the most confident person I have ever met. Don't let fear get the better of you." I felt like a hypocrite as I said that last sentence. I had let fear get the best of me by delaying opening Janice's email.

"You're right," he said. "I'm allowing fear to rule me. I'll write to Clara. What about you, anything new?"

I took a deep breath. "I just saw an email from Janice." My heart pounded with a mixture of excitement and nervousness and the implications of that email became clear.

Janice was someone related to me by blood. We probably even looked alike.

"What did she say?" Timber asked.

"I haven't opened it."

"What are you waiting for?" he said and drummed on the table with his fingers.

"Okay, here goes." I tapped the screen on my phone until the email appeared. It was longer than I expected.

"Read it aloud," Timber said.

"Okay. Dear Amber, first of all, what a pretty name you have. I'm sorry for taking so long to write to you. I had a bit of investigating to do. I didn't know that any of my relatives had given a baby up for adoption.

Anyway, I spoke to my mom and luckily, she did know who it was. Her older sister Audrey gave up a baby for adoption, but no one knew about it except my mom, and their parents. That would be you. We're cousins! I can't wait to meet you, and neither can my mom.

Sadly, my grandparents are no longer with us, but I know they would have loved to meet you too. My mom and I agreed that we would let my Aunty know about you first and let her take it from there. I'm so excited. She'll get in touch with you soon. Oh, and may I have your address please?"

Silence descended the room when I finished reading. Timber and I stared at one another in silence before he finally spoke up.

"It's finally happening," he said, his voice filled with awe. "We get to meet people who share the same DNA as us. Isn't it incredible?"

I gave a shaky smile. His excitement was catching. I couldn't wait to share the latest news with Brody.

"Email her back," Timber said.

"Okay," I said and typed a message out on my phone.

I told Janice how excited I had been to get her message and I also told her a little about myself. For the rest of the afternoon, Timber and I hung out and talked about the future. I liked the thought that soon, Timber and I would have a larger family. It was a comforting thought.

"**W**here are we going?" I said to Brody as he drove to an unnamed destination.

He laughed. "Patience is not one of your strongest points, is it?"

"Nope," I said, grinning.

Brody had texted me that morning to invite me to accompany him somewhere that afternoon. I'd pestered him by text and in person, but he kept his lips sealed about our destination. I relaxed in the car seat and decided to just enjoy the ride.

"Has your mother written or called?" Brody said.

My body tensed. It had been a long ass week waiting for my mother to get in touch. When sending Janice my address, I'd included a phone number and all the other ways she could get in touch with me.

I wasn't active on social media, but I'd started checking my accounts, just in case. Carson had cured me of social media with his messages of harassment. Apart from the anxiety of waiting for my mother to get in touch, everything was going great.

The bakery was coming along nicely, and we had changed the design to make work easier. In a few weeks we would be back in business, and I couldn't wait. Meanwhile, I was servicing a few of my long-term contracts and that was working out well.

The police had reached a dead end with their investigations. They couldn't pin anything on Carson or anyone else for that matter. I refused to let it worry me. Plus, he had stopped lurking in corners and appearing in my vicinity.

Timber and I had agreed that we would install CCTV cameras in and around the bakery. That gave me some level of comfort. It was frightening to imagine that there was someone out there who had torched our bakery.

"Hey, you've gone all quiet on me," Brody said, pulling me back to the present. "What are you thinking?"

"I was wondering why someone would want to burn my bakery," I said. "I don't have any enemies." A thought popped up in my head and as crazy as it was, I wanted to share it with Brody. "But what if it wasn't a personal enemy? What if it was someone who wanted something from me?"

"Like who?" Brody said.

"Like the real estate developer man who kept pestering me about selling," I said, feeling silly as I voiced my thoughts.

Real life was nothing like a movie and what I was saying sounded like something straight out of a detective movie or series.

Brody let out a chuckle. "You're overthinking it," he said. "It could have been something as simple as a mistaken address, have you considered that? Maybe the bakery was not the target."

"You could be right," I said and let out a sigh. "Anyway, it doesn't matter now. At least we're renovating and we'll soon be back at work."

"Exactly," Brody said. "Let's put that sorry business behind us. And we've reached our destination."

We were downtown. "Where exactly have we reached?"

Brody laughed. "You don't give up, do you?"

We got out of the car and crossed to the other side of the road and then walked down the street. When we stopped, I looked up at the building and when it dawned on me where we were, I grinned at Brody.

"The gallery?" I asked.

He nodded. "Let's go in."

I saw the bearded man as soon as I entered. He occupied the place of honor on a stand in the middle of the gallery floor. I stopped and stared at him in awe, and then at Brody.

"You are so talented," I said.

"Thank you."

"Brody?" a man said, coming towards us.

"Hi Fred," Brody said and shook hands with him. "This is my girlfriend, Amber. I'd told you I would bring her around. Amber, this is Fred, he's the owner of this gallery."

Pleasure swamped me. Brody had told the gallery owner that he would bring me. I wanted to play it cool and act like it meant nothing. But it meant the world. It meant that all the feelings swirling inside me were not unreciprocated. Brody felt it too.

Fred gave me a tour of the gallery, but I kept glancing back at the bearded man. He looked so regal and at home. As if he was sitting on a throne and was the owner of the gallery.

I listened to Brody and Fred discuss his production and how often he could have pieces done. Fred also said that he had two serious buyers interested in the bearded man.

As happy as I was to hear that he would be leaving the gallery, I felt a little sad to think that I would never see him again.

"Do you get attached to your pieces once you're done with them," I asked Brody when we left and were headed to the car.

He took my hand. "The only thing I'm attached to right now is you."

AMBER

I slid the pie into the oven and set a timer. I was excited to cook for Brody. I checked the clock on my kitchen wall. Time to call Brody. We had agreed that I should call him in forty-five minutes before we were due to meet as a reminder.

Failure to that, he would work until Hellen went to work the following day. I hit call and waited for him to answer his phone. I was about to give up when Brody answered the phone.

"Hey sweetheart," he said, his voice sounding tired.

"Hi," I said, a huge smile on my face. God, I loved his voice. And his hands and his body. I loved everything about Brody Kruger.

"Is it time to shower and come?" he said.

"Yes. You have forty-five minutes," I teased.

"I'll be there." He blew me a kiss and disconnected the phone.

I had already showered and gotten ready for the evening. I carried my phone with me to the living room and plopped down on the couch. I remembered that I'd promised myself to call Julie. We hadn't spoken in weeks though we'd been texting back and forth on some days.

"Hi Amber," she said, sounding as if she was talking from under a blanket.

"Hi Julie. Are you asleep?"

"It depends on your definition of asleep," she said. "I'm in the blankets." She sniffed and my worry increased.

"What's going on?" I asked.

"Nothing much apart from my hunk left me," she said. "How is it possible to experience heartbreak twice in less than two months?"

"Oh Julie, I'm so sorry. What happened?" Things had been going so well with her and her new guy.

"He said that I was too intense," she said.

"Did he just realize that?" I said, pissed off on her behalf.

She sighed. "That was my reaction at first but now I'm thinking he might have been correct. I moved too fast. I wanted to have what I lost with my fiancé. I should steer clear of men. I don't do them very well."

"I wish I could come over right now but I'm waiting for Brody," I said.

"It's fine, don't worry about it. I'll be fine after a few days of wallowing in misery," she said with a laugh.

"Look, let's meet tomorrow at lunch time. How about that?"

"Sounds good. Thanks Amber. I'm quickly becoming that friend who is always nursing a broken heart."

"No, you're not." We said goodbye and I sat still for a few minutes thinking of how lucky I was to have found Brody.

He didn't play games and he made me know in all sorts of ways that he was serious about us. I swiped my screen and tapped to get into my email. I'd taken to checking my email multiple times during the day. Usually there was nothing new but this time it was different.

There was an email from an official looking email address. Puzzled, I clicked on it. As I read and took in the contents, it felt as though someone was pouring ice water on me. It was from a law firm in Pennsylvania.

Dear Miss. Davies,

Our client, who freely admits that she's your birth mother, has instructed us to write to you advising of her wish not to meet or indeed contact you. That part of her life is over, and she has no wish to revisit it again. After giving up her child for adoption, she forged a new life and has her own family now. They do not know about you, and she wishes it to remain that way.

We've also sent letters to her niece, with whom you have communicated several times. Our client is very adamant that she wishes that no member of her family stays in touch with you. She wishes you well and hopes that this letter is the end of all communication between you and her family.

The trembling started in my feet and rose until my whole body was consumed by shivers. The pain was nothing like I had ever known before. It felt as though my birth mother was right there in the kitchen with me, glaring at me and warning me to stay away from her life.

I bit my lower lip to stop myself from crying. I was not going to cry over a woman I didn't know and who had rejected me. What sort of a person did that to her own flesh and blood?

I jumped to my feet and paced the living room. I walked with my hands around myself. I had never felt as lonely and alone as I did at that moment. I should have followed my instincts and told Timber that he had my blessing to search for his family but that I did not want to search for mine.

My chest burned with anger and dislike for a woman I had never met. I imagined her happy and satisfied in her house, surrounded by children and her husband. People who clearly had no idea that she had given up her firstborn for adoption.

I told myself that it was a good thing that I hadn't met her. A person who lied to her family was not someone I wanted to meet or get to know. Gratitude for my parents and the way they had raised us flooded me.

A wave of grief quickly followed. I wished they had not been taken from us so early. The buzzer rang at the same time as the oven timer. I glanced around in confusion before understanding dawned.

I pressed the button to let Brody in and headed to the kitchen to turn off the oven. I returned to the front door just as he was coming in clutching a beautiful bouquet of flowers. Seeing him smiling at me and looking at me as though he loved me, broke something in me.

"Hi," he said and handed me the flowers. "These are for you."

"Thank you," I said and took them from him.

A need to hold and touch him came over me. I placed the flowers on the coffee table and returned to Brody. I wrapped my hands around his neck and pulled him down for a kiss.

My erratic thoughts grew still as soon as his lips touched mine. I loved his manly scent and I inhaled it greedily as if it was oxygen. The pain in my chest receded and was replaced by pleasure and need.

Brody's hands caressed my back, making round circles and pressing me into him. His body felt so solid, so safe. I loved the hot taste of him, and I quickly deepened the kiss. I caressed his shoulders and arms and moaned into his mouth.

My body felt as if someone had lit a fire inside of me. Brody's hands slipped underneath my dress to cup my ass. Arousal liquids gushed out of me, wetting my panties. As if sensing my growing need for more, Brody broke the kiss and carried me to the bedroom.

"You're so fucking perfect, do you know that" he growled, keeping his eyes locked to mine as he walked us to the bedroom.

He laid me on the bed and draped his body over mine. I grounded my hips against him, loving the feel of his hard cock between my legs. The friction was driving me insane.

He tugged on my lips and then trailed kisses all the way to my neck. Heat sizzled over my skin where his lips touched. He cupped my breasts over my dress and dipped his head down my cleavage, kissing and licking the valley between.

"Take my dress off Brody," I said, desperate to feel his naked skin against mine.

He kept his hungry gaze on me as he pulled down the zipper and pulled the dress over my head. He stared at me for a moment, his eyes lingering on my breasts and then my panties.

"You're the sexiest woman I have ever met," he said.

Tears formed and gathered at the corner of my eyes. It felt good to feel loved and wanted.

That part of her life is over, and she has no wish to revisit it again.

A sob formed and I pushed it down my throat.

"Are you okay?" Brody said, caressing my lips with his fingers.

I nodded and managed a smile. I reached for him and pulled his head down. A moan escaped my lips when he pushed down my bra and his mouth found my nipples. He did delightful things to them, intensifying the ache between my legs.

"That feels so good," I said, arching my back.

"Just the beginning sweetheart," Brody said, tracing his tongue down to my belly while keeping his hands on my nipples.

Desire raged through my body and when he settled between my legs and pulled down my panties, I felt as if I was seconds away from coming. He blew on my pussy and the throbbing intensified.

"You're so wet," Brody said, his voice thick with arousal.

"I want you Brody," I said. "I want you to fill me with your big cock." I needed him to make me forget everything except how good it felt to be fucked by him.

"After I've tasted you," he said and buried his face in my pussy.

Delicious shocks of pleasure shot through me. I writhed under him and cried out in absolute pleasure.

"Oh God, yes," I cried, digging my fingers into his scalp.

His tongue teased my clit and his fingers slid into me and pumped in and out. I raised my hips to meet them, clasping my pussy around his fingers.

"I need to fuck you now Amber," he said, pulling out his fingers.

I opened my eyes and watched him practically tear off his clothes from his body. His cock jerked up and down as he returned to the bed.

"Get on all fours sweetheart," he growled.

I scrambled into position and thrust out my ass enticingly.

"Fuck Amber, I won't last a minute if you do such things," Brody said.

I giggled and spread my legs open.

"Yes babe, just like that," he said and ran a finger up and down my slit, spreading my arousal juices to the rest of my pussy.

"You are so ready," he said and replaced his finger with his cock.

"Oh yes," I cried at the feel of the tip of his cock running up and down my folds, creating a fire in my pussy. "Please Brody."

A hand held my hip and the next thing I felt was his dick slide inch by inch, spreading me open and filling me up completely. When he was buried to the hilt, he paused for a second as if to savor the feeling and then pulled out. Without giving me time to protest, he slammed into me.

Every thrust sent fire and electricity racing through me. Tears flowed down my cheeks and spilt on the bed sheets. My chest almost burst from the intensity of emotion I felt for Brody. My pussy felt as if it was burning in the most delicious way.

Sounds of our bodies slapping against each other filled the room. Brody slapped my left butt cheek lightly sending an orgasm rocking through me. It snuck up on me and shook me with its intensity. I whimpered and cried as Brody kept pumping.

"I'm coming babe," Brody roared and then hot cum filled my pussy.

When it was over, Brody cradled me, holding me tightly. A lid opened and my pent-up feelings burst out. I sobbed into his chest as if my heart had broken.

"Amber, are you alright?" Brody said, panic in his voice.

BRODY

"**P**lease talk to me," I said, fighting down the rising panic. I couldn't figure out what the problem was.

Amber had been fine when I got to her apartment and gave her the flowers. Her sobs gradually subsided and I curbed my worry and waited. I gently stroked her back and when she raised her head, I kissed her forehead.

"You must think I'm insane," she said with a shaky laugh. "Who bursts into tears after sex?"

"I'm worried that my performance was that bad," I teased.

She laughed. "On the contrary. I think it was the best yet."

I grew solemn and held her gaze. "Something's wrong Amber. Please tell me what it is."

Her smile disappeared and a vulnerable expression came over her features. "I got an email from a law firm in Pennsylvania," she said. "It's easier if I show you." She got up and left the bedroom. When she returned, she had her phone with her.

"Here," she said, handing me the phone. She slipped back into bed and propped her head on her arm to watch me as I read.

Horror filled me as I read the formal email. A letter asking Amber to cease and desist from contacting her mother or anyone in her family. I couldn't believe that a person could do that. When I finished reading it, I stared at Amber.

"Is this real?" Pain and anger filled me. I curled my hands into fists. "What kind of a mother would do something like this? Get her lawyers to contact her daughter asking her to stay away." I couldn't sit still. I jumped from the bed and paced the bedroom.

"That was my first thought," Amber said softly.

"I'm sorry Amber," I finally said. It pained me to admit that there was absolutely nothing I could do to make it better. I hated that she had been having a streak of bad luck.

"Me too," she said and added fiercely. "I'm sorry that I allowed Timber to convince me to sign up to search for my relatives. It's as if I instinctively knew that it would not end well."

"Oh sweetheart," I said and went back to bed. The only thing I could do was to hold her, which I did. "I'm really sorry. If I knew that woman, I would strangle her."

Amber giggled. "I believe you would."

"There are some women who should not have been mothers, even if they gave their children away," I said. "My mother would have been in that category too," I said, shocking myself by saying it out aloud. I had thought it many times, but it was not something one said about their mother.

"Your mother sounded absolutely normal to me," Amber said.

"She is on the surface but when you get to know her, you quickly realize how unsuited she is to motherhood," I said, with a trace of bitterness in my voice. "Liz and I were raised by nannies. My mother was and still is a social butterfly. She'd rather have been anywhere else except raising her children."

"Why do you think that was?" Amber asked me.

Her question gave me a pause. I'd never thought about why she had raised us as she had. "My father has always been a philanderer." I took a breath before I continued. "If it wasn't his secretary, it was a woman he had met at the club. There were always other women, and my mother knew about them all. I couldn't understand why she stayed with him and even defended him sometimes."

"Maybe it was because she liked the lifestyle he provided her with," Amber said.

"I would say yes but she's also wealthy on her own terms. She came from a very wealthy family."

"Yes, but what if she likes the security that marriage offers. It's not easy to be divorced and alone," Amber said.

"Maybe." I had never felt sorry for my mother but what Amber said struck a chord in me.

"I can't imagine being married to someone who broke my heart over and over again," Amber said. "She must have gone through a lot of pain in her marriage. No wonder she occupied herself with other things instead of being home."

My view of my mother changed. She wasn't as carefree as she seemed. My father's infidelities still affected her. How could they not when she still loved him? I had no doubt that she did. If she didn't, she wouldn't have come to ask me to join the company. What a mess!

"I've never talked about that with anyone," I said to Amber. "Thank you for helping me look at my mother in a different way. I've always thought of her as a weakling."

"That's the last thing she is," Amber said. "She's just made different choices that the rest of us can't understand."

As we lay talking interspersed with moments of silence, my mind returned to Amber's mom. "How can she not be curious about you?" I asked.

Amber shrugged. "It said why in the email. She's forged a new life for herself. I guess that means that her new family doesn't know about me. I was a secret, and she wants me to remain a secret."

I stared at Amber in admiration and relief that the shattered look was gone. The strong, happy Amber was back. "If only she knew what she's missing."

Amber smiled at me. "Thank you."

I stared down at the figure I had sketched of the lower half of a woman. I smiled as recognition dawned. I had drawn the lower part of Amber's body. Being intimately familiar with it, the sketch flowed easily.

I turned the pages. My notebook was filled with sketches of Amber. I returned to the half body and made a decision to make it my next project. I would call it, All Woman.

A knock on my door interrupted my musings. "Yes?" It was probably Hellen letting me know that lunch is ready.

The door swung open. "Brody, your mother has been trying to reach you. She says that you need to urgently call her back. It's got something to do with your father."

"My father?" I asked." "What happened?"

Hellen shook her head. "Your mother didn't say but she sounded frightened. I've never heard her like that."

"Okay, I'll call right now." I turned on my cell phone and saw ten missed calls from my mother's number.

"I'll be in the kitchen if you need me," Hellen said and left.

I called my mother back and listened as the phone rang and rang. No answer. I called again, and this time, she answered.

"Brody, thank God, I found you," she said, sounding hysterical. "Liz and I are at the hospital. It's your father. He collapsed at home, and I called the ambulance. They're saying it's a heart attack. Oh God, Brody."

"I'm on my way," I said grimly then remembered that I didn't know which hospital they were at. "Where are you?"

"Grendol Hospital," she said.

I disconnected the call and rushed to my bedroom. I would have loved a shower but there simply wasn't any time. I changed out of my overalls and hurried out. I paused at the kitchen and updated Hellen.

"I'll be praying for him," she said tearfully.

"Thanks Hellen," I said and rushed out.

On the way, I tried to imagine my larger-than-life father unconscious or helpless and failed. He wasn't the healthiest person, and he liked his food rich. I knew from my mother that his doctor had warned him several times about his lifestyle.

Of course, my father listened to no one and did as he wished. He was so stubborn. I knew a little about heart attacks and I hoped that it was not a serious one. As I drove, I reached for my phone to call Amber. Then I froze.

I couldn't call her. She would drop what she was doing to meet me at the hospital. That was the last thing I wanted. It was so fucked up. How long was I going to keep her from meeting my father? The answer came as soon as that thought formed.

As long as I could. Sweat formed on my forehead as I recalled Amber's suspicions that my father had something to do with the burning of her bakery. I'd laughed it off as paranoid, but it had left a hole of fear in my chest. I knew then without a doubt that if she found out who my father was, that would be the end of us.

How fucked up was it? My father had a heart attack and I couldn't tell my girlfriend. I got to the hospital and headed to the information desk. I was directed to the fifth floor.

My mother and Liz were huddled in the waiting room. "What are they saying," I asked after hugging each of them.

"No news yet," Liz said.

"Where's William?" I asked.

"Out of town but he's on the way back," Liz said.

"I told you that this might happen," my mother said to me. "It's been too much for him. He's been coming home late and leaving early. I could tell he was stressed at work."

"Mom, that's not a fair thing to say to Brody. He can't just ditch his life and do something he's not interested in. Father has always refused to delegate. That's his biggest problem," Liz said harshly.

Her tone surprised my mother into silence. She went and sat down, leaving me and Liz alone.

"Is Amber coming?" she said. "I know she would want to be here with you."

I touched her elbow. "Let's go down and get some coffee." We excused ourselves from mother and headed to the elevators.

I'd not intended on telling anyone, but I desperately needed someone to confide in. "Amber doesn't know that father has had a heart attack and I don't plan on telling her."

"What? Why?" Liz said, visibly shocked.

I waited until we were out of the elevator and then pulled her to the hallway. "The only way you'll understand is if I tell you the whole story." I told her all of it from when father had planted that seed in me about the pedophile.

Bile rose up my throat as I spoke. Horror drew itself on Liz's features. I left nothing out. When I was done, she stared at me for a few seconds without speaking.

"What is wrong with you and Father?" she finally said. "How can he lie about something like that and you—" she poked my chest with a finger. "How can you be so stupid? You're not a boy to go reacting stupidly like that. Even if the owner of the bakery had really been a pedophile you should know better."

She didn't remember.

"I think I'd probably react the same way again, Liz," I said quietly.

We stared at each other and then her eyes widened and understanding dawned. She clapped a hand on her mouth. "Oh my God Brody, I'm so sorry, I can't believe I forgot about that."

"You were little. I lived through it and knew everything that was going on. That's why it stuck in my head. Father knew how much it had affected me. I saw a therapist for almost a year," I said. "He knew that if he told me that, I'd do something drastic. He wasn't wrong."

Tears filled Liz's eyes and her mouth shook. "Sometimes I hate Father."

"Yeah, you and me both. And Mother expects me to go and work with him. My goal in life is to see as little of him as possible," I said.

"What are you going to do about Amber?" Liz asked. "She's bound to find out."

"I'll plead business for the next couple of weeks," I said.

"I don't mean now," Liz said. "I mean about knowing that the real estate man is your father."

"I'm hoping to put it off for as long as possible."

AMBER

"Are you okay? You seem a little subdued, which is not like you," Timber said.

We were on the way to his mother's place to meet the family. "I'm fine." I wasn't. I missed Brody terribly.

I didn't know what was going on between us. The last two weeks had been horrible. Sort of what Julie had been going through with her man before he told her that it was over. Was that what was happening with Brody?

He replied to my messages hours later and avoided talking to me. He claimed to be busy with work and family stuff. At first, I'd felt left out but as time went on, he became even more elusive, I'd started to feel scared. I had a feeling that we had reached the end of the road and he wasn't telling me.

I didn't want to believe that his feelings had changed so abruptly. I thought he had feelings for me as I did for him. But when someone repeatedly found reasons not to see you, there was no other explanation for it.

"I've never been so nervous in my life," Timber said as he drove.

"More than the time you went to Afghanistan for two years?" I said, remembering the calls he had made home, with the sounds of bombs going off in the distance.

"Yep," he said. "It dawned on me last night that they could very well reject me."

I swallowed down the lump in my throat and shut down thoughts of my mother. "But Claire did write that their mother was looking forward to meeting you?"

"Yes," Timber said. "She said that she had thought about me every day since she gave me up for adoption."

Claire had told Timber the whole story, told to her by their mother. She had been raised in a very strict religious family and when she had gotten pregnant, her parents had insisted that she give up the child for adoption. She had given birth and gone on to college to be a teacher.

As fate would have it, the same young man who had gotten her pregnant was the same one who ended up marrying her. They had tried to get back their baby, but Caroline had signed off the final adoption papers. Timber's father's greatest regret had been not meeting his first-born son.

He had died three years ago from an automobile accident.

"You have nothing to feel nervous about," I said.

"People change their minds when they've had time to think things through," Timber said.

That was true. I remembered Janice's excitement about meeting me until her aunt said no. Timber was so right but that was not what he needed at this moment.

"You're being silly," I said. "If they had a change of heart, they would have already told you."

He fished his phone from the pocket of his button-down shirt and handed it to me. "Check."

I laughed but I checked anyway. "You're ridiculous." I went to his inbox. There were several work-related emails, but nothing from Claire, his sister. "Nothing."

The car navigation system showed that we were near our destination. A sense of excitement came over me. I looked forward to seeing Timber's biological family. I was excited for him and glad it was not me carrying all that tension.

"We're here," Timber said, turning the car into a long drive.

The house was not visible from the road but a few feet on and the drive straightened, and a gorgeous single family detached home appeared. Timber parked the car and we both got out. He took my hand as we walked to the front door, and I squeezed him.

Before either of us could ring the bell, the door flew open and a woman who could only be Timber's sister stood there grinning. She had the same sandy colored hair and brown eyes.

She clamped a hand to her mouth and just stared at him. "Oh my God, you look just like Everly."

"Claire?" Timber said.

She dropped her hand and nodded.

"Can I hug you?" Timber said.

"I was planning on hugging you," Claire said.

Timber stepped forward and they hugged as naturally as if they had been doing it all their lives.

"This is my sister Amber," Timber said, draping an arm around my shoulders.

"That makes her my sister too," Claire said and drew me into a hug.

Timber gave me a slight push and I stifled a laugh. He knew me so well. I disliked hugging and touching strangers. Yes, I know that Brody and I had hooked-up that first time and he'd been a stranger. That had been different though.

The hook-up had been aided by a copious amount of alcohol and seriously unbelievable sexual attraction. Just thinking about Brody made a deep ache form in my chest.

"Come in and meet Mom and Everly," Claire said, moving deeper into the house.

We followed her in.

"I'm not ashamed to say that I was standing right here at this window, looking out for you," Claire said.

"I'd have done the same if our roles had been reversed," Timber said.

They had the same laugh and they even spoke the same. It was fascinating watching them and looking out for similarities. We followed Claire into a large comfortable looking living room.

"Timber," the younger of the two women seated on the sofa said and jumped to her feet. She almost ran across the room, straight into Timber's arms.

Timber laughed. "You must be Everly."

"I am," she said and then broke out into a sob. She clung to him and then stepped back to look at him.

I was touched to see that Timber had tears in his eyes too. The older lady took her time and when she reached Timber, she cupped his face.

"I never ever thought that this day would ever come," she said, her voice thick with emotion.

She looked like a female version of Timber.

"Daniel would have been so happy," she said and then hugged him.

They stood holding each other for a long time. The rest of us watched with tears in our eyes. I couldn't imagine how Caroline was feeling holding her son whom she had last held when he had been a newborn.

They finally drew apart and Timber introduced me to his sister and his mother. They were an easy group to like. We all sat down to talk. Caroline took the lead and explained to Timber again the circumstances that had led to his adoption.

She showed him the only picture she had of him. A newborn with the same sandy colored hair and brown eyes. The photograph itself had aged with being handled too many times.

She also apologetically explained to her daughters why they had decided not to tell them about their older brother. It was an emotional but fun afternoon. It felt good to talk about our parents and how they had raised us.

Caroline had an album ready, full of pictures of her late husband. He had passed on from an automobile accident, a mere three years ago. Caroline told us that his greatest wish had been to meet his first-born child.

I mused over how lucky Timber was. His late father had brothers and a sister and Caroline's own family, apart from her parents, were active in her life too. He had a whole bunch of people related to him and who wanted to get to know him.

My chest expanded painfully as I thought about the letter I had received from my mother's lawyers. We stayed until dinner time and then said goodbye with the promise to visit again for a family get together Timber's family was going to organize. They wanted him to meet everyone.

I couldn't imagine what it felt like to be wanted so much.

"I bet that felt surreal?" I said to Timber on the drive back home.

He was silent for a few seconds before he answered my question. "It was nice, but it made me realize how special you are to me. I like them and I feel something but they're practically strangers."

I was stunned. "I thought you were feeling all the love Timber."

"I don't know how to explain. It's weird. These people look like me, talk like me, hell, they even laugh like me but they're complete strangers. I guess I always thought that when I did finally meet my biological family, I'd feel a sense of rightness.

Of coming home. The same way I feel when I see or hug you."

He slowed down and pulled the car to the side of the road.

"Oh Timber," I said.

He buried his head in his hands and sobbed. I unfastened my seatbelt and hugged him as best as I could from across my seat.

"I'm guessing it will take time to get that feeling with them," I said. "It will come, give it time. And they are such nice people."

After a few minutes, Timber got himself under control. "I can't believe I did that in front of my little sister."

"Hey, you needed to and I'm glad I was here," I said.

"Thanks sis," he said and then stared at me. "You're more than my sister. You're my best friend."

Guilt gnawed at me. I hadn't shared Janice's response with Timber but only because I didn't want to spoil it for him.

"You're my best friend too," I said. "Speaking of which, I did hear from Janice."

Timber's eyes widened and a smile of anticipation pulled at the corners of his mouth. I felt bad for the news I was about to tell him.

"Well, not exactly Janice," I said. "I got an email from my mother's lawyers. She instructed them to let me know that I was not to contact her or any member of her family. Apparently, she's made a new life for herself, and she wishes to forget that part of her life to which I belong." Even after all that time, a lump formed in my throat, threatening to cut off my air.

"Fucking woman!" Timber exploded making me giggle. "What sort of animal is she? Jeez Amber, I'm so sorry. When did this happen?"

I shifted in my seat. "A couple of weeks ago."

"And you didn't tell me?" he said, sounding hurt.

"I didn't want to put a damper on you finding your family," I said.

"Oh Amber, that was so stupid. You know I'm here for you no matter what's going on in my life," Timber said. "So, you handled it all by yourself?"

My chest ached at the reminder of Brody. "No, I talked about it with Brody, and he was great. It was tough at first, but I got over it."

Timber took my hand. "Liar. I'm sorry I wasn't there for you. I can imagine how incredibly painful that must have been. She's not worth knowing."

"I agree with that."

"I'd love to meet Brody. I've heard so much about him and never met him. I'm beginning to think he's your imaginary boyfriend," Brody teased.

"He may very well be," I said. "I haven't seen much of him in the last couple of weeks." I couldn't help the tinge of hysteria in my voice.

I desperately needed some answers. If he wanted to break up with me, then fine. Why not tell me? I wanted to lash out and cry noisily like a child.

"What's going on?" Timber asked.

I told him as much as I knew. Everything had been going well and then boom. He went quiet on me.

"He probably has other things going on in his life," Timber said. "Guys are not so great at sharing. Don't write him off. Just be patient and when he's ready, he'll come back."

I inhaled deeply. "I can do that."

"Yeah, you can," Timber said. "Let's go out for a drink. I could use one and I bet you could also."

"Sounds great. Can I invite Julie?"

"Sure, why not? The more the merrier."

BRODY

God, I missed her. It had been three weeks since I'd seen Amber. We had spoken on the phone several times but that had just left me feeling like a complete asshole.

She had sounded distraught and confused and had stopped short of asking me what the fuck was going on. I didn't want to see her while I was sorting out my life. I couldn't do both. I had to do this first and then go back to Amber. I stared at the papers in front of me and experienced a moment of doubt over the decision that I'd come to.

The phone on the desk rang and I almost jumped. I still hadn't gotten used to working behind a desk with a phone that rang incessantly and which I couldn't turn off or ignore.

"Yes," I said to Beatrice, my father's secretary.

"William is here to see you," she said. I could hear the smile in her voice.

Orion, my father's real estate company, had one thing going for them. They had the best employees and most of them had been with the company for decades. Beatrice had been with Orion since its inception.

"Please tell him to come in," I said. I stood up and when my brother-in-law walked in, we hugged and shook hands even though we had been together at the hospital the previous evening.

"You look good in that chair," William said with a grin.

"I don't feel good," I grumbled. "But I have a plan which I hope you'll love as much as I do."

A skeptical look came over William's face. I knew that for years he had admired my father and had hoped to work together with him. I never understood why my father had never wanted to work with William.

He was hard working and had built his own company up from nothing. The same way my father had. He was also very honest. Maybe that had been the problem.

"Have you seen father this morning?" William asked.

"No but I've spoken to Mom and he's okay," I said.

He's doing a lot better now, but it had been touch and go at the beginning. The doctors had placed five stents in his heart. He'd responded well to treatment, but one thing was clear, he was going to have to change his lifestyle when he recovered.

"Great," William said.

I asked after Amelia. I hadn't seen my niece in weeks.

"A parrot as usual," William said. "I'll tell her that her favorite uncle said hello. How are you doing? And how is the lovely

Miss Amber?"

Hearing her name said out aloud made me miss her even more. "She's well." I couldn't say any more. I didn't know. After we'd exchanged family gossip, I jumped into the reason I'd asked William to meet me in my father's office.

"I'm not sure if you know this, but Orion is in the midst of building this outdoor mall," I said.

William nodded. "I've heard about it. Your father has kept it close to his chest."

I nodded. I'd never heard about it, but it made sense now. What didn't make sense was how my father could have made such a mess of the company finances. He had run out of money to finance the mall even before the work had started.

What had shocked me as I went through the company's affairs was that Orion was also in the bad books of most lending companies.

My father's strategy had been to buy small pieces of property, renovate them and then sell them for a profit. I understood now why he had been so determined to get Amber and Timber's property.

I didn't get why he couldn't have thought to do what I was about to do. If William said no, then I'd have to return to the drawing board. I was banking on the fact that he wanted to grow his company and a partnership with Orion would give him the edge to move up the property ladder.

"It's a good investment, the only problem is that Orion's financial affairs are terrible. The company simply can't afford to build that mall, no matter how much money it will bring in later." I pushed a bunch of papers across the desk to William and gave him time to read it.

He gave nothing away as he read them. When he was done, he looked at me. "I agree, it is a good investment. But it has to be built first. Many good investments have died off before they could take off."

I nodded. "I know. That's why I called you to meet with me. You've done a great job with your company, and I know you want to take it to the next level. I have an idea that will benefit both our companies." I searched William's face and saw nothing but polite interest.

"I want you to come into Orion with your expertise," I said.

He shook his head. "I don't want to work for your father."

"You won't be working for my father. What I'm talking about is a partnership. A fifty-fifty partnership. Orion has the name that attracts big contracts, and you have the trust from investment companies."

"Go on," William said.

I plowed on, relieved that he hadn't dismissed my proposal outrightly. "You'll run the show," I said and gave him more details.

"What about you? Where will you be?" William asked when I finished speaking. "From what I gathered your father might not be coming back to work. Denise has very definite plans for the next ten years."

"Yes, I know." My mom had seemingly changed overnight. It was as if Father's heart attack had brought out her assertive side.

I didn't know how long it was going to last but so far, even Father seemed to be bowing to her wishes.

"I'm not a businessman," I said. "I never have been. I'm happiest being a sculptor."

"You may not like it, but I've seen that you have a knack for it. If I did agree to do this, I'd want you involved, even if only on a consultancy or part time basis," William said.

I curbed my excitement. The thought that I could have my life back was more than exhilarating. William asked questions and I answered them as best as I could. He stayed for an hour and when he was satisfied, he stood up.

"I'll think about it and discuss it with Liz," he said.

"Of course."

I left the office soon after and headed to the hospital. I felt lighter as I drove. I had a feeling that William would take my offer. It offered him an opportunity to play with the big boys and gave me the space to follow my passions. Sculpting and Amber.

My next step was to talk to my mother. It was unfair to give her the job of telling my father, but she was the only one who could judge when the best time was to tell him.

I found a parking space far away from the entrance, but I didn't mind the walk. It gave me time to formulate the little speech I was planning on giving my mother. As it was, I found her strolling the hallway on my father's floor.

"Hello Mom." I kissed her cheek.

She held my shoulders and smiled at me. "You look so handsome in a suit and tie. I knew you would be happy at Orion once you gave it a try."

I held her gaze. "Wearing a shirt and tie makes you happy?" I asked.

"That's not what I mean, and you know it," she said and stepped back to admire me further.

"I'm glad you brought that up, can we talk for a few minutes?" I asked.

"Sure, the doctor is in there with your father. He wanted to speak to him privately."

We went back the way I'd come and headed to the waiting room. There were a few people, but Mom and I found a private spot at the back of the room.

"So, what is it you want to talk about?" she said.

"I want to talk about Orion, Mom," I said. "Nothing has changed about my thoughts on working there. Father's illness has not made me like it any better."

"I can't believe we're back to this," my mother said, a flash of anger coming over her eyes.

"That's because you don't listen to what I say." I took a deep breath when I realized that my voice was raised.

"Most people don't like what they do but they do it anyway, mostly because it brings them good money," she hissed.

"I know that Mom and I'm confident that my work will bring me good money in a couple of years." The skin around my face was tight, as if it had suddenly become too small for my face.

I was barely containing my anger. I reminded myself that my reason for being here was to impart information, not to ask for permission.

"I had a conversation with William, and this was my proposal to him." I told her the whole thing. She was not taking it well, judging by the vein that had popped up on her neck and was throbbing visibly.

"You can't do that," she said when I finished talking. "Your father wanted you, Brody, to run the company."

"Well, then, we have a problem because I won't do it," I said. "I'm not going to spend my life doing something that I don't want to do when I have a choice."

These last weeks had been the most conflicting and hardest of my life. It wasn't just because my father had fallen sick. It was the decisions that I'd been forced to make.

It had been pure torture oscillating between following my duty and following my passion. I pictured the look of joy and satisfaction that Amber usually had on her face when she was working, and I knew that was what I wanted for myself. It didn't matter how long sculpting took before it earned me a proper living.

I was going to do it anyway.

The harsh look left my mother's face and tears filled her eyes. I'd been mentally prepared for both reactions.

She clutched my arm. "Please don't do this Brody. Don't let your father down."

"What about me Mother? When do I get to follow my heart? I spent years being a firefighter just to make father happy and to show him that I was doing something worthwhile. It's time to do something for myself."

She stood up and glared at me. "You're a disappointment Brody Kruger."

I nodded. "I know Mother. But that doesn't bother me as it once would have."

She stalked off and I stood up and followed her to father's room down the hallway. I stopped before I reached the door and fished out my phone. I'd planned to wait until William and I reached an agreement before calling Amber but I couldn't wait any more.

Amber answered on the second ring. "Hi Brody."

Hearing her voice sent a thrill racing through me. "Hi Amber. It feels so good to hear your voice."

I expected her to laugh or say something funny. She kept quiet.

"Are you okay?" I asked.

"I'm fine." Her voice was chillier than I had ever heard it. Had she changed her mind about us? Had I waited too long?

"Would you like to have dinner with me tonight?" I asked. "Please?"

"Brody, I don't want to play games," she said.

The tone of her voice tore at my insides. "I'm not playing games Amber. I promise."

AMBER

I'd told myself that if Brody called me again, I would tell him to delete my number and to never call me again. I couldn't believe that I'd agreed to a dinner date without even bothering to ask him where he had been. I was a fool for love. Wait.

This wasn't love, was it? No way. What I felt for Brody was serious attraction. There was absolutely nothing wrong with being madly, crazily attracted to a man. The important thing was to remember that we were lovers. People who enjoyed each other's company in and out of bed.

I'd fooled myself into thinking that there was something special between us. If Brody had felt the same way, he would not have pushed me out of his life for the last three weeks. He'd have confided in me and together we would have solved it.

But you did not confide in someone with whom you considered purely a lover. To Brody, we weren't friends. Someone jostled me from behind, reminding me that I was standing smack in the middle of the street.

I smiled apologetically at no one in particular and kept walking. Julie had asked me to meet her at our regular coffee shop. She sounded happy. And excited. I couldn't wait to hear what had turned around her mood from the bottom of the pits to bubbling with happiness.

I walked in and saw her at our usual table, and she was not alone. What the heck was Timber doing with her? Frowning, I approached the table.

"Hi," I said and kissed Timber first and then Julie.

"Hi sis," Timber said.

I shot a questioning glance at Julie, and she smiled nervously. A server came around and I ordered a cup of coffee. When I turned back, Timber was holding Julie's hand over the table.

I let out a loud groan. "No, no, no," I said.

They both laughed.

"I'm sorry Amber, I shouldn't have gone home with your brother, or liked him so much that now I'm in a relationship with him," Julie said.

It would have been cute if it hadn't been my brother and my best friend. Worse still, they were the two people I knew who had the worst luck when it came to love. Or they really didn't know how to do the relationship thing. How had they ended up together?

Of course, I'd seen the attraction between them when we'd all met for a drink. I'd have had to be blasé not to have seen it. We had gone dancing after a few drinks, and they had done everything but fuck on that dance floor. Julie and I had laughed about it the following day and I'd thought that was the end of it.

"You can't take all the blame babe," Timber said, looking at Julie as if she was his favorite flavor of ice cream that he wanted to gobble up. "I'm to blame too. I saw you and I couldn't believe what a sexy, gorgeous woman you had turned into. I wanted to—"

"Hey," I snapped, cutting him off. "I'm here."

Julie looked at me with puppy eyes. "Are you very upset?"

The server brought my coffee, and I took a sip before answering. "I'm not upset in the slightest bit. I'm happy for you guys but I need you to understand something. If this goes terribly wrong, I don't want to hear about it from either one of you. Nothing."

They both nodded vigorously and promised not to involve me in any of the drama that might come down the road. I worried that Julie was on the rebound from her two exes, if you could call one of them that, but it wasn't my place to point it out to her.

It was weird to watch them ogling each other but also sweet. It made me miss Brody. Thinking about our date that evening helped somewhat but it also made me sad to think that we couldn't have a simple, easy relationship like Julie and Timber.

I stayed for an hour and then excused myself. Outside, I called my hair stylist and luckily, she was able to squeeze me in. I had no idea why I was going to all this trouble for a man who had seen me naked and first thing in the morning.

Maybe I wanted him to see what he had been missing. I don't know. All I knew was that I wanted to look beautiful. I took a cab to the salon and spent two hours getting my hair and nails done. I couldn't remember the last time I got my nails done but it felt so good, I promised myself to do it more often.

Maybe not my fingernails because of work but my toes would work.

Back in my apartment, I took a long shower and spent hours choosing a dress. I picked the sexiest dress I owned. A cherry red dress with a plunging neckline that fitted me like a second skin and left very little to the imagination. It was so fitting that the only way I could wear it was with nothing underneath.

It was my first time wearing it and when I stared at my reflection I wondered if I had the guts to actually wear it for dinner. It had been a gift from one of my customers who was a designer.

I grinned at my reflection. I looked smoking hot, and I couldn't wait to see Brody's reaction when he saw me. I spent a few minutes putting on mascara and colored lip gloss. When I was done, I felt like the sexiest woman alive. Who knew that dressing sluttish could make you feel so good?

The buzzer rang a few minutes later and rather than let Brody come up, I grabbed my purse and went downstairs.

I pulled open the front door and when I saw Brody, his presence hit me like a heatwave. My breath stopped in my throat. He looked so hot in a white shirt open at the collar revealing the smattering of chest hair that I was so familiar with.

I raised my gaze to his face and inhaled sharply at the raw lust in his eyes as he looked me up and down.

"You look so fucking sexy," he said.

"Thank you," I said, heat pooling at my center. "You look pretty hot yourself."

He offered me his arm. "Shall we?"

I took his arm and we walked to the car. His gaze never left my body, even as he unlocked the car and held the door open for me. I curbed my giggles at the obvious tent in the front of Brody's pants.

He must have adjusted his pants as he walked around the car to the driver's side. When he entered, scents of man and sage filled the car. I ached to be in his arms, pressing myself against his erection and rubbing my nipples against the hardness of his chest.

"Where are we going for dinner?" I asked just to hear the sound of Brody's voice.

I'd missed him so much. But only as a lover. Not as someone I envisioned the future with. Sex was addictive, I'd discovered. My body craved his touch.

"La Ville," Brody said, mentioning one of the top restaurants in the city.

Memories of our first few dates filled my mind and a laugh broke out of me.

"What?" Brody said.

"I'm just remembering the first couple of times we went out together. I was so worried about your finances. I thought you were definitely reckless with money," I admitted.

Brody chuckled. "I remember how reluctant you were to order. You were the first woman I'd met who had a problem with eating in an expensive restaurant."

"A stupidly expensive restaurant you mean?" I quipped.

"It's a lifestyle that grows on you," Brody commented, and we both laughed.

And just like that, the tension that had been between us evaporated and we talked as if those three weeks hadn't happened. There was still a physical barrier and as much as I longed to run my fingers through his hair, something held me back. Fear maybe, with a dose of wariness.

We got to the restaurant and as we walked in, I could feel the eyes on me. It was a little disconcerting. The only person's attention I wanted was Brody's. Not everyone else.

"Every man in this room wants to take you home with him," he said when we sat down.

I spotted an old man surrounded by people who looked like his children and grandchildren, and discreetly gestured in his direction. "Him too?"

Brody laughed. "Especially him. He's probably sure he can become the stud he was before old age caught up with him."

I tried to imagine Brody as an old man.

"What's on your mind?" he said.

"I'm picturing you as an old man," I said and as the image formed in my mind, everything in me longed to be in that picture, old as well. I brought myself out with a sharp reminder. We were lovers. Temporary. Hot and fun while it lasted.

"Oh yeah?" Brody said, tilting his head to look at me. "Are you with me? Because if you're not, it's the wrong picture."

My heart galloped in my chest. I was about to tell him not to say such things when the server came to take our order.

"I passed by the bakery the day before yesterday," Brody said. "It looks ready."

I beamed. "It is. Just a few bits and pieces remaining. We're planning a big party to reopen it. Two weeks from now. I'm so excited."

Brody reached across the table and took my hand. "I'm so happy for you."

I squeezed his hand back. "I have you and the station to thank for that. If it wasn't for you guys, I'd be back to being unemployed."

"You're welcome. How are things on the home front? Timber?" Brody said.

As we ate, we spoke and gossiped like old friends. He was amused to hear that Timber and Julie had hooked up. It gave me hives to think of those two together, but they were adults.

We talked and ate but underneath, desire simmered between us. The single glass of wine we drank after dinner heightened our lust. After Brody took care of the bill, he took my hand, and we left the restaurant.

In the car, he drove us to my place and when we got there, we went in together. We both desperately needed each other and there was no room for pretense. It reminded me of that first time when Brody had taken me to his supposed apartment, and we had sex.

I could feel his eyes burning my back as I opened the door to my apartment. Inside, I strolled straight to my bedroom, with Brody hot on my trail. He closed the door, followed me in and slipped a hand around my waist. He turned me around to face him and then pulled me against him.

I draped my hands on his shoulders and as if in quiet agreement, we slow danced to imaginary music. Brody stared at me intently, dropping his gaze to the front of my dress and then inhaling sharply, as if I was too sexy.

He ran his hands over my bare shoulders. "I dreamed of doing this tonight and the last three weeks."

He had been counting.

"The reality is better than my fantasies," Brody said and brought his mouth to mine.

I closed my eyes and savored the feel of his lips against mine. We touched our lips to each other without moving. I was the first one to move. I parted my lips, inviting Brody to deepen the kiss.

With a growl, he devoured me with his mouth, setting off a wild need in me.

BRODY

I loved her. I loved Amber Davies with every cell in my body. I looked down at her perfect face, into her eyes as she stared at me with big, wary tinged eyes, and I wanted to tell her.

I wanted her to know that she was my everything, that without her, my life was nothing. But I couldn't. First, I had to earn her trust again. She didn't trust me not to disappear without a warning or explanation. I stared at her with love and admiration.

Another woman would have demanded to know where I had been and why I'd not been calling her. Amber had waited for me to voluntarily give an explanation and when I didn't, she had left it alone. I didn't fucking deserve her! But I would earn it. I would earn her love.

"I don't want to remove this dress," I said to her.

She laughed. "That's not quite the reaction I was hoping for when I wore it."

I chuckled. "I'm caught in between. The naked body and the tantalizing effect of the dress." I had draped my body over hers and bent my head to trail kisses along her neck and bare shoulders.

"Your skin tastes so sweet," I murmured, dropping my head to the valley between her breasts. "It should be against the law to be so sexy."

I grazed a nipple over her dress until it was a hard pebble.

"Oh God Brody," she moaned.

I moved to the other nipple and gave it the same treatment, sucking on it over her dress. Amber writhed and wrapped her legs around me.

"I want you, Brody. Now," she said. "We can do the slow thing later."

Despite the heat her words elicited in me, I chuckled while pulling up her dress. "You have to promise to wear this for me again."

"I promise," she said, her voice thick with need.

I loved hearing her like that. Aroused and without an iota of self-consciousness. My woman. She arched her back to give me space to pull her dress over her head. She shrugged out of it, and I took a moment to admire her full breasts, her nipples enlarged.

"So perfect," I murmured.

An impatient look came over her features, jolting me into action. I opened the first two buttons of my shirt and then drew it over my head. Amber unzipped me and I tugged my pants and boxer briefs down.

My cock throbbed painfully, impatient to be buried in her sweet hot pussy. I ignored it and lay on my back, pulling Amber on top of me. I ran my hands over her thighs and ass. Her wetness dripped on my cock as she slid back and forth over it.

She panted and moaned and when she couldn't take the friction anymore, she raised her hips, gripped my cock and sank down on it. She cried out as my cock stretched her, as she slid down until my cock was buried to the hilt.

It had been so long that I'd forgotten how fucking sweet she was and how good we were together. I cupped her breasts and teased her nipples as she moved up and down on my rigid hard cock.

I moved my hands to her waist and moved her faster, up and down, taking her with deep strokes. I grunted as my orgasm got closer and closer.

"Brody," she cried, digging her nails into my belly.

I reached between her legs and rubbed and teased her clit, until moments later, she exploded, my name falling from her lips. I fucked her faster, hammering towards a desperate climax.

When my release came, it felt as if I hadn't been near a woman in decades. I roared in pure pleasure as I poured my seed into her. When it was over, Amber draped her body over mine, keeping my cock nestled in the heat of her pussy.

I stroked her hair and listened to the sounds of our hearts beating in sync.

"How are you feeling sweetheart?" I asked.

She was silent for a moment before she nodded her head. "I missed you."

My heart skipped a beat. The words said so softly and so simply touched a chord in me with their raw honesty. "I missed you too."

~

"**A**re you alright?" Amber said from the bed.

We had spent most of the weekend under the covers, only leaving it to eat and go to the bathroom. We had more than made up for the weeks we had been apart from each other.

I flashed her a reassuring smile. "I'm fine, just thinking of the day ahead and what I need to get done." It was almost the truth. I was working on the All- Woman piece but that was not quite what was on my mind.

William had texted me half an hour earlier to ask if he could come to Orion offices in an hour. That meant that he had made a decision. My confidence that he would say yes had dipped since the last time we'd met. He had everything to gain by agreeing to a partnership.

But he had wanted to speak to his wife, my sister, first. I should have spoken to Liz first and found out what she thought about the idea. My sister was ambitious, and I knew she would be for it. Still, I hated the nervousness that I was feeling.

"What about you?" I said as I dressed.

"I'm meeting with my staff and Timber to go over a few details concerning the bakeries opening day," Amber said, her eyes gleaming with excitement. "You'll come, won't you?"

"Of course, how can you even ask?" I asked.

"I'd like to invite Liz and William," Amber continued.

"They would love that," I said.

"And your parents."

My heart skipped a beat and my heart thumped wildly. Was this how it would always be for me whenever Amber mentioned my parents?

"I'll ask," I said. I kissed her goodbye and left, promising to text or call her later.

I headed home to dress for my meeting with William. For the first time, I wished I had a brother who fit in with my father's ideal son. I'd have been happy to let him inherit Orion and not take a dime for it. No price was too high to pay for my freedom.

I was at Orion offices half an hour later with ten minutes to spare.

"Morning Beatrice," I said as I strolled into the office.

"Morning, Brody," she said, and half stood. "Can I bring you a coffee?"

"Coffee would be great, thanks," I said, feeling like a fraud as I entered my father's office. Beatrice had asked me if there was something she could order, like a rug or any decoration to make it more comfortable for me.

I'd politely declined. Nothing would change the fact that I had zero interest in business, and more so, real estate. Beatrice followed a few minutes later with my coffee.

"Thank you," I said.

"You're welcome," Beatrice said. "How is your father doing?"

"A lot better," I said. "Though if my mother has anything to do with it, he won't be coming back to the office any time soon."

She nodded. "We'll miss him, but his health comes first."

I searched her face for signs of insincerity, but she meant every word. My father was not the easiest man to work for but to his credit, he still inspired loyalty from his staff.

"Please show William in when he comes," I said.

She left and I busied myself with responding to emails in my father's inbox. Excitement coursed through me as the implications of my meeting with William dawned on me afresh. No more guilt trips from my parents plus the freedom to pursue my passion without feeling as if I was letting anyone down.

I loved that I had found someone who was as enthusiastic about my work as I was. The more I got to know Amber, the more I realized how lucky I was to have met her. She was everything I wanted in a woman. Smart, gorgeous, sexy, fun... so much specialness, all in one person.

The phone on my desk rang, rousing me from my musings. I answered it and asked Beatrice to show William in.

I kept a cool face as I greeted William and invited him to sit down. We exchanged pleasantries while all the while my pulse rate was going crazy.

"I'm sure you know why I'm here," William said and smiled.

I nodded. "I'm eager to hear your decision."

His expression turned solemn, and fear clutched at my heart. He had to say yes. The alternative was unthinkable. My gaze bounced around the office. The thought of coming to work at Orion every day was unbearable.

William nodded. "I'm afraid the answer is not the one you want to hear. Liz and I spoke, and we agreed that the partnership you're proposing is not what your parents had in mind for Orion."

"Go on," I said, cursing myself again internally for not speaking with Liz first.

"We both want to do the right thing, which is in this case, to follow your parents' wishes. Liz and I understand that your interests lay elsewhere but we think you should give it a chance. You've never worked here at all. You might like it."

I shook my head and fought to keep my feelings under tight control. I was livid and desperate. "I'm not going to like it. At this point in my life, I know very clearly what I want to do with myself."

"I thought so but your sister thinks that you should give it a shot first. Our proposal is that you give it your all for three months and if you still feel that same, I'll be more than happy to get into that partnership," William said.

I clenched my fists under the table. Dang Liz! The very thing that I loved about her was the very thing I hated right then. Her sense of fairness. I blamed myself too. If only I'd spoken to her, I'd have made her understand there was no chance now nor in the future that I'd ever want to run Orion. It was just not in my cards.

Thoughts of Amber floated to my mind and my heart took on a fast beat again. What was I going to tell her? Did she know my father's company? It was such a fucking mess.

"I'm sorry man, I know that's not what you wanted to hear but I see Liz's point. There's no harm in waiting a few months just to be sure that this is the direction you want to go," William said.

I nodded. "I agree, three months is not a long time but there's the other matter of funding."

"I thought about that, and I've spoken to a few people. They're willing to get into talks with you as long as you're the one running the show and not your father," William said, his face reddening slightly as he said that.

My father had damaged his reputation over the years, and it seemed as if no one wanted to work with him.

"Plus, I'll be coming in on a consultancy basis," William added with a smile and a wink. "After all, we have to make sure everything will be smooth sailing three months from now. I don't expect anything to change."

"I don't either," I said. The only thing that was likely to change was my relationship status.

If Amber found out that Orion was my father's company, that would be the end of us. But that wasn't going to happen.

I would do everything in my power to make sure that she never found out. Three months was not a long time. I could hold it together for three months.

The only thing that was going to suffer was my sculpting.

AMBER

I luxuriated in bed for the next half hour after Brody left. The beddings smelled of him and it felt good to have his scent surrounding me. I couldn't keep a smile from my face. It had been a magical evening and morning. Everything was beginning to look up again.

I reached for my phone and tapped into my work email. There were several inquiries and a few orders. I responded to all of them while in bed and when I was done, I logged into my personal email on a whim.

My hands instantly dampened when I saw a new email from the Lineage company. What now? I was done with that whole business, and I'd managed to put it all behind me. With trembling fingers, I opened the email.

They had found another relation and this time, they thought that the man was my father. Joseph Moore. There was a 99.9% chance that he was my father.

I clicked on his picture to enlarge it. He was a handsome man with startling red hair and a warm expression on his face. Or maybe I was just seeing what I wanted to see.

I couldn't stop staring at his face. The beddings rose up and down with my chest. I stared at his brown eyes which looked exactly like mine. I was a feminine version of my father. A slice of joy went through me at the knowledge that I had not taken after my mother when it came to my looks.

My heartbeat slowed down and my mind cleared up enough for me to think. He looked like a good man, but I was looking at a picture. Looks were deceiving. I bet people who saw my biological mother in the streets thought to themselves what a nice lady she was.

Her words filled my mind and dislike flooded me. I hated feeling that way about someone I had never met but I also knew that the same thing was likely to happen with my father.

He had probably gone on with his life, was married and had a family. There was no space for a daughter who had been adopted at birth and was now a stranger.

I stared at him, regret filling my heart, but I knew what the right thing to do was. I closed the email and set my phone on the table. That part of my life was over. I pushed away the covers and swung my legs to the edge of the bed. It was going to be an exciting day.

I couldn't wait to meet with my staff and brainstorm ideas for the opening party of the bakery. I tidied the bed and my bedroom, and then headed to the shower.

Fifteen minutes later, I was out of the apartment and strolling down the street to the coffee shop where we were all meeting. Joe was already there at a long table that could seat several people.

He stood up when he saw me and opened his arms. Grinning, I walked straight into them, and we hugged.

"How have you been?" he said, drawing back to look into my face.

"I've been well, how about you?" I said as I sat down. "The grandchildren?"

Joe let out a laugh. "They are all well, but they miss their treats from their grandpa."

I laughed too. "Not too long before they'll start getting their treats again." The staff at the bakery were allowed to carry leftover cakes and cookies home.

The server came and we ordered coffee. Tracy and Caroline were next to arrive, and it was another ten minutes before Timber made an appearance. He looked rushed, as if he had just stepped out of bed, which he probably had.

I stifled a giggle.

"Hi everyone," Timber said, and kissed me on the cheek. "I desperately need a coffee. Give me a minute." He went to order coffee himself rather than wait for the server.

"Someone looks like they had a good night," Tracy commented, and we all laughed.

We asked after each other and as we chatted, my chest swelled up with emotion as I glanced at my staff. I'd missed them so much. We had become like family since we started working together.

Timber returned with his coffee, and we dived into the upcoming reopening party. We were all excited for it and we threw ideas back and forth. God, I'd missed this.

"We should have free samples just like we did the very first time we opened the bakery," Caroline said.

My pen flew across the page as I wrote down ideas for the big day. Timber was given the task of advertising on social media as well as hiring a PR company to help with spreading the word across the city.

I couldn't believe our bakery was going to be back in business.

The rest of the team and I worked out a schedule to have our products ready in time for the opening. We would be working with the bakery still closed four days prior to the opening. I couldn't wait to get back to that kitchen.

We ordered a second cup of coffee with sandwiches this time. Time flew as we planned and came up with new recipes. When I looked at the time, three solid hours had gone by.

"You're showing signs of wear and tear," I teased Timber as we strolled towards my apartment.

He grinned. "New love."

I glanced at him. Despite looking tired, he seemed happy and that made me happy too. "I take it things are going well with Julie?"

"Better than well. It's perfect. She's perfect. I feel as if I've finally met my soulmate," Timber gushed.

I was about to roll my eyes when I recalled that I'd had the same thought about Brody a few days after meeting him. Now, everything was mixed up and I didn't know where we stood. The only thing I knew was that sex between us was great and nothing like I'd ever experienced with any other man.

"I'm happy for you. Julie is an awesome person and so are you. You guys are a perfect match," I said, linking my arm through his.

"Thank you, little sis," Timber said. "How are things going with you and Brody?"

I smiled. "A lot better than the last time we spoke. I think you were right; Brody has been going through some stuff even if he hasn't come right out and told me."

"And you're hurt that he hasn't confided in you?" Timber said softly.

My chest squeezed at the truth in Timber's words. "Yes. If someone is close to you, shouldn't they be able to confide in you?"

"Men don't operate like that Amber. It takes a lot of trust for us to confide in someone, even one we love. It takes time to build that trust. For instance, there's so much I wouldn't tell Julie at this point of our relationship. I have to trust her a hundred percent."

I wanted to believe Timber so badly, but I also knew that wasn't the case with Brody and me. We had shared some deep stuff. Things neither of us had ever told another human being. Brody's issue was not trust but I knew it in my gut that he was hiding something from me and that worried me sick.

It frightened me to think that he would end up hurting me as badly as Carson had hurt me. I couldn't face a second heartbreak. The beginnings of a headache started to form. Obsessing over it wasn't going to help.

"I guess you're right," I said to Timber. On a whim, I decided to tell him about the email I had received from the Lineage website.

I'd expected excitement from him, instead, what I got was a muted reaction.

"That's interesting," Timber said.

I stopped walking. "That's not like you bro." He turned to face me, and I searched his face. He looked unusually serious.

He sighed. "I blame myself for the pain you went through the last time. I knew that you were not enthusiastic about finding your biological relatives, but I still pushed you. All it brought was heartache. I don't want to make that mistake again sis."

"Oh Timber, it's all right. It was better to know now rather than in the future. Besides, I got over it." As I spoke, I realized the truthfulness of what I was saying.

Sure, I'd been hurt when I received that horrible email from my mother's lawyers, but I'd gotten over it. She was a stranger and there was not much a stranger could do to hurt you. If it had been someone I knew and I loved on the other hand, the hurt would have lingered for much longer.

"That's good to hear," Timber said. "But I still blame myself."

I squeezed his hand. "Don't. So anyway, what do you think about this new information? Should I pursue it?"

Timber contemplated me without speaking for a few minutes. "I can't tell you what to do sis, but I can tell you this. I'll support whatever decision you make."

I hugged him and held on for a few seconds longer than necessary, feelings of gratitude and love overwhelming me. I drew back. "Thanks for that."

We continued walking and as I turned it over in my mind, a crystal-clear answer came to me. "I won't pursue it. I don't want that roller coaster experience again. My life is full and happy as it is."

"Okay," Timber said and went on to tell me how proud he was of me for making the right decision for me.

We got to my apartment. "No point in asking you to come in," I teased. "I have a feeling that a certain someone is waiting for you."

He grinned. "Yes. I can't believe how happy I feel. It makes me worry that it will be taken away from me at any moment."

"It won't. Don't overthink it, Timber. Just enjoy it," I said.

"Good advice," he said. "Oh, and by the way, I'm going on assignment next week, but I'll be here for the bakery reopening party."

"Awesome," I said.

"Yeah," he said. "It's an exciting one. I'll give you the details when I have them. Meanwhile, can I meet the mysterious

Brody before I leave. I like to know that my sister is in safe hands."

"Sure," I said, excited at the prospect of the two most important men in my life meeting each other. "I'll set up something."

We parted ways and I headed upstairs to my apartment. There was a lot to do with the reopening party in a week's time. As I waited for my laptop to power up, I checked my phone messages.

There was one from Brody.

Brody: *I'm thinking about you. Specifically, how beautiful you looked this morning. I miss you already.*

I smiled like a fool. I read the message over and over again, until I told myself to stop behaving like a lovestruck teen.

Me: *I miss you too.*

I put my phone away and focused on answering business emails. As I worked, thoughts of my father kept sneaking into my mind. Had I behaved like a coward in refusing to contact him? I took a break after half an hour and reached for my phone.

I need a second opinion. I texted Brody and told him about the email.

Brody: *That's pretty exciting.*

Me: *A part of me got excited but another part, the biggest part is terrified. I decided not to contact him. Do you think I should?*

Brody: *I can't tell you what to do sweetheart. Only you know whether you want to risk getting hurt again or it being the most rewarding thing you have ever done.*

The most rewarding thing I had ever done. I hadn't thought of it that way but if, and it was a big if, things turned out okay, having a father figure in my life would be awesome.

AMBER

I stepped out of my apartment and paused to breathe in the cool, early morning air. I raised my eyes to the skies and grinned as I took in the streaks of brilliant orange across the still dark skies. God, it felt good to be going back to work.

True, it would be several days before we opened the bakery to our customers but the fact that we were back to working in the kitchen excited me to no end. As I took my usual route to work, I mused over how much things had changed since the bakery burned down.

My love life had moved from nonexistent to exciting and all because of the fire. Had the bakery not burned down, I wouldn't have met Brody again. We hadn't exchanged numbers after our one night of passion and even though I'd wanted to see him again, we had no way of tracking each other down.

Brody and I were meant to be together, and the universe had conspired to make sure that we ended up together. It made me feel all warm and special inside to think of Brody and me as meant to be together.

Someone cleared their throat behind me, and I let out a shriek and whirled around. The hair behind my neck rose when I clapped my eyes on Carson.

"You again?" I said in disbelief and with more than a sliver of fear. It was too early for people to be about, and a feeling of vulnerability came over me.

My brain did some quick calculations. I couldn't outrun Carson, but I could scream as I ran. Maybe that would scare him off and catch someone's attention. My heart pounded hard in my chest as I took a couple of steps back to increase the distance between us.

He raised his hands in the air. "I'm not going to harm you, Amber. You're the last person in the world I would hurt. Please. Don't be frightened of me."

"What do you want at freaking four in the morning?" I shouted.

"I just wanted to talk to you, I promise. Then I'll go away."

"What?"

He moved closer and I moved back. "I wanted to warn you about your boyfriend."

Carson knew about Brody. "Boyfriend?"

"Yes. Tall, dark, walks as if he owns the world," Carson said with a sneer in his voice.

Fear clogged my throat, then I reminded myself that Carson was no match for Brody who was fitter and stronger than anyone I knew.

When I didn't respond, Carson continued speaking. "He's not who you think he is, Amber. You're not safe with him. He's evil and he's hiding things from you."

"What things?" I found myself asking.

"That's all I'm going to say about that but don't say that I didn't warn you," Carson said.

Before I could respond, he turned around and quickly strode off. I stood watching him until he disappeared round the corner. Confusion came over me. I had no reason to believe a man who had a court order to stay away from me. Except that I'd been having the same thoughts for weeks now.

Brody was hiding something from me. I continued walking, but at a slower pace, the excitement of the day stolen from the encounter with Carson. He had said that Brody was evil and that he was hiding things from me.

I hated the mystery surrounding Brody and yet when we were together, making love, none of that mattered. I desperately wanted to trust him, to believe that he wouldn't hurt me, but I couldn't bear the thought of heartbreak all over again.

But what were my options? I could end things with him but even as I contemplated this option, I knew I couldn't do it. I needed him in my life. In the silence of the early morning, I could finally be honest with myself. Brody had become important in my life.

He made me happy. I wanted more than a physical relationship with him. The realization frightened me. I loved Brody. I'd loved him from the very beginning when he accompanied me in the ambulance to the hospital and he didn't have to. I loved him when he took care of me, insisting on driving me home and making sure that I'd eaten.

I was in trouble and there was nothing I could do about it. Without telling me exactly what Brody was hiding from me, Carson had left me in the dark, just as I had been before he snuck up on me.

I reached the bakery and dug into my handbag to fish out my keys. Joy slowly seeped into me as I inserted the key and turned it.

"Amber?" a deep voice said behind me.

I jumped, turned and flattened myself against the door.

"Relax, it's just me," Timber said, coming out from the shadow.

What was it with people sneaking up on me? "Timber, what are you doing here so early in the morning?"

He grinned. "Did you think you would get to do this alone?"

I fell into his arms, and we hugged. "Thanks, big bro. Shall we?" I said, turning around to open the door.

I flicked on the light and made my way to the kitchen. A feeling of serenity came over me. I had missed my bakery. I moved around the kitchen touching everything, most of which was new. I loved the new smell in the air.

"You did it," Timber said, following close behind me.

"No, we did it," I said and then remembered the generosity of the guys at the firestation.

I knew that Brody had put in a good word for me. Without that, the bakery would have remained shut down for an indefinite period of time. I had such conflicted thoughts about Brody, especially after what Carson told me.

Joe was the next to arrive and his grin brought tears into my eyes. He enveloped me in his arms and shook hands vigorously with Timber.

"Coffee?" he said.

The offer made me feel as if I'd finally come home.

"Yes please," Timber and I said at the same time.

It felt as if we had gone back in time especially when the deliveries started to arrive.

I buzzed around happily overseeing the deliveries and getting the kitchen running. Everyone came in earlier than they used to and there was a celebratory mood in the kitchen as we chatted and worked.

Timber left later for a meeting about an upcoming project. Less than ten minutes after he left, I got a visitor.

I heard his voice before I saw him. Brody.

"I'm looking for Amber," he said to someone at the back door.

"I'm sorry but we're not open for business yet," Caroline said.

My face creased into a smile. I wiped down my flour covered hands on my apron and hurried to the back door. Warmth radiated throughout my body. Carson's words came back to me, and I pushed them to the back of my mind. Excitement over seeing Brody overrode the earlier worries and concerns I'd had.

"It's okay, Caroline," I said when I got to the back entrance. "Hey."

God, he looked handsome in a crisp white shirt tucked into a pair of black chinos. I went straight into his arms and as he circled them around me, I forgot that there was someone else watching us. I raised my face and Brody brought his mouth down and kissed me as if we hadn't seen each other in years.

When we drew apart, Caroline was staring at us with her jaw on the floor. I laughed but felt no shame whatsoever. I took Brody's hand.

"Caroline, I want you to meet my boyfriend, Brody," I said.

She stepped forward and shook Brody's hand. "It's really nice to meet you," she said, trying hard not to show the surprise she was feeling.

I took him inside and introduced him to all my employees and then sat down to drink coffee with him. I felt like a kid showing off her new toy to her friends.

"I can't believe that the day is finally here," Tracy said, rubbing her hands together for warmth.

Summer had given way to autumn, my favorite season. I loved the golds and reds that covered the grass and the inner calm that seemed to come over everybody.

"We are coming back, bigger and better," Caroline said.

"Hear, hear," Joe said and then turned to me. "Do you need help with the door?"

For the first time in a long time, all the guys at the bakery reached work before five in the morning. They looked as if they were doing better than I was. I'd hardly slept the previous night, worrying over everything that could possibly go wrong on our grand reopening.

"I got it," I said as the door swung open.

I turned on the lights and stepped in. I drew in a deep breath before making my way to the kitchen. We had everything under control. Very little baking remained to be done in the morning. All the invitations had gone out and the PR firm we had hired had done a superb job getting word out for our big day.

In the last couple of days, we had a lot of traffic with people coming to check out the bakery even though we were still closed. Joe got the coffee machine going and Caroline headed to the front to get things ready for the day.

Tracy and I changed into our work clothes and carried our coffees to the work area. We went straight to work. My thoughts meandered to Brody as I worked. His sister and her husband had confirmed their attendance, but I hadn't heard anything from his parents.

Maybe they would still show up. I was looking forward to getting to know his family better. At ten I changed out of my work clothes and wore a summery dress and ran a comb through my hair. We were throwing the doors open at noon.

After dressing, I walked to the front of the bakery to inspect the counters. Everything looked yummy and the samples on the top, begged to be popped into someone's mouth. Tracy and I had done a wonderful job with baking decorative little cakes and cookies.

At a quarter to noon, a group of people had already gathered outside the bakery. My instincts were to throw the doors open but the guys insisted that I cool it down and wait for noon. Waiting for the right time was part of the excitement.

At exactly twelve, we ceremoniously opened the doors and our first customers piled in. I helped with the sales as Caroline was almost overwhelmed at the cashier desk. All of our goodies were heavily discounted, and it seemed as if a lot of people wanted to take advantage of that.

After the initial rush, the more leisurely crowd started to stream in as did the familiar faces. Timber arrived with the guests, but he'd warned me that he would be late as he had an assignment that morning.

A firefighter came from the station with everyone's order. We refused to take their money. After everything they had done for us, free cookies and cakes was the least we could do.

I didn't see Brody arrive but as soon as he slipped his hands around my waist from the back, I knew that it was him. I turned around and gave him a light kiss before introducing him to Timber who happened to be passing by taking pictures.

"It's a pleasure to finally meet you," Timber said, pumping Brody's hand. "I must admit that I wasn't sure that you were real."

Brody laughed. Was it my imagination or did his laugh have a ring of nervousness?

"It's a pleasure to meet you too," Brody said.

I spotted William and Liz as they walked through the door, and I left Brody and Timber to chat a little.

"Hi," I said with a wide smile. "Thanks for coming."

"As if we could have missed this," Liz said, drawing me into a hug and a kiss. "I love the décor, it's so gorgeous."

"Thank you," I said, glad that we had decided to change everything including our branding colors.

William gave me a warm smile as we shook hands. "Congrat-ulations. They say the most important thing in business is resilience and I have a feeling you have plenty of it."

"Thank you," I said, heating up from the kind words. "Brody had a lot to do with it to be honest. He's been wonderful since the night of the fire."

Liz excused herself to sample some cake leaving William and me alone.

"We didn't run into each other at the hospital," he said. "We must have been going at completely different times."

"Hospital?" I said, completely lost. I had no idea whatsoever what he was talking about.

"Yes. When Liz and Brody's dad was hospitalized with a heart attack three or so weeks ago?"

Shock and dismay ran through me as the period he was talking about came to my memory. It was the time that Brody had disappeared on me. His father had been sick in hospital fighting for his life and Brody had not breathed a word to me.

A sick feeling rose up my throat. I was a fool. I fought back the tears that threatened to drop from my eyes. Actions were so much louder than words. I turned my face to search for Brody and when I found him, he was looking at me with a hint of a smile.

What was he thinking as he looked at me? That I was just someone to amuse himself with until he got bored?

BRODY

I knew Amber was busy now that the bakery was back in operation but still, how could she be too busy to reply to my texts and my calls? Besides, who was busy all day? I'd sent her three messages over the course of the day and she hadn't responded to any. It was five in the evening, and I knew for a fact that the bakery shut down at three in the afternoon.

Clearly, she was choosing to ignore my messages. I jumped up from my chair and paced the office. Since the opening of the bakery, things had been different between us.

What had I done? I had gone over the whole evening from the moment I'd arrived, and she had kissed me with as much passion as I'd kissed her with. What could have changed? I went over everything that had happened which was no hardship as my eyes had been on her all afternoon as she moved from person to person.

No matter how many times I went through it, I couldn't pinpoint the moment I'd fucked up. Frustration and anger welled up in me. Why was she blanking me out like that?

What hope did we have if we solved our issues by ignoring each other?

I glanced at my watch. I'd planned to stay in the office until six, but I couldn't bear to stay for another hour. I hated every moment I spent in my father's office. I ticked down every day that got me closer to the three-month period that William and I had agreed to.

If it hadn't been for having Amber in my life, it would have felt as if my life had grinded to a stop. Thinking of the wedge that had formed between us made me reach a decision. I was going to find her and make her tell me what the matter was. I had to know and make things right between us.

With my sculpting gone, Amber was the only light in my life. Without her, my life had become an oasis of emptiness, very much like all those years when I drifted aimlessly, never experiencing real joy or purpose in life. The thought of going back to that kind of life filled me with fear and dread.

I returned to my desk and shut down my computer. Beatrice had already left for the day and the only thing to be heard was the click of my shoes on the tiled floors. All I could think of as I drove to the bakery was how desperately I needed to see Amber.

I made myself stay in the car for a few minutes after I shut down the engine, willing myself to calm down. When I felt sufficiently composed, I got out of the car and headed to the back door of the bakery.

It was shut from the inside, which pleased me to see that Amber was taking extra precautions with her safety. I knocked on the door and when there was no response, I pounded on it harder. I was beginning to wonder whether she was in, or she had used the front door to leave.

To my relief, footsteps sounded from the inside before the door swung open. I inhaled sharply at the expression on her face when she saw me. Pain reflected in her eyes, making my chest squeeze painfully. What had I done to cause her that pain?

"Amber," I said.

She raised her right hand as if to ward me off. "I'm sorry Brody, I'm really busy right now."

"You've been busy all week Amber. What's going on? Have I done something wrong?"

A closed look came over her features.

"Please," I said, desperation coming over me. "Please tell me. I miss you."

Something like anger flashed across her eyes.

"Come in," she said coldly.

I followed her in. I expected to sit at the bar stools in the kitchen but instead, Amber led me to her office. She sat behind her desk, folded her arms across her chest and indicated that I should sit down too.

I sat down, feeling as if I was at a particularly difficult interview. My heart raced but there was also relief that she was willing to talk to me.

"I don't know what I did to upset you, Amber. Things changed on the day of the reopening, and I can't figure out what it is that I did, and you won't tell me." My voice shook with the anguish that I felt.

She stared at me without speaking for so long that I thought she wasn't going to answer my question. Then I noticed that her eyes were filling up with tears and all I wanted at that moment was to crush her into my arms.

"Your father was fighting for his life, and you didn't tell me."

I froze. Fuck. That was the last thing I had expected and when I unfroze, I scrambled for a response and came up with nothing. How had she known about that? The answer came to me. William. It couldn't have been Liz because she knew that I'd kept that away from Amber, but William didn't know.

I could have kicked myself. Why hadn't I thought of asking William not to say anything to Amber or even better, not invite them to the party?

"Why are you suddenly quiet?" Amber said coldly.

Panic clutching at my throat, it dawned on me that it was my moment to speak the truth. Tell her the whole truth. A sweat broke out on my back. I visualized the horror that she would feel when I told her that the despicable real estate man was my father.

And I knew I couldn't tell her. Not the whole truth anyway.

"My father and I don't get along and he's not a pleasant man," I said, going for half the truth. "He finds a way to spoil every good thing that I have going. I didn't want to introduce him to you. You're too good Amber."

The guarded look left her eyes.

"I told you about my sculpting. He belittled it until I stopped doing it. It's always been like that since I was a child. It was his way or nothing. He's always known the right things to say to demean you and make what you want to do seem silly."

"Oh Brody. Your father doesn't have any power over me," Amber said.

I inhaled deeply. "I know but I never wanted to subject you to him," I said, meaning every word. If my father and Amber never met, I'd remain a happy man.

She stared at me, a vulnerable expression on her face. "Are you sure there's nothing else you're hiding?"

Guilt bubbled up inside my chest. I hated that I was keeping things from her, but I told myself that it was for us that I was doing it. I was protecting us.

"There is," I said. And a stricken look came over her.

"What?"

"I love you, Amber. I love you with all of my being. I've fallen in love with you."

Her right hand flew to her mouth to clamp it. Tears filled her eyes. "You do?" she finally said.

I nodded. "I've loved you since that first night we slept together. I knew you were different and special, and I wanted you in my life forever."

"Oh Brody," she said and stood up.

By the time she went around her desk, I had pushed my chair back and she straddled me and sat down on my lap without hesitation. I wrapped my hands around her and pulled her closer. I raised my head to kiss her neck. I groaned aloud at the sweet, intoxicating womanly smell of her.

Her body felt so soft, and so perfect. I held her tightly, careful not to crush her with the power of emotion I felt. She pulled back after a moment, cupped my cheeks and held my gaze.

"I've missed you, Brody. I was so afraid that it meant you only saw me as someone to distract yourself with," Amber said, her voice shaky.

"How could you think that sweetheart?" I asked. "You're everything to me Amber. You've filled my life in a way I never thought another human being could."

Instead of responding, Amber brought her mouth to mine and hungrily kissed me. She moved her hands to the back of my head and held me captive as if there was a risk that I was going to get away. It was fucking sweet and even though she hadn't reciprocated when I told her that I loved her, her actions told me what I needed to know.

Our heavy breaths filled the air as the kiss and our caresses grew more frenzied. I reached for the hair band that held her hair and pulled it loose, and then combed my fingers through her hair. I'd missed every single part of her.

Amber inched forward, crushing her breasts against my face. Taking the cue, I buried my head in her cleavage and cupped her breasts over her top. She made whimpering sounds that made my cock throb painfully.

Impatient with the material keeping me away from Amber's bare skin, I lifted her shirt off and tossed it to the floor. Greedily, I pulled down the cups of her bra and took one hard nipple into my mouth and sucked on it as though my life depended on it.

Amber made noises that left me in no doubt that I was doing the right thing. I moved to the other nipple and gave it the same attention. My cock grew impossibly hard as Amber ground onto me. I caressed her thighs pulling her skirt up as I did so, until my hands were at the top of her thighs.

I grazed my fingers lightly along the edges of her panties and she let out sweet torturous sounds. Fuck, she was hot. And sweet and sexy. Guilt bubbled up again, but I shut it down. Whatever lies I'd told were only to protect us.

"I want you Brody," Amber said, raising her hips to unzip me.

She wasn't making any progress with the zipper, and I took over. Stepping away from my lap, Amber yanked down her panties and tossed them on her desk, then returned to her position, while bunching up her dress around her waist.

My pants and boxer briefs were down by then and my cock stood jutting out of my body, jerking back and forth. I expected Amber to tease me but instead, she raised her hips, wrapped a hand around my cock and then slowly lowered herself on it.

A primal grunt left my mouth as her pussy walls gave way to my steel hard cock. I lowered my hands to her hips, holding her in place and then pushed up, fucking her in slow, deep strokes.

"Oh God," Amber cried, and dug her fingers in my shoulders.

I tightened my hold on her hips and slammed her on my cock. Tears flowed down her cheeks.

"You Look so fucking gorgeous Amber," I said, my voice thick and barely unrecognizable.

Her eyes, despite being wet with tears, gleamed with passion and heat. I felt like the luckiest man alive. She was mine and we had our whole lives ahead of us. Then a voice snuck into my brain and reminded me about the lies that sat between us.

She didn't know that my father was the man she despised. Another reminder pushed its way into my thoughts. I had burned her bakery. A fresh coat of sweat broke out on my back, soaking my shirt.

I hadn't thought of that in weeks. I'd managed to convince myself that we were like any other couple. I forced my thoughts back to the present, to how hot Amber looked when she was about to come.

She moved up and down on my cock, her breath coming out in noisy pants. I reached between us and found her clit. I rubbed her sensitive, swollen nub. Amber hissed into my ear.

"Oh my God," she cried. "I'm going to..."

Her body jerked and her pussy clenched my cock hard.

"Yes babe, come," I growled.

Seeing her in the throes of pleasure like that splintered the last of my control and I let go. I came hard and fast, filling her pussy with my seed. Amber kept moving up and down on my cock, slowing down with every second.

At last, she went still and lay her head on my shoulder. I wrapped my hands around her waist, and we sat for a long time without moving or talking.

I grinned as I became aware of our surroundings. "Do you realize that we've just made love in your office?" I asked. "You'll never be able to work here without laughing."

"Without growing hot for you, you mean," Amber said in a lazy voice.

AMBER

"Please Brody," I cried out, gripping his scalp tighter than I should but unable to loosen my hold.

How was it possible not to have enough of a man's body? We were in Brody's bed, and he was between my legs doing things that rendered me incapable of coherent thought. He circled my clit with his tongue, mercilessly teasing it until I thought I'd grow mad with lust.

I rocked my hips against his mouth and sensing the desperation to come that I was feeling, Brody thrust his tongue deep inside me and fucked me with it. He hit a spot that made me cry out harder.

"Again," I said, and he did it again and again, toppling me over the edge.

I threw my hands back to grip the headboard as a tsunami of an orgasm swallowed me whole. I shook and trembled and let out streams of words that made no sense.

Before I could recover, Brody rose from his position and the next thing I knew, my legs were being hoisted onto his shoulders and his cock was prodding my entrance.

"You're insatiable," I said to him with a light laugh.

"Only when with you," Brody said, meeting my gaze as he spoke.

Pleasure swamped me. Another kind of pleasure started in my pussy as he rubbed the head of his cock up and down my folds, spreading my juices all over me.

My voice was hoarse from all the screaming I'd done in the office and since we got home. Deep noises rose up my throat as his cock slid up and down. He spread my pussy open with his cock and then slid it in.

"Fuck Amber," Brody growled, as he filled me to the brim.

"Fuck me Brody," I cried, raising my hips as much as I could with my legs on his shoulders.

Brody moaned and thrust into me, falling into a fast, sweet rhythm. I would have paid for sex with Brody. I'd never thought that sex could be that good. It didn't take long before my body was awash with overlapping waves of pleasure.

It felt as though I was melting into him. I fisted the bed sheets as my orgasm crested and then crashed down on me. I tightened my inner muscles wanting Brody to ride the orgasm with me.

He let out a deep growl and pumped faster until he came with a shuddering cry.

~

midnight snack," Brody said as he set a chicken sandwich and a glass of milk on the island in front of me.

"Literally," I said with a giggle.

We had dozed off, woken up and made love again and when we were finished, hunger had brought us to his massive kitchen in search of food.

"I love Hellen," I said as I bit into the tasty sandwich.

Brody laughed. "I'll let her know tomorrow morning," he said.

"She doesn't come in on Saturdays," I reminded him.

"That's what you do to me Miss Amber, you make me forget everything except how beautiful you are," Brody said.

"Flirt," I said, flushing with pleasure. Brody was perfect. Inside and outside of bed.

And he had said that he loved me. I still couldn't wrap my head around that. From thinking that I was an item that he used and then discarded until the next time, to him saying that he loved me. Every time I thought of that, I wanted to cry.

"Hey," he said, reaching across the island to cup my cheek. "You look sad. What are you thinking?"

"You said you loved me," I said.

He nodded. "With all of my being, Amber Davies. You deserve to be loved."

I inhaled deeply and gathered my courage. It was frightening to think about it, let alone say it. But I needed to. I couldn't let fear stop me from experiencing what I knew would be the greatest love of my life.

I took his hand from my cheek and sandwiched it in mine. "I love you too Brody."

A look of wonder and joy came over his features. "Really?"

I nodded. "Really. And you too deserve to be loved by everyone who knows you. You're the most special man I have ever met."

"Oh Amber," he said. "You don't know how much I've longed to hear those words from you." He stood up and came around to my side and held me close.

I rested my head on his chest.

"I would kiss you but we both know how that will end and I need you to eat," Brody said and stepped back.

I laughed. "I agree. We cannot be trusted."

Brody returned to his stool, and we continued to eat, while exchanging sappy looks every few minutes. I loved being in love. I'd forgotten the feeling of completeness and indescribable joy one felt when you loved someone.

"Have you received any more emails from the Lineage website?" Brody asked.

I hesitated before answering. I'd been thinking about my biological father despite all my efforts to banish that chapter from my mind. "I haven't except the one about my father. It's been on my mind a lot and a part of me is inching towards reaching out. But I'm scared."

Brody nodded. "After what happened the last time, you have every reason to be scared."

"I'm not a coward, but so far I've behaved like one." I hadn't been honest with myself when it came to my biological family. "I always said that I wasn't interested in knowing my biological relatives, but I think it's fear of rejection that always held me back."

Brody nodded and waited for me to continue.

I inhaled a deep, almost painful breath. "But the worst has already happened. My own biological mother rejected me." As the truth of what I was saying dawned on me, a feeling of freedom filled me. "Been there, done that. So, what if this man who is my father rejects me, I'll survive. I have you and Timber and my friends."

Brody stared at me. "I admire you so much Amber. You're the bravest human being I know. I'm so proud of you sweetheart."

Relief surged through me. I wanted his encouragement. I needed him to tell me that I was making the right decision, but Brody had done more than that, he had let me work it out all by myself.

"Thank you," I said. Excitement grew inside me as I came to a decision. "I'm going to write to him. I don't want to have any regrets in my life. Whichever way it goes, I'll know that I tried."

"I'll get my laptop," Brody said and rose to his feet.

I laughed. "Now? He'll think I'm insane."

"He'll see it in the morning. Can you imagine what an awesome day tomorrow will be for your father? Hearing from his daughter?" Brody said as he left the kitchen.

I wished that was true, but I was not going to indulge myself in fantasies and set myself up for disappointment. I sipped my milk as I waited for Brody to return with his laptop.

"Here you go," he said moments later.

I flipped it open and turned on the power. I ignored my trembling hands and logged onto my email.

I found the email I'd received from the Lineage people and found the picture of my dad. Despite telling myself not to get overly excited, the pace of my heart picked up and I couldn't help envisaging his arms around me in a warm hug. Swallowing hard, I turned the screen to face Brody.

"That's him," I said, my voice coming out choked as unexpected emotions overwhelmed me.

"You have his eyes and hair Amber," Brody said, his voice filled with wonder, that made me laugh.

"I know. It's weird," I said. "I have no doubt that he's my biological father."

"Wow," Brody said, still staring at the picture. "His name is Joseph Moore."

I nodded. Brody pushed the laptop back to me.

"Worried that I'll change my mind?" I asked.

"Yes," Brody said. "Plus, I have a good feeling about this one."

I clung to his words as I opened a fresh page and started typing. I read aloud as I typed. I introduced myself, told him the tale of how my brother and I had made the decision to seek out our biological relatives after the death of our parents.

It felt weird to be telling a total stranger details about my life, but I reminded myself that he was not a stranger. Not in the real sense. He was my father. The man whose genes and looks I carried.

AMBER

After the last round of baking, my feet were aching, and it was time for my break. It was lunch time, and our rush hour was over. I poured myself a mug of coffee, grabbed one of the sandwiches that Tracy had made for everyone to eat at their convenience.

I carried my food to the front of the bakery and joined the others at the table.

"We've run out of the chocolate almond cookies," Caroline said as I took a large bite of my ham sandwich.

"Really?" I said, happy that the twist we had added to the chocolate almond cookies were a hit.

"We had customers who came back for more," she continued.

"We'll increase them tomorrow," I said happily in the direction the bakery was going. It was odd but since opening, business just kept growing.

It was as if the fire was turning out to be the best thing that had ever happened to Crusty Cookies. Our reopening party had been featured in the news bulletins and just like that we had become a favorite in the city. When we looked at the books, Timber and I could not believe our eyes.

We were keeping our fingers crossed that the upward trajectory didn't stop.

We talked shop as we ate and just as we were finishing up, the front door opened and a man whom I recognized instantly strolled in. He confidently walked up to the counter and Caroline shot to her feet and moved behind the counter.

I stayed absolutely still and listened to the conversation between them. He didn't pretend to be a customer.

"Hello, I'm looking for Amber Davies," he said in a deep warm voice.

"Oh, she's right there," Caroline said, pointing at me.

He turned to face me and when our gaze met, a wide smile came over his features. I found myself smiling back. The rest of the guys got up and excused themselves, leaving me alone at the table.

Joseph Moore. My dad. My heart pounded like mad when he cut across the room to come to the table. I scrambled to my feet and when he reached me, we stood and stared at one another.

My heart pounded hard in my chest. What should I do? Hug him, shake his hand? He solved it by closing the distance between us and resting his hand lightly on my shoulder. I noticed then that his eyes had filled up and that removed the apprehension that I felt.

"Hi," I said.

"Hi," he said in a voice that had thickened with emotion.

My chest expanded to painful proportions.

"I hope it's okay that I just showed up," he said, a worried look coming over his features.

We had emailed back and forth twice, and I'd told him about myself, and he had done the same. He had never married, and he didn't have any children and he hadn't known that I existed.

"It's more than okay. I'm glad you did. Please sit down," I said. When he sat down, I continued. "What can I get you? We do a mean cup of coffee."

He chuckled. "Maybe later. Right now, I want to get to have my fill of my daughter. I can't believe I'm saying those words. My daughter."

We both laughed as I sat down on the chair directly opposite him. We sat staring at one another without an ounce of self-consciousness.

"You're so beautiful," he said. "And an unexpected gift."

"Thank you."

"You've done well for yourself," he said, throwing a glance around the bakery.

"Thank you," I said. "I started it with my brother."

"Timber?" my father said.

I was beginning to think of him as my father. "Yes." I told him the whole tale of how the bakery had been burned down and how close I'd come to losing my life, if it weren't for Brody.

"I'd like to meet that young man and thank him," he said.

I couldn't believe how comfortable I felt with him and how much I told him about myself. I spoke so fast I became breathless. When I paused for air, I let out a laugh of embarrassment.

"I've been talking nonstop for fifteen minutes," I told him.

"I can't remember having so much fun in such a long time. Please keep going," he said. "I want to know everything about you."

I wished that Brody was there to share this moment with me. Joseph listened attentively and even asked questions.

"Your turn," I said what seemed hours later. "Tell me about yourself."

"Well, I'm a retired banker and I like to spend my days golfing with my friends. There's five of us and we've known each other for more than fifty years," he said, his eyes brimming with joy.

Even though he had no family, he seemed like a man who was content with his life. As he told me about his life, my thoughts drifted to the connection with the woman who had instructed her lawyers to write to me a cease-and-desist letter. How could such an obviously warm person have made a baby with someone like her.

"I had contact with my birth mother," I said, choosing my words carefully.

"Oh," he said. "You spoke to Susan?"

I didn't miss the wary note that came to his voice. It gave me the courage to tell him what had happened. His skin paled lightly as I spoke.

"I can't say that I'm entirely surprised," he said. "You asked in your last email how your biological mother and I met. I preferred to tell you in person rather than in an email."

For some reason, my heart started pounding hard in my chest. I didn't know what to expect but I couldn't wrap my head around the two of them being a couple.

"We met in college even though we were from two different sides of the world. She was from a wealthy family, and I was in college on scholarship."

I nodded for him to go on.

"Needless to say, it got serious pretty fast and in our last year of college she took me home to meet her parents. We were so excited about the future. I couldn't wait to make her my wife." His eyes took on a faraway wistful look.

My heart lurched at the tone of his voice. He had obviously loved her.

"The only thing her parents wanted to know was who my parents were. They hated me as soon as I opened my mouth and told them that my mother was a single parent."

"Why?" He was talking about a world that I was unfamiliar with. I'd never met people who judged a person based on who their parents were.

"They wanted Susan to get married to someone in their circle, not some guy whose last name wasn't known."

"That's horrible."

"Yes, it was. Anyway, they forbade Susan from seeing me again and she, being an obedient child, followed her parents' wishes. She wrote me a letter and left it under my door. That was the last time I saw her."

He sounded so sad. My chest ached and my eyes hurt with unshed tears.

"She never told you that she was pregnant?" I asked.

He shook his head. "If she had told me, there was no way I'd have given you up. I'd have raised you myself."

He said it so fiercely that I didn't doubt him for a second. It filled me with both pride and pain.

"Sorry to interrupt, but you guys must need some coffee," Caroline said, appearing at the table.

We both ordered coffee and then returned to our conversation. The afternoon flew by, and only later did I remember to check my phone to see whether Brody had messaged me. He had. Each subsequent one had carried a note of worry.

The last message had me smiling. He had called the official bakery line and Caroline had told him that I was okay and was speaking to a nice-looking older man.

"I'd like to meet the person who put that smile on your face," Joseph said.

My face heated up. "His name is Brody and he's my boyfriend. He's the one who rescued me on the night of the fire."

～

247

"I can't wait for you to meet him, Brody," I said, pacing up and down Brody's kitchen as he warmed the dinner that Hellen had left.

I was too excited to settle down. The last few hours had changed my life. The impact of it in my life was beginning to dawn on me. I had found my biological father!

"Can you believe that I've found my dad?" I said, stopping to let the words sink in.

"And he's not an asshole," Brody said solemnly.

I knew he was thinking about his dad. "He's definitely not that." I longed to meet his dad too, but it wasn't fair to push Brody when he clearly wasn't ready.

He was still working many hours at his father's company. I'd tried hinting that I'd love to see where he worked but Brody had dismissed it by saying it was temporary and not worth the trouble.

"You deserve all the happiness in the world," Brody said, pulling our plates of food from the microwave. He set them on the island and tugged at my hand to sit down.

I barely took note of what I was forking into my mouth. I was still on a high, as if I'd spent the whole afternoon sipping on margaritas.

"I've never seen you like this," Brody said, a smile on his face.

I swallowed the food in my mouth without being sure whether I'd chewed it. "I've never felt like this. As if my existence suddenly makes sense." Realizing what I'd said, I quickly corrected myself. "Not that it didn't make sense before."

"You don't have to explain," Brody said gently. "I understand what you mean. This is not about me and you. It's about connecting with your dad. The man whose genes you carry."

Relief surged through me. "Exactly. It feels serene. This feeling that I've had all afternoon is what Timber was searching for. As if the world has righted itself. Does that make sense?"

"Perfectly. I think it's human nature to want to feel connected to our roots to feel fulfilled," Brody said.

I raised my hand and used my fingers to tick off. "That's one, the other is meaningful relationships and work."

"I agree," Brody said. "When one of them is missing, we feel lost."

I ate silently as I contemplated the list we had come up with. I raised my gaze to Brody. "Have you had time to work on your sculpting?"

A fleeting look of sadness crossed his eyes, but it disappeared in the next few seconds. "Work is taking up more time than I expected. I haven't gone to my studio in weeks."

"How much longer do you have to work there?" I said, careful not to ask too many invasive questions.

Despite our growing closeness, there was a gray area between us especially when it came to Brody's father. I usually asked him about his health and each time Brody said that he was improving but he rarely gave me any other details.

It frustrated me but I was learning to respect his wishes. If he wasn't comfortable talking about this father, then I wasn't going to push him.

"A couple of months," he said, his voice coated with misery.

"Will he be well enough to return to work?" I asked and held my breath.

"It doesn't matter," Brody said, a hard note creeping into his voice. "I can't do it for longer than that."

I could tell by the tone of his voice that we had reached the end of how far Brody was willing to go.

"So, when do I get to meet your father? Did you tell him that you have a boyfriend?"

I grinned. "It was one of the first things that I told him. And that my boyfriend is my hero. He saved my life."

BRODY

"We'll give you our dates in a couple of weeks," I told one of the contractors for my father's dream project of an outdoor mall.

I raked my fingers through my hair and tuned him out as he grumbled about his disrupted schedule. I didn't want to begin a project that I wasn't going to complete. That and as far as I was concerned, that project was William's. I only had to keep things running for a few more weeks and I was free from Orion.

There were smaller projects in the works and those kept the company busy. That kept me busy too, but I resented every minute that I was away from my beloved art studio. Both Hellen and Amber had noticed my sour mood in the last month. It was becoming harder and harder to pretend that I was okay.

Working a job where your heart just isn't in it is like watching your soul slowly die off. I finished the call and as soon as it ended, Beatrice put another call through without letting me know first who it was.

That was not like her at all, and I answered with a scowl on my face. "Hello, Brody Kruger here."

"Hello Brody."

My muscles loosened on hearing my mother's voice. "Hello Mother. How is everything going? Father, okay?"

"He's very okay," she continued in a tight voice that meant she was displeased with someone. "In fact, we are on the way to the office."

"Oh. Did the doctor say it's okay for Dad to be at the office?" I asked.

"I think that man is working in cahoots with your father. He said it can't do any harm and is good for your father's mental health. For the record, I don't agree with that. I think your father should be resting some more."

To be fair, Father had improved considerably in the last month. He even took daily walks which had done wonders for his fitness. We were of course pleased by the progress that he was making but my mother and I were both afraid it meant he would come back to work.

For me it would be good news. Sort of. I would happily hand over Orion to him without a backward glance. On the other hand, he was still my father, and I knew that work was not good for him in the long run, especially after seeing what a mess he had made of it in the last couple of years.

Orion needed fresh blood. It needed William. Like everybody else in my family, I wanted Orion to survive and thrive, but it wasn't going to do so in the hands of my father.

"Maybe he just wants to make sure that everything is going well," I said.

"No, he's talking about coming back to work full time," she said. "I need you to talk to him and knock some sense into him."

Before I could respond with a sarcastic comment about how he never listened to me, my mother disconnected the call. I spent the next ten minutes before they arrived musing over what I'd tell my father. By the time they arrived, I had a plan in place.

I would tell him the truth in front of my mother.

He was wheeled in by his nurse with my mother closely following behind. In charge these days, she directed the nurse where to park the wheelchair and then asked him to leave us until she called him.

"It took a heart attack to get you to sit there," my father said when the three of us were alone.

I smiled at the attempt at a joke. "I'm here temporarily," I said and ignored the bad look my mother was directing my way.

"I've been hoping that when I recover, we could continue working together. Just like I'd always wanted," my father said. "What projects have you been working on?"

I inhaled deeply and updated him on what we had been doing. His face grew pinched as I spoke. Finally, he waved a hand away.

"Those are small potatoes, and you know that, Brody. What about the mall? Any progress with funding?"

I shook my head. His cheeks reddened.

I shifted my gaze from him to my mother. "Father, you know as well as I do what bad shape Orion is in. The reason your mall stalled was because of the bad name the company has with lenders. You've made bad decisions in the past which have made investors lose confidence in you and the company."

A stricken look came over my mother's features. She turned to look at her husband. "Is that true?"

"He's exaggerating as usual," my father said. "I should have known better than to hope that Brody will do anything here. I bore a loser of a son and it's time I accepted that."

Anger swarmed me until I remembered that my father's words didn't have the power to hurt me anymore. I was a grown man with a beautiful girlfriend who would one day become my wife. I didn't need my father's approval on how to live my life.

"You can't come back to work David," my mother said. "This is what caused the heart attack in the first place."

"Mother is right. Orion has become a stressful environment for you, but I have a solution. I spoke to William and he's willing to come in as a partner."

"Over my dead body," my father thundered. "I'm not giving away half of my company."

"You don't have a choice, Father. William is your best bet. He has the funding and the expertise. Either that or be prepared for bankruptcy," I said, keeping my voice firm and emotionless.

My father seemed to slump into his chair. He stayed that way for a few seconds and then he looked up at me. "Is it that bakery girl who is influencing you?"

It took a moment to realize that he was talking about Amber. "Amber? Of course not. She has nothing to do with this."

My mood was upbeat as I drove from work that evening and headed to the bakery. Amber and I had fallen into a routine where we had a cup of coffee after work and then went home together. We alternated between her place and mine.

I'd also gotten to know her biological father and he had turned out to be the kind of father everyone dreamed of having. He was a perfect balance of a parent and a friend. It pleased me to no end to see Amber so happy. I couldn't wait for my life to return to normal, then Amber and I could continue with our own lives without me putting her off every time she wanted to visit me at Orion.

That conversation with my parents was the beginning of resolving things once and for all. We hadn't reached any conclusions with regards to the company but now my parents clearly understood that my future was not in Orion, no matter how many insults my father heaped on me.

I parked my car and went around to the back parking lot. The service door was slightly ajar and as I stepped in, laughter filled my ears. I paused at the doorway and smiled.

"I can't believe how I suddenly have this large family," Joseph was saying. "Life is really full of delightful surprises."

I made out Amber, Timber and his girlfriend Julia's voices. Listening to them talking made me feel the dysfunctional nature of my family. Joseph had known Amber for a little more than a month and in that time, they had become a family. He had even informally adopted Timber as his son when he heard that Timber's biological father had died before the two men ever met.

I roused myself and entered the kitchen. Amber was the first to see me. She jumped up from her chair and came to me. "Brody! You were the missing ingredient in the party."

"As I'm sure you can tell from Amber's reaction," Timber teased.

I held Amber close and then kissed her lightly on the cheek. We held hands as we moved to the table where everyone was seated. I shook hands with the men and Julia gave me a hug.

"Coffee?" Amber said.

"I'd love some thank you," I said as I sat down.

We exchanged pleasantries while Amber poured me the coffee.

"How's it going at the real estate company?" Timber asked. "Amber tells me you're not too keen on it."

"Yes, but I won't be there for much longer. My brother-in-law who is in the same industry will take over and I can go back to my own work."

Joseph politely asked me what I did and when I told him about my sculpting, he immediately ordered a piece without seeing my workmanship.

"I trust my daughter's taste," he said when I protested. He winked at Amber who laughed in response.

Later, after everyone had left, Amber and I washed up and then stood at the sink kissing.

"I feel like a teenager," she said laughing.

"I feel like that all the time around you," I said.

She cocked her head to one side. "You look a lot more relaxed today. Is it true what you said? William will soon take over and you can go back to your sculpting."

"Yes," I said, while debating whether to tell her about my parents' earlier visit to the office. "My parents came to the office today and we discussed it. I'm not cut out for that life-style, and I think that finally my father gets it." Calling it a discussion was stretching the truth a bit.

It had been more like accusations flung back and forth.

"That is good news," Amber said and pulled my neck down for another light kiss.

"You smell and taste so good," I said, lowering my head to plant kisses on her neck.

Amber laughed softly. "Only you would say that. I smell and taste of flour and spices."

"The best perfumes are made from spices," I countered, dropping my hands to cup her breasts.

She let out a long low moan when my fingers found her nipples. I teased them over her blouse and when that wasn't enough, I pulled up her blouse and pulled down the cups of her bra.

I inhaled the scent of her skin and brought my mouth down to lick and suck her nipples. I loved how hard they already were from my earlier teasing. With every gentle bite, Amber let out a sharp cry and gripped my head tighter.

I dropped one hand between her legs and inhaled sharply at the dampness of her pants. I rubbed her sweet pussy, and her cries grew louder. I hadn't planned on having sex in her kitchen but a sudden urgency to fuck her came over me. I couldn't wait for us to get home.

I pulled down her pants and panties, and she kicked them off. I turned her around and caressed her gorgeous ass with one hand while fumbling to unzip my pants with the other.

"I'm sorry Amber for rushing, but I want you now," I said, pulling my cock out.

"I want you now too Brody," she said, gripping the counter.

I pulled her back by her hips and when she was at the perfect angle, I aligned the tip of my cock to her entrance and slowly eased it in. She was hot and so fucking wet; I almost came as soon as her inner walls clenched around my cock.

"Fuck, fuck, fuck," Amber cried when my cock filled her to the brim. "Please."

"You're so perfect babe," I said as I pulled out and then rammed my cock into her again.

I found a rhythm that suited us both, carrying us closer to orgasm. I circled her hip and snaked my hand between her legs until I found her clit. I stroked her a few times before Amber's body started convulsing as she came noisily.

I returned my hand to her hips and closed my eyes to revel in my own release. I pounded home, bursting into her and filling her with my seed.

AMBER

I'd opted for a summery dress with long high heeled boots and a warm coat for dinner at Brody's. I had a feeling that something special was going to happen tonight. Brody had been pretty mysterious about why he was being formal about us having dinner together at home.

I didn't want to overthink things, but I couldn't help but think, what if he wanted to propose? No, that was silly of me. It was too soon. I felt as if Brody and I had been in a relationship for years while in reality, it was not more than three months.

It was just a dinner for two people who loved each other. I grabbed my purse and rather than request for an Uber before I left my apartment, I decided to enjoy a short walk first.

It was a beautiful evening. The air was crisp and deliciously cold. It made you think of a fire in the chimney, and a mug of hot chocolate. As I turned away from the building door, I noticed a fancy black car with tinted windows parked by the side of the road.

I was about to walk on when the door opened and a young woman in a nurse's uniform opened the door.

"Miss Amber Davies?" she said, with a warm disarming smile.

"Yes, that's me," I found myself saying as I walked towards her.

She opened the door further. "There's someone here who wants a word with you."

Timber would have killed me if he saw me. All his lessons on safety and taking care of myself flew out the window as I peered into the car, led by curiosity. As soon as I saw the occupant, I recoiled and stepped back as though I had been slapped.

The man never gave up! He must have noticed that my bakery was up and running so there was no way I was going to sell the building. I was about to turn and walk away without saying a word when something struck me.

"How did you know where I live?" I said to him.

"My son told me," he said.

"What?"

"Brody Kruger. He's my son. My name is David Kruger."

The world slowed down as I tried to make sense of his words. A sickening, icy numbness crept across my skin. There had to be a mistake. He could not be my Brody's father. I shook my head. "No."

I shook so badly; my legs almost gave way. He smiled and the resemblance between their smiles struck me like lightning. I inched closer to study his face. He wasn't lying. He was Brody's father. Nausea rose up my throat. I reached out to clutch the car, feeling as if someone had cut off my legs.

"I see that as usual my son kept you in the dark," he said. "I'd like a word with you. Please. Come in, just for a few minutes. I'm still too weak to stand otherwise I'd be out of this damn car."

My instincts screamed at me to get away from him but where was I going to go? To Brody's place for the romantic dinner he was making for us and pretend that everything was okay between us?

Against my better judgment, I entered the car. I clasped my hands together to keep them from shaking.

"Brody wants to leave the company," his father said.

I relaxed a little. Brody had become a stranger to me the moment his father had introduced himself. I remembered all the things I had said to Brody about the despicable real estate man, and my face heated up. Even if the two men did not get along, he was still his father.

And it must have hurt Brody on some level to hear me speak that way about him. I sneaked a look at him and wondered how such a man could have fathered a good person like Brody.

"He wants to return to that nonsense of sculpting. I need you to talk some sense into him. He'll listen to you."

I stared at him incredulously. "How is it that Brody is your son, and you don't know him, even after all these years? He's not cut out to be a businessman. He's very gifted in sculpting and that's what makes him happy."

He stared at me shrewdly. "Will you say the same thing when he can't afford to pay for your child's private tuition fee?"

"What?"

"Look, you're a smart young woman. At least I hope you are. You like a good life, don't you? With Brody at the company, you'll never have to lift a pretty finger for the rest of your life. Just like my wife. You'll have a good life doing the things you love doing."

Which planet did he live on where women didn't enjoy working? "I love working."

"Only because you have to. Wait until you get a chance not to," he said with a chuckle.

As I stared at him, it dawned on me that we were from two different worlds, and he was never going to believe that not all women wanted to be taken care of. He interpreted my silence to mean that he was making progress and he kept at it.

I understood then why Brody had done everything he could to keep his father away from me. Obviously, there was the fact that he had been trying to bully me into selling my beloved building, then there was the kind of person he was.

I felt sorry for Brody, having to grow up with such a man as his father. I could only imagine the horrors he had endured under his father. The hurtful words and the sneer that his father seemed to have perfected.

"I love Brody and I want him to do whatever makes him happy. This may come as a surprise to you, but not all of us need millions of dollars to be happy. Some of us are content with just enough."

He stared at me as though I was the one from space.

"I wish you a quick recovery," I said and got out of the car.

As I walked away, a bitter taste filled my mouth and I realized I was crying. Not for anything that Mr. Kruger had said, but for Brody. How tough it must have been to hide his father from his girlfriend knowing that if she found out, she could very well end their relationship.

I loved Brody but finding out who his father was made me love him even more. Interspersed with that love were feelings of protectiveness that made me want to wrap my arms around him and keep him safe.

I walked until my feelings were not so raw and I wasn't crying every few minutes. I flagged down a cab and when I got in, I gave him Brody's address. On the way, I checked my phone and found a message from Brody asking if I was okay.

I texted him back, letting him know that I was on the way. Fifteen minutes later, I was getting out of the cab.

"Good evening," the night doorman said with a low bow as he held the door open for me.

"Good evening," I said, feeling like a different person from who I'd been the last time I'd been to Brody's place.

I really knew him now. Every piece felt as though it had fallen into place now that I knew who his father was. I had a good feeling that from now on our relationship would move to another level.

I rode the elevator to the penthouse to find Brody waiting for me by his front door. Seeing him with all the hidden parts of him now out in the open made me feel as if a dam had burst inside of me. Love and desire for him overwhelmed me.

"Hey you," he said.

"Hi," I said and went straight to him. I threw my arms around his neck and rose on tiptoe to kiss him.

I nudged his lips open for a deeper kiss and stroked his neck, running my fingers all over his back. Heat consumed my body, and I pressed my chest against his, loving the friction between us.

I wanted to do more but the little semblance of common sense I possessed at that moment reminded me we were in a semi-public place. I pulled away, took Brody's hand and led him into the apartment.

"What's going on?" Brody asked in an amused tone as I led him down the hallway to his bedroom.

"You'll see," I said, mysteriously.

In his bedroom, I made him stand still as I undid the buttons of his shirt one by one. When they were all undone, I scraped my nails over his muscular chest, teasing the hairs that covered him.

He inhaled sharply, the amusement gone from his eyes. I pushed the shirt from his shoulders and Brody shrugged out of it. He raised his hands to reach for me, but I firmly returned them to his side. His belt was next to go followed by his pants.

I knelt down and trailed kisses up his masculine thighs. I couldn't get enough of the scent of him as I peppered kisses further and further up. His boxer briefs tented so much, they looked as though they were going to split in the middle.

I reached up, grabbed the hem and slowly pulled down his briefs. I took a moment to admire his beautiful cock, filled with dark veins that ran lengthwise. I pulled down his briefs the rest of the way and he stepped out of them.

I wrapped my hand around his cock and slowly stroked it before I stuck out my tongue and tasted the pearly precum sitting on the tip of it.

"Fuck Amber," Brody hisses, placing his hands on his hips.

I sucked at his cock as if it was a lollipop enjoying the grunts and noises of pleasure that he was making. He let out a deep growl when I took all of it into my mouth and suctioned the tip.

He rocked into my mouth, slowly at first and then he picked up speed. I kept one hand cradling his balls and when they tightened and I sensed that Brody was about to come, I pulled away and concentrated my attention on peppering kisses on his thighs and the v above his cock.

I stifled a laugh at the groan of frustration he let out. I stood as I kissed him, and then took him and led him to the bed. As he lay on his back watching me with his dark eyes, I slowly peeled off my clothes. My pussy throbbed as I pulled down my panties and I had to fight the temptation to touch myself. It was about Brody tonight, I reminded myself.

When I was completely naked, I joined Brody on the bed, covering his body with mine. I stroked his face and then brought my mouth to his. His hands moved to cup and squeeze my ass.

"You feel so fucking good," Brody said between kisses.

"So do you," I said. "I want to make love to you tonight."

"I like the sound of that," he said in a deep, affected voice.

BRODY

"I love this making love thing," I said to Amber as she loved me with her tongue and lips.

She let out a soft laugh and then straddled me. So far, I'd not been allowed to touch her but now I took the opportunity to sit up and touch her. I pulled her closer and went for her mouth, capturing her lips in a tantalizing, teasing kiss. She raised herself slightly and rubbed her wet pussy up and down my cock.

I caressed her ass and hips, then brought my mouth to take a nipple into my mouth. I swirled my tongue around it and then lightly grazed it with my teeth. When I did the same thing to the other nipple, Amber became undone.

"I want this cock inside me," she said, gripping the base of it. She slowly lowered herself on it, letting out sweet soft moans as she took more and more of me.

I let myself fall back on the bed but kept my hands on her breasts. "You're so beautiful, I can't believe that you're mine."

Her eyes were filled with heat as she focused her gaze on me. "I'm yours Brody. Please take me."

I pulled her to lie on me and then flipped us around so that I was on top. I smoothed her hair away from her face before bracing my hands on either side of her. I looked down at her. "I love you, Amber. So fucking much."

"I love you too Brody."

Joy exploded in my chest. Those words were like sweet music to my ears. "Ready for a wild ride?"

She grinned. "Yes sir."

I plunged into her, instantly wiping the grin from her face. She cried out and dug her fingers into my shoulders. With every thrust, I plowed deeper and harder. Amber wrapped her sexy legs around me, drawing me closer.

"I'm going to come Brody," Amber cried out, throwing her hands to the sides as if to anchor herself.

I fucked her deep and hard, taking us both to the edge and then we were tumbling over it as we screamed out our releases. Pleasure rippled through me, both from my release and watching Amber's eyes roll over as she came.

"What brought that on?" I asked her later when we had gotten our breaths back.

She shot me an amused look. "Are you complaining?"

"No, I just want to replicate it another time, but I gotta know what brought it on."

"It was events out of your control," Amber said. "Now how about that dinner."

I knew when I was being gently put off, having done it myself more times than I could count. "Let's go see if it's been ruined." I excused myself to go to the bathroom first and when I returned to the bedroom, I carried two white robes.

"Thanks," Amber said as she wore hers. "What did you make for dinner?"

"Italian spiced pork chops with roasted potatoes and veggies," I said.

"Yum. Fancy," she said, already making her way towards the kitchen.

I laughed and followed her. "I love a woman who loves sex and food."

"In that order," Amber threw over her shoulder.

In the kitchen, we warmed the food then sat in our bathrobes feeding each other. I'd never done anything like that with a woman. Come to think of it, I'd never done a lot of the things I did with Amber with another woman.

"Some wine?" I asked Amber when we finished eating.

"Yes please. The perfect ending to a perfect evening," she said, letting out a luxurious sigh.

"Who said the evening is over?" I asked.

Amber yawned noisily. "My body."

I chuckled as I grabbed a chardonnay from the fridge, uncorked it and carried it to the table. I poured us two glasses and suggested a toast.

"To us and a wonderful future together," I said.

270

We clinked glasses and sealed it with a light brush of our lips. A thoughtful expression came to her face as she sipped on her wine.

"I wasn't sure whether to tell you this or not, but I don't want any secrets between us," she said.

I went absolutely still. Any mention of the word secret had my heart racing. It reminded me of the secrets between us.

Amber locked gazes with me. "I met your father today."

All the air left my lungs. I had to have misunderstood what Amber had said. Afraid of saying the wrong thing, I kept quiet and waited for her to continue.

"Your father is the real estate man that used to pester me about selling, isn't he?" she said.

My head felt as if it was made from cement as I nodded. My mouth was fucking stuck together. Either that or my brain had stopped sending speaking signals to my mouth.

"He was parked outside my building. He had come to ask me to talk you into continuing to work at Orion. To quote him, 'I'm sure you like the finer things in life.'"

I cringed and mumbled curses at my father. What the fuck was wrong with him? Sweat coated my skin. Then something else struck me. Even after finding out who my father was, Amber had still come.

"He's not a very pleasant man but I had no right to say the things I said about him. I'm really sorry."

"You only spoke the truth, Amber. Besides, you didn't know he was my father and even if you did, you were right. The fact that he's my father doesn't make me blind to his faults. I know what kind of a man my father is."

"I just want to tell you that I understood why you chose not to tell me the truth," she said.

I wanted to weep. How could a woman be so fucking perfect for me? Amber had met my father and had not been intimidated by his presence or wealth. Very few people could stand up to him.

"You were frightened of losing me," Amber said, her eyes brimming with tears.

I nodded. A shot of guilt raced through me. She still didn't know everything. Knowing the identity of my father was the least explosive of the two. As perfect as Amber was, the other secret was unforgivable. Destroying her business and then pretending to be the hero afterwards?

"Let's go back to bed," I told her, unable to bear her gorgeous trusting eyes on me, any longer.

We took turns using the bathroom and then cuddled up in my bed to sleep. Amber fell asleep in my arms within five minutes of entering the bed. My mind refused to settle down enough to sleep. All I could think about was what had transpired between Amber and my father.

Finally, I felt my eyelids growing heavy and I gave in to the lure of sleep.

At first, I was sure that I was dreaming. The smell of gas filled my nostrils. The hairs at the back of my neck stood up and I woke up fully, with my heart pounding hard in my chest.

I woke up so violently that Amber immediately stirred. "What's wrong?" she asked sleepily.

Before I could answer, the bedroom door swung open, and the room flooded with light. A man stood in my bedroom, staring at Amber as she scrambled to sit up. Then he raised a gun and aimed it at Amber. I raised my hand without thinking about it and tried to pull Amber behind me.

"Carson, what the hell are you doing?" Amber said.

Fuck! It was her crazed ex-boyfriend. We were in trouble. Psychopaths didn't break into their ex-girlfriend's boyfriend's apartment to say hello or good morning.

"I warned you about him and you wouldn't listen," Carson said in an angry voice.

"It's my life Carson and how I choose to live it is none of your business," Amber said. "You're not supposed to be near me, Carson. You're breaking the law."

Despite the precarious situation we were in, admiration rose inside me. Her crazy ex was waving a gun at her and Amber didn't sound scared one bit.

"I'll always love you, Amber. No matter what the court or anybody says. It's my duty to protect you."

Carson shifted his gun and attention to me. "I told you he's evil Amber, but you wouldn't believe me, and you allowed him to fuck you."

"Get the fuck out!" I said with barely controlled anger. I didn't do well with threats to myself or my woman.

He grinned. "Or what? I'm not going anywhere until I finish doing what brought me here."

My mind worked fast. We needed a distraction. Something to make him drop the gun. The next words he said made my blood turn to ice.

"Did your boyfriend tell you that he's the one who burned down your beloved bakery?"

Silence followed his question. I could feel Amber's glance turn to me. Sweat formed on my brow.

"Brody, is it true?" Amber asked in a shaky voice, her eyes as big as saucers.

I swallowed.

"Please tell me he's lying," she begged.

"He can't tell you that beautiful because he knows that I speak only the truth," Carson crowed, triumph in his voice. "I was there on the night of the fire. I saw him break in the back door, enter like a damn thief, and set the bakery on fire."

"Brody?" Amber urged, a note of hysteria in her voice. "Say something."

"That's not how it happened. It's not the whole story," I muttered. Jesus, I sounded so lame.

Amber staggered back. "Who are you, Brody?" she shouted.

"I love you Amber and I would not do anything deliberately to hurt you. That night was a mistake. I didn't know the bakery was yours."

"Were you the one who lit the fire?" she asked, her voice cold and hard.

"I—"

"Did *you* light the fire?" she asked in a cold, dead voice.

"Yes."

At that moment, I knew that it was over between us. The one thing that I'd lived in fear of happening finally had. But we were still in danger. There was a mad man waving a gun at us. There was no way I was going to let him harm Amber.

Without a warning, I lunged out of the bed, catching Carson by surprise. While listening to Amber and me, he had dropped his guard and the gun was loosely held on his side. His eyes widened in surprise, but before he recovered enough to raise it, my body had knocked the gun off.

It fell to the ground, closely followed by Carson and me crashing next to it.

"Run Amber!" I shouted to her, as I grabbed Carson's hand to keep him from reaching for the gun.

Time slowed down as we wrestled on the floor, each trying to keep the other from reaching the gun. With my foot, I kicked the gun deeper under the bed at the same time that Carson kicked my balls, rendering me immobile with agony for a few seconds.

He seized that moment to scramble to his feet. Amber! I ignored the searing pain, crawled under the bed until I reached the gun. Then I stumbled after him. Panic rose up my chest as the smell of gas grew stronger.

"Don't do this Carson, please," Amber said as I burst into the kitchen.

She was near the door while he stood at the other end holding a lighter in his hand. I moved to stand in front of Amber, and I gestured at her to inch out of the room.

Carson had a manic look on his face, and I knew he was going to flick the lighter.

"Drop it!" I shouted.

He swung his gaze to me and let out a loud manic laugh. "It's over Brody. Let's see whether your father's millions are going to help you now huh?"

I made a split decision. I squeezed the trigger. The next thing I knew, a blast of heat hit me, and I was flying in the air. "Amber!" That was the last thing I said, before the world went black and I lost consciousness.

AMBER

"Oh my God," I cried over and over again. I stood rooted to the spot, with the operator on the other end asking me questions. Something that sounded like a gunshot followed by an explosion had gone off and I knew that Carson had carried out his threat.

I dropped the phone and fighting the scream rising up my throat I ran to the kitchen. I saw Brody as soon as I stepped in. He was crumpled up on the ground and the kitchen was on fire. A fire alarm went off. Shards of glass lay everywhere, and the heat was almost unbearable.

I had to wake Brody up. I knelt next to him and shook him violently. He didn't stir.

"Brody please," I cried. "Okay. Calm down. You need to pull him." He was so much heavier that I was but there was no choice. I had to get him out or lose him. Already the kitchen was full of smoke and breathing was becoming difficult.

I got up, grabbed his hands and pulled with all my strength. I'll never know how I did it, but inch by inch, he moved until we were out of the kitchen and in the living room. A minute later, I was opening the door for the firefighters and paramedics.

I sunk to the floor when I saw them. "Brody needs help," I cried pointing at where he lay.

"Don't worry we'll take care of him," someone said, while two others grabbed me by each arm and helped me out of the apartment.

I tried to tell them that I wasn't injured as they carried me to an ambulance.

"We'll need to check you out," one of the paramedics said in an infuriatingly calm voice.

"Brody's the one who's been hurt," I said tearfully. I recalled the shot I'd heard but I consoled myself with the fact that I hadn't seen any blood when I dragged Brody out.

"He's being taken care of. I promise."

I lay my head down and I allowed myself to relax. Brody was in safe hands. I shut my eyes tightly and pushed away the disturbing video playing in my head of the last couple of hours.

All that time, I'd thought I was safe, but Carson had been watching me and planning. Timber had never stopped worrying about Carson and I thought he was being paranoid. Oh God. Bile rose up my throat.

I sat up. "I need to vomit."

Someone placed a vomit bag in front of me and I shoved my face inside. I threw up, feeling as if I was retching my guts out. When the heaving in my stomach ceased, I took the tissue offered by someone I couldn't see and cleaned myself up.

~

It was the second day, and they still hadn't allowed me to see Brody. They said only his direct family were allowed into his room. I sat in the waiting room wringing my hands and waiting for Liz to come out and tell me how Brody was.

The previous day, he had been in a lot of pain and had been knocked out by painkillers. I shot to my feet when I saw Liz's figure returning to the waiting room.

"He's asking for you," Liz said.

"Thank you," I said, rushing out. The last two days had been a nightmare with not knowing how badly hurt Brody was.

My hands shook as I turned the knob of the door. I stepped in to find him half sitting in bed, with a white bandage wrapped around half of his head.

"Oh Brody," I cried.

"I look worse than I am," he said. "Just a few burns but they told me that those will heal completely."

Relief flooded me. He was going to be okay. "I'm so glad. I was so worried, and they wouldn't let me see you yesterday."

I went and stood by his bed, but I didn't kiss him. How could I when there had been so many lies between us. I loved Brody. I had no doubt about it.

"I'm sorry," he said, his eyes wet. "I'm sorry I was not honest with you from the beginning."

"What happened?" I asked. I hadn't planned on having that conversation now but seeing that Brody had brought it up, I desperately needed to know.

"My father and I had been in the car together and he had asked the driver to slow down in front of your bakery. He pointed out a man taking pictures outside the bakery and told me that he was moving into town and that he was a known pedophile."

"That was Timber," I said, stunned at the accusation.

"I pieced that together later but at the time, all I could think was he must not be allowed to remain in our town. My father knew that I would react that way. He knew my hatred for pedophiles."

Brody told me about Liz's childhood friend who had been kidnapped then killed by a pedophile. My chest squeezed with pain as I listened to his narration of what had happened all those years ago.

As he spoke, I understood then why he reacted as he did.

"I know I shouldn't have reacted instinctively, and I should have known better than to take my father's word. I know that now. That was the biggest mistake I've ever made. Can you ever forgive me? Is there hope for us?"

I wanted so badly to say yes. But he had burned my bakery! He had committed arson. But worse than that, he had lied to me and not just once or twice. How could I ever trust him again?

"I forgive you Brody," I said. "Your heart was in the right place. But I can't do this." My voice choked.

"Please don't say that Amber. You're the best thing that has ever happened to me. I love you with everything I've got."

"Love is not enough Brody. We have to be able to trust each other and I don't know if I can ever trust you again. You lied to me over and over again. I already forgave you for lying about who your father is. But this one is too big. You committed arson, Brody."

I didn't tell him that Timber had been so angry that he had wanted us to go to the police immediately. Julie and I had talked sense into him. We had made him see that Brody was a good person, but his impulsive reactions were the ones to blame for what had happened.

He nodded. "I don't deserve you, Amber. You're a good person. You deserve a person who's got their shit together."

Tears flooded my eyes. "You're a good person too Brody but there's been too many secrets between us. Too many lies. I can't live like that."

"I'm really sorry."

"I also know now that the fire station doesn't have a fund for victims of fires," I said.

"I wanted to help but I knew you wouldn't have agreed to take money from me. It was my fault that you had lost your livelihood and it was my responsibility to make sure your bakery was up and running again, no matter what."

"I'll pay it back," I said.

"No Amber. I owed you more than a hundred grand. I owe you much, much more. Please."

The pain in my heart grew to unbearable proportions. I had to leave. I looked at Brody. "I would have forgiven you anything if only you would have trusted me enough to tell me the truth."

He stared at me without speaking until I turned and left the room. I found Liz in the waiting room. She stood up and came to me.

"He meant well you know," she said.

She had known about the fire and had been horrified by it but there was nothing she or anyone could have done about it. She obviously couldn't have told me. Her first loyalty was to her brother and that's the way it's supposed to be.

"I know he meant well, but that doesn't excuse the fact that he kept so many things from me," I said.

"I know," Liz said, looking at me with sad eyes. "You two were so great together." Her eyes flooded with tears. "I'll miss you Amber, but I'll be dropping in at the bakery every so often. I hope it's okay."

"Of course, it's okay," I said.

We hugged and said goodbye. Outside, I got into my car and drove to the bakery but when I got there, I couldn't go in. I needed to speak to someone who understood. Someone who could look at both sides with compassion. I knew the right person to talk to.

I drove back in the opposite direction from the one I'd come from and headed to my dad's place. I had been there before for dinner. As I got nearer, I wondered whether it was a good idea to show up without telling him.

Even though he was my dad, I didn't know how he felt about a lot of things. Like his privacy.

My anxiety disappeared as soon as he opened the door and saw me. His face lit up in the kind of joy you couldn't fake.

"Amber!" he said, pulling me into a hug. "What a great surprise. Come on in."

"Hi," I said almost shyly. I'd not figured out what to call him and sort of avoided calling him anything directly.

I followed him into the house to the living room. He was surprisingly neat for a man, but I guess being single all his life, he had gotten used to taking care of himself.

"Can I make you some coffee my dear," he said and at his kind tone, my self-control disintegrated.

I burst into tears, and he immediately came to me and held me. I cried noisily on his shoulder and when I calmed down a little, he took my hand and led me to the couch.

"It can't be that bad," he said.

The whole story poured out of me as he held my hand. His face grew pinched, and I could tell that he was trying very hard to control his anger.

"I'm with Timber here," he said and when he saw my face, he added. "I'm sorry and I think very highly of Brody. I like him too, but the bakery was someone's livelihood. It doesn't matter how angry you are, there's no excuse for taking the law into your own hands."

I'd never seen him so upset. "Brody really regrets reacting that way. He has learned the hard way." I sniffed when it hit me afresh that it was over between us.

The future I had dreamed of had been snatched from me. I told my father all this. How I felt betrayed by all the lies.

"I have to say that he has really gone to a lot of trouble to keep you," my father said and then flashed a quick frown. "I don't agree with his methods, but you have to admit that the man was determined."

I chuckled despite the circumstances. "Can you imagine keeping the identity of your father from your girlfriend?"

My father shook his head. "I can't imagine the pressure he must have been under." He sobered up. "I've never been glad that someone has lost their lives but I'm glad that Carson has. The world is a better place without him."

I shuddered when I pictured his eyes which had flashed with madness. "Me too."

My father closed the distance between us and pulled me under his arm and held me. "I'm just so thankful that you are okay. I couldn't bear to lose you when I've just found you. I love you, Amber."

"I love you too, Dad," I said.

BRODY

I sighed in frustration as I surveyed the work I'd been doing all day. My all-woman piece was not coming out as I'd envisioned. I resisted the urge to throw it to the wall. I'd formally stopped working at Orion to give all my attention to my artwork, but I seemed to have frozen.

I couldn't feel the piece. Footsteps rushing down the hallway caught my attention and I looked towards the door as a knock came on it.

"Brody?"

"Come in, Hellen," I said.

"Your sister just called. She said to tell you to meet her at the intensive care ward in the hospital. Your father had a stroke."

I let out a stream of curses. This was exactly what the doctors had warned my father about. He had dismissed their warnings and had continued going to the office and taking on a lot of stress in the process. I thought of my mother and wished I could protect her from this.

She had begged and even taken away my father's cell phone. Nothing had worked. Now this. As I dressed, thoughts of Amber filled my mind. I needed to hear her voice. I needed her strength. I inhaled deeply and reminded myself that wishing for things that weren't going to happen was a waste of my time.

It felt as if I was reliving the past as I hurried out of my studio and to my bedroom to change out of my work clothes. We had been warned that a stroke after a heart attack could make my father a vegetable or could be fatal. I shuddered now as the two prospects loomed closer.

I drove as fast as I could to the hospital without breaking the speed limit. I was lucky to get a parking spot near the entrance. I sprinted in and took an elevator to the intensive care floor.

I saw my sister as soon as I stepped out of the elevator.

"He's not doing too good Brody," she said, coming to me.

I gave her a quick hug. "What are the doctors saying?"

We spoke as we walked.

"An artery has ruptured deep in his brain. Too deep to be operated on," Liz said, her voice choking with a sob.

My father was hooked to a life support machine and the only sign that he was alive was the rise and fall of his chest. My mother stood by his side, her face white and her hands clenched into fists.

I went to her and pulled her into a side hug. She turned to me and then buried her head in my chest. Her body wracked with sobs. I'd never seen her that way.

"It's going to be okay, Mom," I said.

She raised her gaze to mine. "No, it's not. I told him that this was going to happen if he wasn't careful."

"You did the best you could," I said and held her again. "Father always does what he wants and nothing anyone says makes a difference." I felt no bitterness as I said this. I'd come to terms with who my father was.

No one was ever going to change him, but it also meant that I had to chart my own path, not to be carried by the tornado that my father was. I was proud of myself because I'd left Orion against my parents' wishes and I was following my dreams.

We stayed at the hospital for the rest of the day, but my father's condition didn't change. They did a battery of tests to check for a response.

Three days later, the doctors called us for a meeting and informed us that my father was brain dead. There was no hope that he would regain consciousness. They wanted our consent to turn off the life support machine.

Despite being the strong one, the one who comforted my sister and my mother, I still hadn't come to terms with my father's death. I'd even gone to the morgue and seen him, but I couldn't equate the lifeless body lying there as that of my father.

The full force of losing him hit me on the eve of his funeral. I sat on the floor of my studio and cried like a child. Despite the differences we'd had between us, he was still my father, and I felt the loss deeply and painfully.

I cried for the relationship we never had and would never have. I cried for the lost years. I don't know how long I sat there but a loud knock on my door roused me from the bubble of grief. I poured water on my face and went to answer it, knowing it was either my mother, Liz or William.

I opened the door and inhaled sharply when I saw Amber standing there. I blinked several times, unsure whether my brain was playing tricks on me.

"May I come in?" she said.

"Yes." I stood to the side to let her in. As she went by, she left behind her signature vanilla scent that evoked all sorts of memories.

Amber on top of me, with her eyes gleaming with passion as she rode me. Amber curled up on my chest as she lay asleep. A laughing Amber, with her head thrown back and her gorgeous mane of red hair flying around her face.

I hadn't known it was possible to miss someone the way I had missed her. Seeing her gave me hope. A buoyancy that I hadn't felt in a long time filled me. I didn't want to have my heart broken again but her coming had to mean something.

I shut the door and followed her into the living room. She patted the couch space next to her and I went and sat down.

She smiled gently. "I'm sorry about your father, Brody. I read about it in the papers."

"Thanks. We're grateful that he went peacefully and didn't experience any pain."

The seed of hope in my chest shrunk. Had she only come to offer her condolences?

"I had another reason for coming," Amber continued. She laced her fingers together on her lap. "I miss you, Brody."

My heart rose and then thundered so loudly in my chest that I couldn't hear myself think. What was she saying exactly?

"I love you Brody and I know I'll never feel that way about another man. You did something very wrong, but you meant well, and your heart was in the right place."

I had to touch her. I took her small hand and sandwiched it into mine. "I don't deserve you, Amber."

She smiled amid tears. "We deserve each other."

"I love you so much," I said. "You make my life full and happy. I pray and hope that you'll be able to forgive me one day."

"I've already forgiven you Brody, but you must promise to never lie to me again. Even by omission," Amber said, her eyes wide with vulnerability.

I was sure my eyes reflected the same vulnerability. "I promise."

She stood up and came and sat on my lap. We clung to each other like two drowning people. I held her so tightly, I was afraid I was going to crush her. Needing more, I stood up and carried her down the hallway to my bedroom.

"I've missed this," Amber said as I lay her on the bed.

"I've missed everything," I said as I lay next to her. "When you left me, you took with you my ability to sculpt."

"You haven't been working?" Amber said.

"I have, but it doesn't have the magic it usually has. I have a feeling that problem is gone forever."

She smiled. "So, I'm your muse huh?"

I nodded. "Yes, you are. Which means I have to make sure that you're mine forever."

"I am," Amber said and brought her mouth to mine.

We kissed slowly and unhurriedly. Until then, I didn't know it was possible for someone's heart to expand and contract at the same time from happiness.

The following day, as we laid my father to rest, I felt strong and ready to say goodbye. Amber stayed glued to my side and later as we entertained close friends in my parents' home, she flitted between me, my mother, Liz and William, making sure we were all okay.

"She's a wonderful girl, Brody. Don't mess up," my mother said to me just as we were about to leave.

"I won't mother. I promise."

EPILOGUE

AMBER

One Year Later

I was a nervous wreck even though it was the second time we were doing it. The difference however was that our second bakery was in a prominent spot in the new mall that Orion had built.

William and Brody had brought Mr. Kruger's dream of an outdoor mall to life. William had taken over the company but had insisted on keeping Brody as a consultant. I'd been touched when they had given Timber and me the choice of one of the retail spaces.

We had trained new staff to run the new bakery but today, we were all in Crusty Cookies for the opening of the bakery. Timber was busy taking pictures while I was in and out of the kitchen, making sure that everything would be ready when we opened the doors at nine.

"Amber," Caroline said, rushing into the kitchen. "There's a TV crew outside," she squealed. "I'm going to be on TV."

We all laughed, and the tension of the morning dissipated. My father draped an arm around me.

"I'm so proud of you," he said.

I leaned into him. "Thanks Dad."

Brody came in through the back entrance at that moment. He looked so handsome and suave in a black suit and crisp white shirt.

"You look beautiful," he said, kissing me lightly on the mouth.

I'd chosen a semi-casual sky blue dress to match the signature colors of the mall. "Thank you. You look handsome too."

Brody shook hands with my dad and then went around the kitchen teasing everyone. We had become like one big family and Brody and my dad fit right in.

We opened the doors at nine on the dot to a big crowd and a lot of cheering. Me, Timber and the staff got interviewed by several TV stations which was fun. The day passed in a whirlwind of socializing and selling a lot of cookies and cakes.

A few hours later as I was walking through the throngs of people, I noticed my dad speaking to a woman. She had her back to me but something about her seemed familiar. As if I knew her.

My father's stance caught my attention too. He seemed to concentrate too much on her. They stood close to each other and whatever they were talking about looked intense. They stood a little way from everyone else.

I found myself moving towards them. As I got closer, something about the woman made the hairs at the back of my neck stand up. For no reason at all, my heart started galloping in my chest.

My dad looked up, saw me and he seemed to freeze. He swung his gaze to the woman and said something that made her turn her head to look at me. Even without being told, I knew who she was.

"What is she doing here?" I asked my father when I reached them.

I refused to look at her. I didn't care to know what she looked like or whether we shared any features. The feelings of rejection came rushing back as did my anger.

"She just wanted to see you once Amber," my father said. "Please."

The pleading tone in my father's voice made me turn to look at her. I'd not expected to feel anything but when my gaze met hers, sympathy came over me. Fear flickered in her eyes. What was she frightened of? She was the one who had her lawyers warn me off?

"I'm sorry I'm not the person you thought I would be," she said in a voice that sounded eerily like mine.

"I never had any preconceived ideas about who you were." I couldn't believe that I was having a conversation with the woman who had given birth to me.

She looked at my father as if for help.

"I don't understand why you wanted to see me after that scathing letter," I said, genuinely puzzled.

I felt nothing for her. Not anger, or even curiosity. She was just the vessel that I'd used to get into this world.

"I didn't want to do that but if my husband knew." She made a noise like a sniff. "He has political ambitions, you know. He can't afford to have anything ruin his chances."

"Does he know about me?"

She shook her head. "The only people who knew about you were my parents and they are both gone now."

"Do you have other children?" I knew the answer to that, and I also knew that hearing it would hurt me, but I wanted to know.

She shook her head. "No. Douglas and I didn't have any children."

I felt as if I'd been punched. She didn't have any children and she had rejected the only one she had.

"I know this is hard to believe but I do love you and I wish you all the best in life even though I'm not a part of it," she said.

Footsteps sounded behind me and seconds later, Brody draped his arm around my shoulders. "Are you okay Amber?"

I smiled at him. "I'm fine. Completely fine." I turned and took Brody with me, and we headed back to the party.

"Who was that?" Brody asked.

"No one important," I said. "I'll tell you about it later." Walking away, it felt as if I'd left behind all the things that had held me back and caused me pain and suffering.

In her rejection of me, my biological mother had hurt herself more than she had hurt me. She had picked her husband's political ambitions over getting to know her own daughter.

Sometime in the evening, as the ceremony was winding down, a hush and then a cheer sounded. As I craned my neck to see what was happening, the crowd of people parted in front of me like the parting of the Red Sea.

Then I saw Brody. On his knee. Holding a jewelry box.

My legs threatened to buckle under me. Oh my God. He was going to propose. I made my legs move to get closer to Brody. When I met his gaze, everything in me went still and I forgot that I was in the middle of a crowd. All that mattered was Brody.

"Amber Davies. From the first moment I met you, I knew that my life had changed. You were tailored made for me. I want you to be the mother of my children and the woman I grow old with. Amber Davies, will you marry me?"

We had been through so much together and as I looked into his eyes, I saw the same thought reflected there. We had come so close to losing each other. We had almost lost our lives at the hands of a psychopath. We had been there for each other in the most important moments of our lives.

I'd held Brody's hand when he lost his father and buried him. He had been there for me in my quest to find my father. I had encouraged Brody when he started a new career, and now his name was beginning to be known in the art world.

We knew each other as much as two people could and we still loved each other, warts and all. I couldn't think of anyone else I would have said yes to. Only Brody.

I don't know how I moved from where I'd been standing into Brody's arms. I knelt in front of him and fell into his arms. He wrapped me up and held me close. In Brody's arms, we became one. Our hearts beat in sync and the thought that I would experience the same feeling of peace and security made me want to cry with joy.

"Yes, I'll be your wife," I cried, tears streaming down my face.

"I love you so much," Brody said, his words barely audible as a cheer went up reminding me that we were in the middle of a crowd.

Brody stood up, taking me with him, then kissed me to more cheers and catcalls. The crowd moved closer as our friends and loved ones hugged and congratulated us.

COMING NEXT: SAMPLE CHAPTERS

THE FORGOTTEN PACT

Chapter One
Clarissa

I can't help but smile as I get off the bus at the bus station and look around. I wasn't sure how I would feel coming back here after all of these years, but with the familiar scent of jasmine in the air welcoming me home, I'm so glad I'm here. It's like stepping back in time, back into my childhood. All at once, I feel a rush of nostalgia go through me. I feel as though it's been forever since I was here and yet at the same time, I feel as though I've never been away from the place.

I leave the bus stop and start walking through the town. The apartment I've rented isn't far from the bus stop and it's a nice enough day. I was all set to take a cab to my apartment building, but I find that I want to walk, to soak up the atmosphere of the town and reminisce somewhat. Most of my things have already been sent to my apartment with the moving company and I only have a weekend bag with me so it's not like I'm laden down with luggage.

It's been fourteen years since my dad got offered a job in Italy. I was fifteen and of course I hated the idea of moving away, but as a child, I didn't get a say in the matter and before I knew it, I was in Rome. Rome is a beautiful place and looking back now, I'm glad we went. It will always hold a special place in my heart, but it's no St. Augustine. This feels like coming home in a way that returning to Rome after college just didn't.

I smile to myself as I pass the park we used to play in when we were kids. We would spend hours there in the summer and on weekends and evenings after school.

Nothing much has changed in the park. I can see the swing set, the top of the slide, the duck pond and the bandstand. The trees are taller, and the flower beds are different, but aside from that, it almost feels like I've gone back in time rather than just come back to town. I suppose that's part of the appeal of a small town like St. Augustine – nothing changes, meaning people will always feel at home here, even if that hasn't technically been true for almost a decade and a half.

I round the corner at the edge of the park and my smile widens when I see the large oak tree with our tire swing still attached to it. The tree has grown a lot over the years and the tire swing is now too high for any kids to be able to play on it, but the fact it's still there is amazing to me.

The tire swing reminds me of long, hot summer days when Gabe, my best friend at the time, and I would come down here and spend all day on that swing, daring each other to go higher and higher. I miss those days and I miss Gabe. We were inseparable for years before I was whisked off to Italy. We made the odd call to each other after my family and I moved away but long-distance calls are so expensive and both of our parents used to moan at us about the phone bills and eventually, we just lost touch.

I hope he's still here somewhere in town, so I get to see him again. It's been so long, and we would have so much to catch up on. He could no doubt tell me about his successful career, his beautiful wife and adorable children. And in turn, I could tell him about my failed career and my cheating ex-boyfriend.

I wonder if he remembers that night in the bandstand. The night we… I smile and shake away the memory. I really don't need to go back there. He probably won't remember it and even if he does, so what? It's not like it's actually going to happen.

I realize I've walked the rest of the way to my new apartment building without really noticing anything more around me while I was lost in thought. I feel a surge of excitement go through me as I open the main door and head for the elevator. For all of the things here that are so familiar to me, this is still a fresh start for me, and I can't wait to start on my new life and leave the old one – the one where I get cheated on and get my heart broken – very firmly behind me.

I step out of the elevator on the ninth floor and walk down the hallway. It's a nice hallway, carpeted in dark blue. The carpet is clean as are the cream-colored walls and the pleasant smells I catch in the air as they drift out of people's apartments, food cooking, laundry detergent, something sweet and fruity that may or may not be a candle burning. It's definitely an improvement on the apartments in my last place.

When Michael cheated on me, I felt as though my world had ended. I thought we were in love, but I was wrong. I was in love. Michael claimed to be in love with me but the fact that he would fuck some skanky little secretary from the office told me otherwise. Despite loving Michael, I still had enough self-respect that there was no way I was staying in a relationship with him after that. The place we were living in was his and I moved out the very day I found out about his affair.

I remember walking the streets with a suitcase containing my clothes and my makeup and my toiletries – the only things that were actually mine. Everything else in the apartment was Michael's – I had given up all my furniture, everything I owned really when I moved in with him. As I walked, I tried to work out what the hell I was supposed to do next.

The rain started then and within minutes, I was soaked through to the skin. I was shivering in the cold with my hair sticking to my scalp, the rain mixing with my tears and streaking my makeup. I checked into a hotel for the night. It was all I could think of to do at that time. I didn't want to turn up at a friend's place looking so disheveled.

The next morning, I extended my stay while I worked out where I was going to go and what I was going to do. The first thing I did was call my boss and tell him I quit. I couldn't face going back to the office after what Michael had done. I knew I was the victim, and he was the one who should feel ashamed, but knowing that didn't change the way I felt. I couldn't stand the thought of going back to work and having them all laughing at me behind my back and talking about me. I would be the one they pitied. The one who couldn't keep her man satisfied. No thank you. I had more than enough to worry about without bringing that onto myself.

I began searching for another job pretty much instantly but word travels quickly through the finance sector and my boss had no qualms about telling other firms that I had left him in the lurch and refused to work my notice period. Naturally he didn't bother to tell them why. No finance company would touch me after that. And because of the way I left my job, I didn't get a pto payout and staying at the hotel was eating my money like there was no tomorrow.

I had enough left for a deposit and a month's rent on a decent apartment and then I would be out of money. I began looking for both an apartment and a job outside of my comfort zone. I found both, neither of which exactly filled me with joy. I found a job waiting tables – something I really didn't enjoy in the least. After a few weeks there though, an opportunity opened up to work behind the bar instead. I took the opportunity and I loved it. My job situation felt much better, but my home life was still in shambles.

I had massively underestimated the cost of rent in the city and the only apartment that I could afford was a tiny thing. The living room also functioned as a dining room and a bedroom and it had a little kitchenette at the end, which meant that every time I cooked on the small stove, I risked setting my bedding on fire – that's how small the room was. The bathroom was so small that if I gained so much as a pound, I didn't think I'd fit in my shower, and it wasn't like I was overweight to begin with.

My apartment's size was the least of my worries there though. My neighbors posed a bigger problem. The hallway leading to my apartment was covered in graffiti and smears of what could have been blood or feces – I didn't know which and I didn't want to know. It smelled of stale urine and boiled vegetables left to rot. The smells drifting from the other apartments told me that my neighbors were stoners or worse.

Six months I put up with that before I finally knew I'd had as much of the place as I could take. I had never felt as low as I did the night my circumstances really hit me. I opened a bottle of wine and that was my first mistake. The second bottle was my second mistake, but by far my biggest mistake was when I called Michael. In my drunken state, I had decided to call him and really make him understand what he had done to me when he betrayed me. I wanted him to feel my pain. Somehow though, I ended up in tears telling him how my life had gone so wrong lately and before I knew it, he was at my door. From there, it didn't take much before he was in my bed.

The next morning, I felt regret like I had never felt before. My head was banging, I felt nauseous and worse than that, I felt ashamed of myself. Was I really so low that throwing myself at Michael had been an option?

I knew then I had to get away from the city, away from my shit hole apartment, away from my dead-end job and most importantly, away from Michael. And that's when I made the decision to come back to St. Augustine. For the same monthly rent, I have an apartment in a nice block that seems to house nice, normal people who don't smear shit up the walls and smoke drugs.

Chapter Two
Clarissa

I fish my key back out of my purse and unlock the door to apartment thirty-six. I take a deep breath, steeling myself for whatever might lay inside. I've only seen the apartment in the realtor's photos and of course they are trained to make anything look good. I close my eyes, push the door open and step inside. I open my eyes and relief floods me.

I'm standing in a short hallway with four doors leading off it. So far so good. Doors mean rooms, separate rooms for separate things. I poke my head in the first one and find a bathroom. It's small but nowhere near as small as my old one. The shower is over a bath rather than in a cubicle and I imagine myself having long, lazy bubble baths with music playing, surrounded by candles and I smile at the image.

Buoyed up by the decent bathroom, I move on, feeling more confident that the place is going to be ok. I open the door opposite the bathroom and find myself in a large, open plan room. Again, it's an arrangement of the living room, dining room and kitchen but it is so much better than what I'm used to.

The kitchen is a full-sized kitchen with a breakfast bar with tall stools sectioning it off from the rest of the room. The dining area is equipped with a small wooden table and two chairs, and the living area has a large beige couch, a coffee table, two recliners and a TV on the wall. There's plenty of room, or at least there will be when I get around to unpacking all the boxes the movers have unceremoniously dumped in the middle of the living room.

I can't stop myself from smiling as I back out of the living room and view the other two doors. I open the one next to the living room and find a good-sized linen closet with shelves. I'm pleased about that as I never seem to have enough storage space. Finally, I open the door at the end of the hallway. I find a good-sized bedroom with a double bed, a wardrobe and a small cabinet beside the bed. I go right into the room and move over to the window, smiling to myself when I look out and see that I can see the park from here.

I spend the rest of the day unpacking my weekend bag and my boxes and by the time I flop down on the couch with a pizza, I feel like I've had a productive day. All my things are unpacked and put away and already the apartment is beginning to feel like home. I just know I'll be happy here.

As I eat my dinner, I think about what I'm going to do for work. I don't have any savings – getting this place took the last money I had. I know I could go back to my old job working as a personal assistant in the finance sector. After all, I haven't worked in the area for a while now, I have kept up with the changing trends, and I can't see my old boss feeling the need to try to sabotage me all the way over here. I just won't put his name on my resume.

At the minute though, I need an income and I need it fast. I don't want to rush into a bad job in a place I'm less than happy because I want this to work in the long term. I don't want to end up taking something I'm not happy with just because I have bills to pay. I decide that for now, I'm going to try and find a bar job to tide me over while I do some research on local finance companies and see what the sector has to offer in and around St. Augustine.

I finish my dinner and think for a moment. I go through to the bathroom and brush my teeth and then my short black hair. I use the toilet and then I leave the bathroom and grab my jacket and my purse. I head out of the apartment, locking the door behind me. There really is no better time to go looking for bar work than now – that time when the night-time drinkers are starting to come out and the pub is busy enough that the manager isn't trying to do paperwork undisturbed but not so busy that taking the chance to ask about an opportunity might be a nuisance.

It's a fairly nice night and I set off walking towards the main street. It's only a ten-minute walk but it takes me slightly longer than that as I go into two bars on the way. Both of them are deathly quiet and unsurprisingly, neither of them is currently looking for any new staff. I make my way onto the main street. This is the one part of the town that has changed considerably.

The shops I remember from my childhood are mostly gone, replaced with boutique clothing stores, convenience stores and a cute looking little thrift shop that I make a note to come back to when it's open. I vaguely remember my father drinking around here, a place called Landers or something like that. The spot where I remembered it being is now an Indian restaurant. There are still several bars along the street though, so I don't let myself get disheartened just yet.

I feel a smile creep over my face when I see a help wanted sign in the window of the next bar I come to. I stand back slightly and look up at the sign above the door. The sign tells me that the bar is called The Marlow Bar and Grill. It looks fairly small but respectable and I pull the door open and step inside.

The place is lit by dim hanging lights and candles. The atmosphere is intimate and cozy, the tables far enough apart to give the diners some privacy. The smell of grilling meat in the air makes my stomach rumble despite the fact I've just eaten. The hostess smiles at me from behind her lectern as I approach her.

"Hi. Welcome to The Marlow Bar and Grill. Do you have a reservation with us this evening?" she asks.

"No. I'm actually interested in the job you have advertised in the window for bar staff," I say.

"The position is actually to join the team of wait staff. If you're still interested I can grab the manager for you?" she says.

I think for a moment. Am I interested? I think back to my old job waitressing. The burnt arms. The drunken gropes. The yelling and complaining about things that weren't even my fault half of the time. The tables that stiffed me on tips and left me with a choice between heating and food. The people who barked their drink orders at me rather than returning my polite hello. No. I'm not interested. I can't go back to that. I smile and shake my head.

"No thank you," I say. "But can I leave my contact details in case a bar job opens up?"

"Of course," the hostess says.

She hands me a pen and a piece of paper. Her smile has never slipped the whole time we spoke, and she still smiles as I scribble down my details and hand her back the paper and the pen.

"Thanks," I say, although something tells me that as soon as I leave she will throw away the piece of paper I hand back to her.

Turning around I leave and continue my wandering. The next two places I try aren't hiring and I'm starting to get massively deflated. I keep walking though, interested to see what else has changed on the main street. I pass a bar and debate going inside but I decide against it. I'll try again tomorrow. I can only take so much rejection in one night.

I pass an opening that I think is a side street. I peer down it to see if it's home to any more shops and see it's no more than an alley really, but I work out that if I walk down it, I'll cut my walk home in half. I start to head into the alley when the building on the other side of it catches my eye. It's another pub and I can't help but smile when I see the name of the place, The Black Swan. When we were kids, Gabe always said he would buy a bar and call it The Black Swan. Could it possibly be his bar? Has he actually followed through on his dream?

I don't suppose it's going to be his bar. Chances are he's not even in town anymore. Still though, I am curious. If it is his bar, it would be great to see a friendly face and catch up with him. Maybe he has a wife now. Children too. It would be great to have a ready-made little family to befriend.

I push the door open. The bar is fairly busy but it's not rowdy yet and I can hear the jukebox playing over the sound of the chatter coming from the tables. I hear the clink of balls as a group huddle around a pool table. A cheer goes up as one of the players sinks the black ball and wins the game. I find myself smiling as the winner does a little victory dance around the table.

I head for the bar, already liking the friendly atmosphere here. As I reach the bar, I open my mouth to ask if Gabe is by any chance the manager here when the sign behind the bartender's head catches my eye: bar staff wanted.

"Hi," I say when the bartender comes towards me. "I'd like to apply for the job."

I nod towards the sign and the bartender smiles at me.

"Great," he says. He turns away from me. "Penny. You're needed up here." He turns back to me. "Penny's in charge. She will have a chat with you."

"Thanks," I say with a smile.

So, it's Penny's bar not Gabe's bar. Oh well. I never truly believed it would be his. But still, the coincidence makes me think it might be a sign that this is the bar I was meant to find a job in.

A short, red-haired woman appears through a door behind the bar. The bartender nods towards me and she walks across the bar area. She lifts the divider between the bar and the public area and steps around to me. She smiles widely and offers her hand. I take it and we shake hands.

"Hi. I'm Penny. You're interested in the bartender position?" she says.

I nod.

"Clarissa Blayde. And yes, I'm very much interested," I say, returning Penny's smile.

"Have you got ten minutes to have a quick chat?" Penny asks.

"Like an interview?" I ask. I look down at my jeans and shake my head. "I'm not dressed for an interview."

"Well, the fact you recognize that gives you brownie points," Penny says. "And I won't judge you for not dressing for something you didn't know was going to happen."

"Then I'm free to chat," I say.

Penny leads me to a small table away from the bar in a quieter area of the room. We sit down and she smiles again.

"Do you have any bartending experience?" she asks me.

"Yes," I reply, telling her about my old job and how I moved from waiting tables to bartending and loved it. She listens intently and then she nods her head.

"Ok Clarissa, I'm going to level with you here. I am seriously short-staffed right now and I need someone who can hit the ground running. You will obviously be shown how to work the cash register and that kind of thing, but I will expect you to work on your own initiative quickly. Is that something you feel comfortable with?" Penny asks.

That's the moment I know I have the job, but I don't want to come across as too cocky, so I resist the urge to smile. Instead, I nod.

"Of course. In my old bar job, I was often the only bartender working and many nights I was the last person to leave, meaning I was responsible for securing the premises," I say. And then I play my ace. "And having just moved here today, I don't have anywhere I need to give notice so I can start whenever you need me to."

"So, you're saying you could start tomorrow evening?" Penny asks.

"Sure," I say, nodding my head.

"Then you're hired," Penny says.

"Thank you," I say.

"Bring your paperwork and everything along tomorrow. Around six thirty so I can go through your paperwork and then give you a quick tour and you can start your shift at seven. Rebecca will be working with you, she'll show you the ropes and help you out if you have any questions or anything," Penny says. "There's no specific uniform but we ask all staff members to wear black. Whether that's pants or a skirt with a top or a dress is up to you."

"Ok," I say.

It all sounds pretty standard, and I am excited to start working. Suddenly I don't want to leave the warm, happy atmosphere of the bar and go back to my empty apartment and I'm trying to work out whether it would be appropriate for me to stay after this and have a drink when I realize that a shadow has fallen over the table and Penny is talking to me and gesturing towards the shadow. I've already missed the first part of what she said.

" ...this is Gabe Kerrey. He owns the bar," Penny finishes.

I look up, knowing the shock is clear to see on my face. I find myself looking into the eyes of Gabe. My old best friend Gabe. I'm not surprised by the rush of warmth I feel when I see him. I am surprised by the rush of wetness I feel in my pussy though as my muscles clench deliciously at the sight of him.

Gabe has changed more than anything else in St. Augustine. He has gotten smoking hot. Gone is the scrawny kid with the broken, old-fashioned glasses. Before me stands a man solid with muscles, the kind of sculpted body I just want to run my hands all over. His broken, old-fashioned glasses are gone, replaced by trendy black framed ones. His eyes haven't changed. Their brown depths still hold warmth and a sparkle of joy and playfulness.

And when he smiles, it's like going back in time. The way his lip curls up at the side, something I always noticed but didn't really pay any attention to, now is something that makes me shift in my seat as my clit tingles.

I swallow hard, aware that I've been staring at Gabe for far too long. But he stares back at me, and I can't bring myself to look away from him in case it isn't real, and he vanishes again if I do. The seconds stretch into what feels like minutes although it can't really be that long. Penny clears her throat, sounding uncomfortable and that breaks the spell. Gabe looks away and I can finally move my eyes again.

"I'm sorry," Gabe says. "I'm just shocked to see Clarissa, that's all. Did you say you hired her Penny?"

"Umm… yes. Is that a problem?" Penny asks, her discomfort dragging on.

"Quite the opposite," Gabe says. He pulls out one of the spare chairs at the table and sits down. "Clarissa is originally from St. Augustine. She and I were best friends as children."

"Oh, small world," Penny says, her discomfort leaving her. She smiles at me. "You get extra points for not name dropping."

"Well in the interest of complete honesty I had no idea Gabe owned the bar," I say.

"What, even after seeing the name?" Gabe says before Penny can respond.

"Well, I did stop and think twice, and when I first came in, I half expected to see you behind the bar, but then I assumed Penny was the owner," I admit.

"So, you did remember?" Gabe says.

He looks at me, his gaze is intense and once more, I find myself unable to look away. I can feel my cheeks flushing as I nod.

"Of course, I remember," I say, surprised at how husky my voice sounds all of a sudden.

"That's good, because I remember everything," he drawls. He is smiling, but I feel a shiver go through me as his eyes bore into mine. "Every dream we shared, and... every promise we made."

"I do too," I say, my voice barely above a whisper.

Pre-Order your copy here:
The Forgotten Pact

ABOUT THE AUTHOR

Thank you so much for reading!
If you have enjoyed the book and would like to leave a
precious review for me, please kindly do so here:

The Fire Between Us

Please click on the link below to receive info about my latest
releases and giveaways.
NEVER MISS A THING

Or
come and say hello here:

ALSO BY IONA ROSE

12022436R00187